DEATH
ON
STANLEY
DOCK

DEATH ON STANLEY DOCK

A MURDERS ON THE MERSEY MYSTERY

NICKY NIELSEN

To Dee who gave inspiration and ideas
To Blondie who gave her name
To the scousers of Liverpool who gave me a home

Chapter One

Hatred drove my first blade. Hatred not of the individual, but of the circumstance. Now, the blade falls with purpose rather than blind rage. She whimpers. I feel her dying breath condensing on the palm of my hand. She has served her purpose. The night smells of honeysuckle and decay. Her limbs are thin, birdlike. I carve her up as I would a chicken for supper. It's getting harder these days. I'm not as young as I once was. The rum burns my throat. The tobacco smoke stings my eyes. And there she lies. Her eyes stare up at the canopy, but see nothing. Blood pools in the long grass by her shoulders, her thighs. and around the soles of her feet. I exhale. I'm exhausted but exhilarated. The need has been satisfied, at least for now.

Maybe the effect will last longer this time. How many times has it been this year? I cannot remember anymore. Too much rum, perhaps. They all become one, after a while.

I sit and listen to the sounds of the fading night. The warblers and blackbirds have begun to call out. The slow rhythmic sounds of the muddy waters lapping against the bank puts me into a trance. Then the high-pitched chirping scream of a fox sparrow cuts through my pleasant reverie. Energy surges through me from the swamp and from the blood, and from her eyes with their dimming light.

I'm dripping with her blood. Sweat runs in rivulets down my back. I kneel and reach down to scoop up handfuls of brackish water to wash myself. I do not let my hands linger in the water too long. The sovereigns of the swamp are on their way to devour her remains. I can hear their tails hitting the water. In the twilight, they are nothing but ripples on the surface of the murky waters. Ripples hiding teeth, power, and death just out of sight.

I pick up my shirt, jacket, and vest from the ground. An ebony walking cane leans against the scarred trunk of a sycamore. In my jacket pocket, I carry a bone comb and a small jar of pomade. I apply it to my moustache. From bloodthirsty savage to pillar of the community. It doesn't take much, just the right jacket, accent, and manner. I take a last look at the girl, then I turn and walk down a narrow path leading through the dense thicket and brush. The mosquitoes descend like a black cloud. Not even the smoke from my cigar can drive the beasts away, but I barely feel their bite. I'm still too full of the night's experiences.

After fifteen minutes, I emerge onto a wider gravel road. I turn right, setting off at a brisk trot back towards the distant lights on the horizon that marks Savannah. The old town is like me. On the surface, civilized. A city of widows, learned scholars, and well-behaved children with golden hair. However, when darkness descends over the city's large mansions, villas, and manicured squares with their dainty floral displays, another creature emerges. Savannah lets go of her inhibitions and her fine manners with wild parties fuelled by rum and fine cigars. Sugar and tobacco made her rich. Sugar, tobacco, cotton, and the blood and suffering of her slaves. Although the Yankee tyrant long ago gave the slaves their freedom, the citizens of Savannah still remember the old times. They make sure that the former slaves stay away from the city centre in their squalid slums on the outskirts, well away from polite society.

I move through one of these neighbourhoods now as I approach the city, but I'm not afraid. The residents know well what would happen should they attack a white man. The revenge of Savannah's refined bourgeoisie would be merciless and instantaneous. For insurance, I carry a small Philadelphia Derringer pistol in my pocket, but I've never needed it. I hope never to need it either. I prefer the blade to the bullet. It is far more intimate.

Chapter Two

Liverpool, October 25th 1891

As the sun rose over the slate roof tiles of the city, the tenements of Liverpool came alive. First with the cries and screams of babies and young children, hungry and eager to be fed. Then with the scolding of the mothers as they stoked fires in rusty ranges and stoves bringing pots of water and oats to the boil. If times were good, they would add a small spoon of sugar or maybe a dollop of cream to enrich the porridge. If times were hard, the porridge was little more than oat-flavoured water. The final sounds were the slamming of doors as the men, young and old, left the tenements, fortified with porridge and maybe a measure of gin, to make their ways to the wrought iron gates of the docks.

The men wore faded linen shirts in beige, brown, or grey and jackets shiny with wear, grease, and age. Newsboys, applejacks, ivy's, and boilerman caps were the preferred headwear, though some donned heavily worn and frayed broad-brimmed slouch hats. Every man who could do so grew a heavy moustache greased with lambs' fat, or heavy mutton chops to keep out the freezing wind.

As they trudged down the cobbled streets towards the docks, they walked in small groups, chatting and gossiping. However, when they arrived at the dock gates, all alliances were broken, all friendships temporarily put on hold. The gates were kept securely locked, and in front of each, stood three men, a foreman and two roughs carrying heavy cudgels. The foreman held a heavy brass ring with small, perforated tin badges. Each badge guaranteed one day's labour at the docks and one day's pay. The pay depended on the difficulty of the offloading, on the type of ship arriving, and the cargo it carried. But any pay was better than none, and soon the broad avenue that ran parallel to the dock gates was filled with hundreds of day labourers, jostling to get as close to the foreman as possible in the hope of catching his eye.

The foreman in charge of the Trafalgar Dock, a short man with a pockmarked face and a thatch of ginger hair, consulted a short list in his hand.

"Alright, you 'orrible lot," he bellowed, and the waiting masses gradually fell silent. "It's your lucky day. We got three ships arriving. Two rum runners from Cuba and a Ruski trader carrying pickled herring from Kaliningrad. We need seventy men, no more and no less. And be warned, I won't hire no piss artists. I'll not see the cargo drunk out from under my nose."

Angry mutters broke out among the waiting men. There was well over two hundred of them waiting in front of the gates. Most of them would go home with nothing in their pockets, and tomorrow their families would eat watery porridge for breakfast.

"Come on, Flanagan, you tight-fisted bastard," one of the men in the front row shouted. "Three ships need a hundred men, easy. Maybe more."

The foreman scanned the faces in the crowd until he found the man who had spoken up.

"And just for that, William Ellis, you can get away right now. I won't pay a good day's wage to an instigator."

The young William Ellis opened his mouth to argue back, but one of the guards flanking the foreman took a step forward, raising his cudgel. The young man looked for a moment to be considering his options, then turned and pushed angrily through the crowd. It flowed seamlessly in to take over the free space he left.

"Alright," the foreman continued. "Unless there's any more bull from you lot maybe we can get started."

He carefully folded up the list of arriving vessels and put it in his back pocket. Then he detached one of the thin tin badges from the ring he carried on his belt.

"First man," he shouted, holding the badge aloft and scanning the front row. His eyes fell on a brawny Irishman with broad shoulders and a livid white scar running the full length of his face. "You," he shouted, waving the man forward. "Name?"

"Cope," the man said, a deep rumble in his voice. "Brendan Cope."

The foreman shoved the badge at him.

"Through the gate, to the right, give your details to Mr Griffiths. Second man!"

The ghastly lottery continued. As the number of tin badges on the foreman's belt dwindled, the crowd grew increasingly fractious. The youngest and the oldest were pushed mercilessly to the back, sometimes helped along with swift fists and kicks. Robbed of any opportunity to earn a wage, they set off to the nearest gin palace. They would spend what coin they had on drink, and maybe a cheap whore to soothe their wounded pride. The next morning, the dance would start afresh, the daily battle for a handful of shillings.

While the men in the crowd occasionally dealt out harsh reprisals on those who tried to cut in front of them, or push them out of the way, the situation rarely escalated to a full riot. The reason for this was three men who stood nonchalantly fifty feet away from the gates. They wore silver-buttoned overcoats and heavy boots, black helmets, and carried rosewood truncheons, brass bells, and a whistle strung about their necks.

The three were constables from the Rose Hill Precinct, the northern division of the Liverpool Constabulary. Their job was to keep the peace, even if that meant doling out a fair portion of instantaneous justice with their truncheons and steel-toed boots.

As they waited for the foreman to continue his daily task, the men in the crowd glanced nervously at the constables with their impassive faces and hands casually resting on the handles of their bells. As the foreman reached his twentieth badge, the constables glanced up as a two-horse growler clattered down the street. It stopped in front of them, its steel-rimmed wheels throwing up a brief shower of sparks against the granite cobbles. The door swung open, and a dark-haired man with short-clipped sideburns jumped out. He stretched, reached into the pocket of his vest, and pulled out a battered brass snuffbox, flipping the lid open and taking out a pinch before strolling over to the constables.

The new arrival was dressed in a short tweed sack coat with a dark burgundy vest and a white shirt, its collar stained and grimy. He had evidently attempted to tie a black bowtie about his neck, but had hurried the task, and the edges of the tie were already beginning to unravel. His hair was short, and when he turned to glance at the men in the crowd, they saw that the top of the man's left ear was missing, giving his face a strangely asymmetrical appearance. Some of the men nodded or waved in greeting. He raised a hand lazily in return before turning to the constables.

"How's it looking, boys?" he asked. "Any trouble?"

The three constables stood to attention.

"Detective sergeant," one of them replied, touching his forelock, "Not much to report. Not much beyond the usual."

"I see Flanagan's on the gate," Detective Sergeant Thomas O'Callaghan said, glancing in the direction of the short ginger-haired man. "He's a stingy bastard. I'm surprised none of them have tried to nut him yet."

"William Ellis came pretty close," one of the constables said with a frown. "He went off in the end, but he didn't look best pleased."

"William Ellis," O'Callaghan said thoughtfully. "Willy Ellis? That short lad who lives down Barton Street? His wife works as a scullery maid."

"That's the one, sir," one of the constables replied. O'Callaghan's knowledge of the citizens of Liverpool and their varied sins was encyclopaedic.

"He drinks in the Lion Tavern, doesn't he?"

The constables nodded.

"Make sure you mention it to the patrolmen when they go out on the beat," O'Callaghan said. "Sounds like he's had a rough morning, and by tonight he'll be spoiling for a fight if the gin doesn't put him to bed first. Better if one of the boys can head it off early."

The detective sergeant looked around. The foreman and his guards had finally finished and retreated behind the iron fences that surrounded the dock. The men left outside with no tin badge, gradually began to disperse. Old friends met up and alliances re-formed, at least until tomorrow.

"It's getting worse," O'Callaghan said quietly.

"Soon the bloody owners won't need more than a handful of men to offload if they keep buying all those hellish machines," one of the constables said darkly.

"I heard," the youngest constable piped up. "That the owners at Hutchinson's have bought a dozen steam cranes from a factory up in Newcastle. They're laying tracks on the dock. One of me mates told me that the cranes can lift cotton bales straight from the ship to a train cart and then send it to Manchester." His voice was tinged with a mixture of disgust and grudging admiration.

"Aye," O'Callaghan replied. "And another hundred men will be out of work. As if we didn't have enough to worry about. If this goes on for much longer, we'll have another strike. Or worse."

During the previous year, the docks had been rocked by a series of labour strikes. The dockers, stevedores and day labourers had joined ranks and stayed at home. They had refused to lift another bale of cotton or barrel of rum before the dockyard owners, the ship owners and directors agreed to pay them a set minimum wage for a day's work. Before the strike, workers could be hired for as little as a single hour a day, paid a pittance and dismissed on the spot. The strike saw to it that the workers who gained one of the little tin badges were guaranteed at least six hours of pay, even if the off-loading took less time. In reality, though, the owners had simply begun to hire fewer men, terrified as they were of hiring too many and ending up having to pay them for nothing.

In many ways, the strikes had made the situation worse. The encroaching industrialisation simply added another headache for the overstretched constabulary. As many as half the grown men in the city of Liverpool depended on the docks for their livelihood. And as more and more of the owners brought in steam cranes, locomotives, and other machines designed to replace or reduce human labour, those men found it impossible to earn a daily wage. And O'Callaghan knew well that if a man saw his family starve, his children cry themselves to sleep with hunger, and his wife growing weaker and more ashen-faced by the day, there was nothing on God's green earth he would not do to remedy the situation. These men, cut off from honest work, became housebreakers or cutpurses, smugglers, and fraudsters. Eventually, they landed up in the cells of the Rose Hill station or, if their crime was bad enough, they ended their days in the gloomy courtyard of Kirkdale Gaol, swinging at the end of a rope.

"Don't worry, sir," one of the constables said, smiling and patting his heavy truncheon. "Any sign of trouble and we'll take care of it right away."

O'Callaghan's thin lips twitched as he looked at the constable.

"I don't fancy your chances against a couple hundred angry men, Oakley. Not even with that truncheon of yours. We've all seen what desperate men can do."

He tapped his mutilated ear and grinned.

"Some of us have felt it too."

The constables laughed. O'Callaghan had joined the Liverpool Constabulary at eighteen. Within two weeks on the force, he had found himself drawn into a tavern brawl that had spilled into the street. After blowing his whistle for reinforcements, O'Callaghan had joined in the fray with his truncheon. Suddenly, one of the heaviest drinkers, rendered half-mad and half-blind by several bottles of gin, had drawn a wickedly sharp folding knife and lunged at the young constable. He had missed O'Callaghan's neck, instead cutting the constable's left ear with enough force to sever the upper portion entirely. Bleeding and screaming with pain, O'Callaghan had retreated from the fight as arriving constables overpowered the brute.

The detective sergeant looked with a frown towards the dispersing crowd of labourers. On the river, ships coming from distant ports with strange-sounding names drifted serenely passed.

Chapter Three

Captain Porter Knightly could not remember a more fraught crossing. The Royal Mail paddle steamer *King Orry* had departed the port of Le Havre on schedule, as she had a dozen times before. She was crewed by fifty veteran sailors, and there had been no issue docking the ship's nine-hundred passengers before departing the port. However, as soon as *King Orry* was out of sight of land, the problems had begun. A crewmember had fallen from the braces and broken his neck on the very first day of the voyage. Then, a dozen first-class passengers were taken violently ill with food poisoning on the third evening. The following morning, a routine inspection of the vessel's ballast chambers revealed an unacceptable level of seepage, requiring Captain Knightley to supervise emergency repairs and reduce the speed of his ship. The directors of the Royal Mail Company did not look favourably upon officers who fell behind schedule, and he knew that his every order and decision would be subjected to critical scrutiny the moment he set foot on land.

Finally, there had been the explosion. Knightley had been on the bridge when the *King Orry* lurched as though hit by a rogue wave. He only had time to look questioningly at Mr Stebbins, the ship's first mate, before a roar, as loud as a frigate's broadside, had temporarily deafened him. Smoke billowed from every rivet-hole of the steamers large central paddle, which, along with three masts, provided her forward thrust. As Mr Stebbins grabbed the speaking tube and frantically called to the engine room, Knightley jumped down the stairs to the upper deck. With the speed of a much younger man, he barrelled through the ship's narrow corridors and down the internal stairwell that led to the engine room. He had not needed to enter the room to realise how serious the situation was. The explosion had blown the door to the engine room clean off its hinges. It had bent the inch-thick iron outwards like the punch of a giant's fist. Smoke billowed from the room. Smoke and screams.

Knightley rallied the dozen sailors who had arrived to investigate. Together, they manhandled the ship's fire hose, attached directly to the bilge pumps, into the engine room, dousing the fire with seawater. As the flames died down and the smoke cleared, Knightley had to suppress an urge to vomit. One of the ship's four boilers had exploded, sending white-hot, twisted metal scything through the air. A headless torso of one of the stokers lay in the corner of the room. A pair of bodiless legs lay in the other. Four other men were scattered about the floor, three of them moving. The fourth, Knightley knew at a glance, would never move again. An iron bolt, the size of a walnut, had punched clean through his chest and embedded itself in the opposite wall. Blood mingled with seawater, running towards the gratings set along the starboard wall, gradually washing back into the bilges.

The three wounded sailors were carried onto the deck. Passengers were milling about, panicking, shouting, and demanding information, crowding the captain and his men. Knightley had been forced to pull out his Webley and fire it into the air to clear a path. Retching and shitting first-class passengers filled the ship's infirmary, so the captain had ordered the three wounded men taken to his stateroom. He needed no medical training to realise how bad their situation was. All three had large, gaping wounds in their arms, torsos and legs. Angry red patches showed where the steam from the boiler had touched their skin. One man had no hair on his head, his fine drooping moustache reduced to a scorched stubble.

Dr Burges, the ship's surgeon, had arrived in a blind panic. There was too much for one man to do. Certainly, too much for a man as fond of whiskey as Dr Burges. And then, Captain Knightley thought darkly, and then there had been that woman. As Burges did his best to stop the three stokers bleeding out, a gentle knock at the door of the stateroom had revealed a tall, blonde woman in her late twenties. Knightley recognised her vaguely as one of the ship's first-class passengers. In clipped tones overlaid with a faint Nordic accent, the woman had introduced herself as Sophia Amalie Steenberg. With those basic niceties out of the way, she had pushed past the captain and demanded a spare needle and thread from the ship's surgeon. Dr Burges, his eyes still blurry from the previous night's overindulgence, had complied out of pure shock. Before either man could intervene, the young woman had expertly threaded the needle and begun to stitch up a large wound in the thigh of one of the stokers. As she worked, she curtly ordered two of Knightley's sailors to bring pots of boiling water from the kitchen. To the captain's surprise, the men had obeyed. Then she proceeded to quiz the doctor on what medicines he had available, rattling off a dizzying array of medicaments, which would be needed to help the wounded men.

At that point, shaking off his initial bemusement, Knightley had demanded answers from the woman. She calmly told him that she was a trained surgeon, and when he scoffed at this ludicrous statement, she told him to send a man to her stateroom. In it, he would find a leather satchel and inside the satchel, a letter and certificate from the Royal Danish Society of Medicine. Knightley was readying himself to physically eject the deranged woman from the temporary infirmary, but then he thought back to his younger days. A veteran of the Ashanti Wars, he remembered well that on the battlefield, when limbs were severed by assegai and arrows lodged in soft, yielding flesh, you could not turn your nose up at an extra pair of hands to stitch and bandage. Regardless of what sex those hands were.

Knightley had to admit, now, that the young woman had proved to be an asset. She had worked tirelessly with Dr Burges for the remainder of the voyage, only leaving the injured stokers to eat and sleep. While one of the stokers had died from his injuries on the third day after the accident, the remaining two men were now awake. It would be a long time before they recovered, but they would at least live to see their families greet them on Prince's Dock.

Knightley turned his thoughts from the tribulations of the voyage and focused his gaze on the shoreline. The *Orry* had arrived at the mouth of the River Mersey during the night guided by the glow of the New Brighton

Lighthouse standing on a granite outcropping fifty yards from the sandy beaches of the northern Wirral Peninsula. Behind the lighthouse, the captain had clearly been able to make out the flickering lights from the narrow windows of Fort Perch, a sandstone behemoth, which guarded the entrance to the port of Liverpool. The fort's eighteen 32-pound canons were kept primed at all times, ready to unleash a storm of fire on any hostile ship approaching the river mouth.

Knightley had ordered his vessel anchored, and as dawn came, the fort's commander despatched a pilot in a small dinghy to guide *King Orry* up the river towards the Prince's Dock. With the dawn came also the passengers. They lined the rails of the ship, first-, second-class, and steerage mingling together, straining to catch a glimpse of their destination.

The smoke and smog from the factories, workshops, and foundries that lined the banks of the Mersey obstructed the view of the city at first. As the daylight began to dispel the grey shadows of dawn, a stiff breeze sprang up from the west and the miasma gradually cleared. From his post on the raised quarterdeck, Knightley could hear the excited chatter of the passengers like so many starlings, as the city gradually came into view.

Liverpool was not a beautiful city. But it was bustling and overflowing with sheer energy. Even from the river, the susurration of tens of thousands of people talking, yelling, laughing, crying, and living carried clearly. The city stood on sloping ground leading towards the river. Dozens of docks, some intended for dry goods, some for wet, and some for passengers, lined the east bank. Behind and between them were shipyards, tenements, factories, and the occasional church, its spire reaching towards the heavens. Bells tolled, street vendors haggled with customers, stevedores and dockworkers cursed as they unloaded bales of cotton, barrels of rum, wine, brandy, sacks of sugar, and baulks of timber.

On the city's higher ground, manicured parks, tree-lined avenues, and sturdy brick houses replaced the wooden tenements and hovels closer to the water; the homes of the city's merchants. They made their living by the sea, by the grime and dirt of the docks and riverside, Knightley thought. Nevertheless, they lived far enough away from it to avoid its smell. Instead, when a ship crossed by Fort Perch, the garrison sparky would send a message to her owners via the Central Telegraph Office. By the time their vessel docked, they would already be waiting to oversee her offload and interview her skipper.

Knightley sighed. He knew full well that the Postmaster or one of his deputies would be waiting on the dock, in a foul mood and expecting an explanation as to why the *King Orry* was arriving at a crawl, a full four days behind schedule. Every one of the two hundred and thirty-eight postbags she carried in her hold now contained nothing but delayed mail and old news. Knightley was not entirely certain what excuses he could make. The Post Office did not accept bad luck as a justification for delayed mail.

"Take her in will you, Mr Stebbins?" Knightley said as he emptied the cup of tea his steward had brought to him the moment he arrived on the quarterdeck.

"Yessir," Stebbins replied.

As Captain Knightley walked down the gangway to the starboard deck, he heard the sailors hanging in the braces break into song and smiled.

Leave her, Johnny, leave her. Oh, leave her, Johnny, leave her. For the voyage was long and the wages low. And it's time for us to leave her.

Around him, those of the passengers who knew the tune joined in.

The captain made his way down to the first-class dining room, a luxuriously appointed space that was as wide as the full width of the ship. It was illuminated with gas lamps set along the walls, and a huge, gently swaying cut glass and crystal chandelier. Round mahogany tables and chairs upholstered with red velvet provided comfort for the diners as they ate the three sit-down meals a day provided by the ship's galley.

Now, though, so close to land, the room was almost empty. One of the ship's stewards was busily packing the silver cutlery into canvas bags, carefully counting out each utensil. It would not do to run out of forks or spoons halfway through their return journey. Aside from the steward, the only two people in the room were the young blonde woman and Dr Burges, who sat by a table in the corner, eating mock turtle soup.

"Miss Steenberg," Knightley greeted her stiffly. She looked up at him, the azure blue of her eyes and her steely glare nailing him to the spot.

"Captain," she said, gesturing to one of the empty chairs next to her. "I hear we're approaching port."

"We should tie up in less than two hours," he said. "You may want to go and pack your things."

"That has already been done," she said. "I've spoken with Dr Burges, and we've agreed that the two men are in a stable enough condition to move. They'll live. But it'll be months before they can go back to sea."

Knightley glanced towards the doctor, who shrugged and nodded. He was around sixty years of age with nicotine-stained sideburns and a weedy moustache. His eyes were red-rimmed and watery.

"There'll be a berth for them on my ship when they're ready to return," Knightley said. "And I'll speak to the General Post Office. They'll see to it that their families don't starve in the meantime."

"Good," the woman replied.

The three sat in uncomfortable silence. Miss Steenberg finished her soup and started on a cold meat pie. As the silence dragged on, Captain Knightley found himself distractedly tapping his feet. He shook his head slightly and composed himself.

"If you don't mind me asking, miss, what precisely is your business in Liverpool?"

The woman cast a mildly annoyed glance at him. Then she took a sip of water and cleared her throat.

"I'm not settling here, Captain, if that's what you're asking. Nor am I meeting my intended."

"Well, a woman travelling alone. Usually, that happens only for one reason."

"I'm in Liverpool until the *Britannic* sails for New York in two weeks' time."

"A long journey. You've come from Sweden?"

A brief smile flashed across her face.

"Denmark, actually. But it's an honest mistake."

"Yes, I remember the..." he trailed off.

"Ah, so you did send someone to my cabin to examine my medical certificate. I wondered."

"I meant no disrespect, of course," Captain Knightley said hurriedly. "Merely out of concern for my men."

"I understand, Captain. A woman surgeon is a rare beast. I'm sure a man of the sea such as yourself has seen more mermaids than female doctors."

Knightley smiled ruefully despite himself. He glanced at Dr Burges. The older man was looking intently at Sophia, a mixture of disdain and puzzlement in his eyes.

"Whether a mermaid or a sawbones, miss, I want to thank you for your assistance," Knightley said.

For the first time, the young woman's delicate features broke into a genuine smile.

"I'm sure you must be eager to come ashore after this particular journey, Captain," she said. "Should you ever find yourself in need of a surgeon in New York, do remember my name."

"Speaking of going ashore, miss, can I assume that you have arranged for an escort to meet you on the dock?" Knightley asked. "Liverpool's docks are notorious. They're infested with cutpurses and brawlers of all kinds, and that's without mentioning the stevedores, dockers, and their ilk."

"Please don't concern yourself on my account," she said. "I'll be staying in the Adelphi Hotel along with most of the other first-class passengers while we wait for the *Britannic* to board."

The Adelphi Hotel in the centre of Liverpool was, with its soaring gothic façade and luxuriously appointed rooms, the grandest hotel outside of London. It played host to only the richest clientele, an eclectic mix of American stockbrokers and railway tycoons, politicians, the nouveau riche and nobility of all sorts from Lithuanian Grand Dukes to Canadian lumber barons and plantation owners from Barbados.

"Very well," Captain Knightley said, getting to his feet. "I'm sure the hotel will send a growler to pick you up at the dock."

The young woman looked puzzled.

"Growler?" she asked.

Knightley laughed.

"Begging your pardon, miss, I forgot you're not a native speaker of our language. A growler is our name for a small carriage. The Adelphi employs a fleet of them to ferry their guests from the docks to the city centre."

"I shall remember the term," she said. She, too, got to her feet and faced the grizzled sea captain. Standing nearly six feet, she was only slightly shorter than he and, in a light blue crinoline dress with dark blonde hair framing her oval face, she struck a fine figure.

"I don't expect we'll meet again," she said. "But I should like to thank you as well. For your faith in me."

Knightley reached up and touched his hand to the brim of his cap.

"Fair winds and fortunate travels, miss," he said before turning around and departing the first-class dining hall.

* * *

A soft knock at the door startled Sophia out of her reverie. The Danish surgeon had collapsed into a heavily upholstered wingback chair the very moment one of the Adelphi's porters had put down her luggage and left her alone in her spacious suite. The stress of the journey, the backbreaking work in Paris, and the years she had spent in Copenhagen fighting for the recognition of her peers had washed over her. She wanted sleep, but at the same time, she felt too tense. She glanced towards the door, for a moment believing she had imagined the gentle knocking.

"Yes?" she said hesitantly after a few seconds of silence. Then she cleared her throat and straightened her back. "Enter," she said, more forcefully.

The door to her room swung open, and a young, skinny girl stepped in, curtseying nervously. She wore a simple black dress and a heavily starched white apron. Her white lace engageantes and mobcap identified her as one of the hotel's chambermaids. Each of the hotel's top-floor suites had a resident maidservant to help the guests unpack and dress.

"Excuse me, miss," the maid said, "I've come to help you get settled in."

Sophia looked closely at the girl. She had a pretty face, slightly pointed with a dusting of freckles across an upturned nose. Her hair was a deep auburn and tied in two modest plaits, rolled into coils and fastened around her head like a halo. Her mobcap seemed to balance somewhat precariously atop this gilded crown.

"Very well," Sophia said, pointing to one of a pair of green leather and wood steam trunks standing by the suite's four-person dining table. "You can hang the dresses in the wardrobe by the bed. Leave the other trunk packed. I won't be here long."

The maid bobbed another curtsy, crossed the room, opened the trunk, and carefully removed Sophia's dresses one by one. Sophia ran a hand across her face, rubbing her tired eyes as the girl worked methodically. However, as she lifted the second, she stopped suddenly, frowned, and cleared her throat. Sophia looked at her.

"Yes?" she asked.

"I'm sorry, miss," the maid said, lifting out a rectangular rosewood case with brass fittings. "This must be your husband's. Where would you like me to put it?"

The case was a common design, one familiar to anyone who had ever visited any medical practitioner. It contained a surgical kit, a selection of scalpels, knives, and a short saw for amputations. It also included rolls of bandages, pliers, needles, and thread, as well as a selection of useful medicaments such as opium and laudanum. Sophia smiled.

"Just leave it on the table and finish up with the clothes."

The maid looked at her curiously, but did not ask any further questions. When she had emptied the trunk, she looked around the room.

"Did the porter bring up the rest of your luggage, miss?"

Most of the guests who visited the Adelphi travelled with dozens of trunks, large leather satchels, suitcases, sacks, and sometimes even wooden crates containing furniture and antiquities with which they could further enrich their suites and rooms.

"I'm travelling light," Sophia said. "But you can run me a bath before you go."

"Yes, miss."

Sophia got up and walked to the dining table as she heard the gilded brass faucets turning in the bathroom, and water splashing merrily into the clawfoot bath. Boilers in the basement of the hotel ensured that guests always had hot water whenever they required it, and each room was fitted with the newest flushing lavatories and porcelain washbasins.

The surgical kit opened with two soft clicks and revealed the array of viciously sharp blades, each one carefully cleaned and boiled in a mixture of distilled water and vinegar. They gleamed like jewels as they lay on their black velvet bed. Sophia ran a hand over the ivory handle of the slightly curved bone saw. She felt a heavy lump in her throat. She pressed her eyes tightly shut but could feel the creeping warmth of tears amassing in the corners of her eyes.

The sound of the running water stopped, and she heard the footsteps of the maid as she entered the living room.

"Will there be anything further, miss?" she asked. Sophia did not turn around.

"No," she said, trying to keep her voice from cracking. "Thank you."

"If there's anything at all, just push the button by your bed and I'll be right up."

"Yes," Sophia said, not trusting her voice with any longer sentences. After a few moments of awkward silence, she heard the maid walk to the door, open it, and step into the corridor. As soon as the door closed, Sophia relaxed her abdomen, and a soft moan escaped between her lips.

Outside the tall, arched windows of the suite, the sunlight gradually faded. The lamplighters walked their rounds, setting the gas-powered streetlamps across the centre of the city ablaze. The cries of vendors subsided as they made their way home to count the day's takings. Sophia lay in the bath until the water grew cold. Then she rose, dried herself off, and collapsed on the bed, too tired to eat or to think any further about the past or the future. Before the bells on St Stephen's tolled ten o'clock, she was fast asleep.

Chapter Four

Thomas O'Callaghan awoke. He had not been disturbed by a sound, but by unaccustomed silence. Ordinarily, his life consisted of nothing but noise. From the shouted orders of the custody officers, the clamour of the constables readying themselves for the beat, to the screams and curses of criminals captured and brought to justice. In the absence of sound, his body tensed in expectation of an attack, even in his deepest sleep. He twisted around on the narrow bed and found that his night terrors had again seen him tangled in his sheets like a fly in a spider's web. He punched and jerked himself free of the clawing linen and stumbled to his feet. The greyish light filtering in through the room's cracked window told him the time as effectively as any watch. Not quite night, not yet dawn. A magical hour where the crimes of the night had subsided, but the business of the day had yet to begin.

He stretched his naked frame and walked across the room to a tin washbasin standing on a rickety table. Aside from a chest of drawers, a narrow wardrobe, two mismatched chairs, and his bed, the table constituted the only furniture in the room. The city did not pay its constables and junior detectives well, and having grown up as one of seven brothers in a family of dockworkers, Thomas had no inherited wealth. He swished water around his mouth and spat it into an empty chamber pot standing by his bed. Then he picked up a thin leather cord and strung it around his neck. A single gilded button hung from its glimmer, setting it apart from every other item in the room.

He splashed cold water on his face and pulled on a pair of long underwear.

He put on his boots and left his lodgings via the back stairs. He finished his morning ablutions in the soiled and foul-smelling loo, a wooden shed built in a small courtyard. The three-story house he inhabited with a dozen other families was built of crumbling recycled bricks from Newcastle and rotting timbers left over from the construction of Navy frigates in one of the Birkenhead shipyards.

When he got back to his room, he heard the first noise of the day and sighed. A man's voice raised in anger. Through the thin plaster walls, Thomas could hear every word of the argument. A woman tried to defend herself in a softer voice, meek and apologetic. Her softer tones did not, however, dissuade her husband. It never did. Within five minutes, Thomas heard the first unmistakable sound of fists hitting soft flesh. He sighed, pulled on his shirt and trousers, and grabbed his truncheon.

As he left his room, he nearly collided with a short, thin woman who came rushing out of the neighbouring apartment, her head in her hands. Thomas grabbed her by the shoulder and twisted her face towards the single tallow candle set in a holder on the wall. The right side of the woman's face was bruised purple.

"Bastard," Thomas muttered.

"Please just leave it," the woman pleaded, grabbing a hold of Thomas' shirt as he tried to push past her. "He didn't do nothing wrong."

Thomas stopped and looked at his neighbour. She was young. Not twenty years of age, and the slight bulge around her middle showed that she was already pregnant. She had lived for less than two months next to Thomas with her new husband. Even in that short time, the detective had grown used to waking up in the early hours to screams and the sound of fists and boots. While it was not depressingly common for men to beat and hurt their wives and children, common assault, threats of death, and grievous bodily harm had nevertheless been crimes in the country for nearly three decades. And that included harm caused to spouses and family members.

"Mary," Thomas said sternly, "This can't go on. He'll end up killing you one of these days."

"Please," she said, tears now running freely down her bruised face. Thomas shook his head and pushed her gently aside. He used the butt of his truncheon to push open the flimsy and ill-fitted wooden door to the flat. It was as clean as any of the rooms in the building could ever be. Mary kept a tidy house and waged a constant war against the mice, the rats, and the cockroaches that infested the whole neighbourhood. Her husband, a young, skinny lad with shoulder-length black hair, sat on the room's only chair, swigging heavily from a glass bottle.

"I think you've had enough, John," Thomas said, closing the door behind him. John looked up through bleary eyes.

"Go to hell, bizzie," he said and spat on the floor.

Thomas sighed inwardly. The Liverpool Constabulary were not popular among many in the wider population, and the varied nicknames the force had been given reflected that hostility. Where police in London were known as peelers or bobbies after Sir Robert Peel who founded the Metropolitan Police Force, Liverpool constables were called bizzies, a nickname born from the perception that the men on the force were always too busy to assist when needed, but happy to poke their noses in where they were not welcome. The busybodies who were always busy with the wrong things.

"That's right, I am. And I'm a bizzie who's just about had it with waking up to the sounds of fighting and wailing every damn morning."

He crossed the room in two steps and smashed his heavy truncheon against the scrubbed wooden table an inch from John's hand. The swiftness of his movement and the loud crack of the truncheon shocked the younger man, who overbalanced and fell off his chair. He sprawled like an overturned tortoise, the bottle of gin rolling and spilling the remainder of its contents across the floorboards. Before he could get back up, Thomas put a heavy boot on his chest.

"I've tried talking to you man to man, my lad, but I don't think you understood me, so I'll try again. If I see another bruise on your wife's face, I'll have a word with a couple of mates who've spent plenty of nights in my cells. And I'll ask them to wait for you when you stumble home from the pub, and they'll beat seven kinds of hell out of you. Do you understand what I'm saying to you?"

Thomas had leaned closer and closer to the man on the floor as he spoke. He saw a flicker of fear in the man's eyes, made blurred and dull by drink.

"I asked you a question, lad."

"Y-yes," the prone man stammered. "I understand."

Thomas straightened up, removed his foot from John's chest, and stretched out his hand.

"Good," he said, "Let me give you a hand there. You don't want to be lying around on a cold floor. You might catch your death."

As Thomas left the small, well-scrubbed room, he passed by the young Mary huddled in a corner of the corridor. She glanced fearfully at him, her eyes flitting to the missing portion of his ear, but he merely smiled and tugged his forelock in greeting as he passed her.

"It's a tough world, Mary," he said. "Get tougher."

A couple of pennies became a ham sandwich, sold from a barrow at the end of the street. The fog of the evening was giving way to a weak sun as Thomas arrived at the Rose Hill station house, still chewing on his breakfast. A couple of constables from the night watch saluted him as he went into the cavernous front office littered with desks, chairs, and benches. Constables sat reading the newspaper or going through arrest reports. The duty sergeant, an elderly and burly Scot, waved at Thomas from behind his desk.

"Morning, sir," he roared.

"Sergeant Fraser," Thomas said with a smile, "Quiet night?"

"I wouldn't say that, sir, I wouldn't say that at all." Duncan Fraser had grown up the son of a farmer and moonshine distiller on the Isle of Arran, but a wanderlust had convinced the young Duncan to sign on to a merchant vessel as a cabin boy. The ship was hardly out of sight of land before the young lad realised that he did not have the temperament for a life at sea. Rather than suffer for the full journey, he had jumped ship at the first available port, Liverpool, as luck would have it. There he had made a career first as an expert pickpocket, later as a famous bareknuckle fighter before joining the force. His considerable knowledge of the city's underworld and his talents in the boxing ring stood him in good stead, and within a few years, he had become a respected officer.

"What's been going on?"

Fraser consulted the large leather-bound incident book.

"We've got a couple of muggers in the cells," he said, "Nothing much for you to do, detective. We nabbed them with the loot still in their pockets. Pretty open and shut. Then we had a couple of street brawls, but the buggers ran off before we could nick them."

"Doesn't sound too much out of the ordinary," Thomas said.

"We got a murder too," Fraser said grimly. Thomas sighed. Life was often cheap in the city, and murders common. Nevertheless, that did not make them any easier to deal with. Usually, they happened when bar fights went too far, or when a husband hit his wife a little too hard. Around the docks, when the sailors came ashore with a pocket full of pay and months' worth of pent-up aggression and energy, a brawl could become a killing in the blink of an eye.

"Who's the victim?"

"A lad by the name of Pat Hannigan, do you know him?"

"Name rings a bell. Haven't we had him in here before?"

Fraser nodded.

"He's a bit of a fighter. Likes a drink and a punch-up. Liked, I should say."

"Someone hit him back too hard?"

"Something like that. He got shanked in the throat during a fight outside Rosie's Tavern last night."

"Did anyone see who did it?"

"Street was full of people. Someone must've seen."

Thomas nodded.

"Send a couple of constables down to Rosie's. If they can't find anyone willing to talk, then one of the barmaids must have seen who Pat was fighting if the trouble started in the bar."

Thomas paused and glanced towards the cracked plaster ceiling, tapping his hand on the duty sergeant's desk.

"He lived with his old mother, didn't he? Somewhere around St Vincent de Paul?"

Fraser shrugged.

"Don't know about that, sir," he said, "But one of the constables will know. I'll put out the word, and when we find out, we'll send down a runner to fetch his old ma."

"Make sure they leave her with family or neighbours when they bring her back home," Thomas said. "The lad may have been a nuisance, but his ma won't see it like that."

"Understood."

Thomas clapped his hands together.

"Right," he said. "And where's the esteemed detective inspector Muldoon?"

"A runner came for him about an hour ago, and he ran out of here going hell for leather."

Thomas frowned. It was not like the old inspector to move at anything above a casual stroll. William Haskins Muldoon had been heading the detectives working out of Rose Hill for nearly twenty-five years. He was a small man, and so fat as to appear almost spherical. The sight of his black bowler hat bobbing up and down as he walked the streets of Liverpool was a familiar one. He wore the hat at all times, Thomas knew, to conceal a steadily growing bald spot, and never moved at speed if he could avoid it to disguise a pain in his right knee that got worse and worse every winter.

"That's not like him," Thomas said. "I wonder what's got him all riled up."

"Didn't tell me a thing, sir," Fraser said.

"Well, I'm sure he'll send for me if he needs me," Thomas said. "In the meantime, has the morning dock shift gone out?"

Fraser opened his mouth to respond, but was distracted by the sound of the watch house door crashing open. Thomas turned to see a young constable, his face beetroot red, panting and clutching a stitch in his side. The young man looked around wildly, spotted Thomas, and waved frantically, his mouth opening and closing as he fought for air.

"Sweet Jesus lad, breathe easy," Thomas said, crossing the floor and patting the young constable on the back.

"M-Muldoon," the young man croaked. "Inspector Muldoon needs you. It's urgent."

"What's happened?"

"He didn't say, sir," the constable held his hand tightly to the stitch in his side. "Just sent me to fetch you. He's down on Stanley Dock."

Thomas glanced at Sergeant Fraser. His face looked grim. Inspector Muldoon did not go in for theatrics. To send a runner halfway through the city meant that something serious had happened. Thomas squared his shoulders.

"I'd better go and see what he wants," he said to Fraser.

"Right you are, sir."

Thomas left the station house at a fast pace, but when he heard the heavy door, he broke into a run, sprinting through the city's cobbled streets and paved boulevards, heading for the river.

Chapter Five

At the entrance to Stanley Dock, Thomas saw the heavy iron gates bolted shut. Rather than the usual guards, a swarm of constables stood in front of the gates, many of them arguing with dockers and stevedores who had evidently been thrown unceremoniously from the dock by the arriving police.

"There's two ships loaded to the gunwales with tobacco," moaned the dock foreman. "They're lying right outside the dock and now you bastards won't let them land and unload. We'll all be behind schedule."

"I told you, sir," one of the constables replied testily, "You can tell them to unload at the bottom of the river for all I care. The inspector's orders were clear. No one sets foot on the dock until we've finished."

Thomas pushed his way through the angry crowd and caught the eye of one of the constables standing closest to the gate. He raised his truncheon threateningly at the foreman, who took a step back. Thomas slipped into the gap created by his hasty retreat and was half-pushed, half-pulled behind the line of constables. Two of them manhandled the heavy chains from the gate and pushed it open wide enough to admit him.

Stanley Dock was one of the newest of the city's dockyards. It comprised a long sandstone pier fronted by redbrick warehouses. The heavy scent of tobacco revealed what was stored in the padlocked buildings. Most of the tobacco smoked across the United Kingdom came from Virginia and Cuba, and almost every tobacco leaf passed through Stanley Dock and the port of Liverpool.

The dock was eerily quiet, without the usual bustle of arriving ships, sailors, and dockers milling about and working at cross purposes. Thomas glanced down the long pier and saw a knot of constables standing outside the furthest of the warehouses and the only one with its tall wooden double doors thrown wide open.

Uncharacteristically, the constables stood in silence. Their faces were pale and drawn. As he drew closer, Thomas noted a pile of vomit by the side of the door. One of the constables was still wiping his mouth with a handkerchief.

His eyes took a moment to adjust to the gloom of the building. The storeroom was full of bales of tobacco, stacked floor to ceiling, except for a narrow passage that ran from the doors to the opposite wall. A low and narrow backdoor stood unbolted and slightly ajar. In the middle of the passage were two men, standing close together.

Thomas recognised the shape of Inspector Muldoon easily enough. The elderly detective had temporarily removed his bowler and was wiping a handkerchief across his gleaming bald patch. A persistent clicking, which echoed around the room, revealed the identity of the second man, Mr Joshua Watson, one of the photographers, attached to the Rose Hill station. After much cajoling, the enterprising photographer and sketch artist had persuaded the police commissioner to invest in a single camera of a type recently invented by the Kodak Company in America. This small box-shaped camera allowed Mr Watson to take photographs directly on a thin roll of cellulite film, and, with the aid of a dark room in the basement of the Rose Hill station house, he could produce perfect photographs mounted on square pieces of pasteboard in less than an hour.

Muldoon looked up at the sound of Thomas' footsteps. He did not raise his hand in greeting, made no sign of recognition at all. His usually ruddy face looked sickly and pale.

It was a young girl. She was lying on her back, her hands by her side, stiffly as though she was standing to attention. She was naked, her light blue dress bundled up and placed under her head like a pillow. Blood had pooled around her shoulders, and as Thomas drew closer, he saw that both of her arms had been separated entirely from the torso. Thomas felt a rush of blood to his head, but he forced himself to keep moving steadily forwards. As Muldoon stepped aside, Thomas saw the girl's stomach and abdomen with horrifying clarity.

He reached the doorway before he threw up, the acidic bile coming in a coughing splutter that burnt his throat and eyes. The young girl's stomach had been opened like a silk purse from one side to the other. The killer had removed her intestines, placing them neatly in a pile below the abdomen.

Thomas breathed heavily, leaning against the doorframe. He glanced up and saw the constables staring at him. There was no ridicule in their stares, but he recognised the drawn expressions. He had seen such expressions before. For a horrible moment, he could smell the clawing smog of London even on this windy dock. In a flash, he saw Constable Watkins; the young man's face seemingly hovering before him in the air. Watkins' face was marred by sheer horror as Thomas ran towards him, his bell raised and ringing wildly. Then the discarded pile of humanity lying in a corner of Mitre Square. Even now, three years later, the corpse of the Eddowes woman visited him in his night terrors.

"Don't feel too bad, lad," he heard Muldoon say as the inspector put a hand on Thomas' shoulder. "I lost my breakfast when I saw her as well."

"Her arms…"

"Both cut off at the shoulders. And someone gutted her like a freshly caught haddock."

Thomas shook his head, trying to clear it. Then he drew a deep, shuddering breath and turned back to face the corpse. He walked slowly forward and then knelt by the side of the girl's head. He stared into her eyes. The killer had left them open, staring eternally towards the heavy wooden beams that supported the warehouse roof.

The girl had been pretty. Her eyes were pale blue, now covered in a greyish film of death. Her hair was deep auburn and had been tied into plaits and arranged decoratively around her head. Her nose had a slight upward tilt, and her pale skin dusted with sprinkling of light brown freckles. She could be no more than eighteen, Thomas thought. His eyes slowly travelled down her mutilated body, taking in the deep slash across the throat that had killed her. The cut was so deep that the white bone of the spine showed through the wound. He touched the fabric of her dress. Then he looked down and frowned.

"Where are her shoes?" he asked. "It was bloody cold last night. Was she carried here?"

Muldoon pointed towards the end wall of the warehouse.

"There's a pair of lady's shoes lying down there," he said, "The killer must have removed them. Or maybe she took them off herself."

"How in the name of all the devils in hell did she get in here?" Thomas asked. "I thought the docks were supposed to be kept locked tight. There's a fortune in tobacco in here."

Muldoon gestured angrily towards a subdued group of four men standing apart from the constables, the lapels of their heavy great coats turned up against the wind.

"The night watchmen have an understanding with some of the whores," Muldoon said. "They let them in with their clients for a few hours each night in exchange for a cut of the takings."

Thomas looked over his shoulder towards the broken body.

"She was a whore then?"

Muldoon nodded.

"The lad who found her recognised her," he gestured to one of the watchmen, "Says her name's Polly Wilkes. She works as a maid up at the Adelphi. In the daytime at any rate. He lets her in a couple of nights a week."

"Did he see who she was with?"

Muldoon shook his head.

"She was definitely with a client, but whoever he was, he didn't want to be seen. He stayed in the shadows. And our lad was more interested in Polly's money than whoever was paying her."

Thomas swore softly under his breath.

"You sure it wasn't one of them? One of the watchmen, I mean."

Muldoon looked intently at Thomas. The detective inspector's pale grey eyes were hard and infused with intent. He might have allowed the advancing years to make him a little soft. But now he seemed like a bloodhound who had scented blood again after many years in a comfortable kennel.

"You and I both know what this looks like, Thomas. Who it looks like."

Thomas shuddered. In the distance, the bells of St Stephen's called the faithful to mass. In the rhythmic thuds of the bell, as though through ghostly echoes, he could hear the thunder of heavy boots, the blowing of whistles, the frantic calls for help.

"It's been nearly three years, sir," he said quietly. "And two hundred miles."

"The Yard always suspected he'd been nicked for something else and that's why he stopped carving up whores. What if he's been let out and decided to skip Whitechapel?"

Thomas gazed towards the entrance to the dock. A growing flotilla of merchant vessels lay at anchor, impatiently waiting permission to offload their cargoes. Sailors, like tiny sparrows at this distance, crowded the rigging and sheets, gazing towards Stanley Dock, no doubt gossiping eagerly about the nature of the delay.

"This can't get out," Thomas said. "We can't let the papers know."

"You won't be able to stop it, Thomas," Muldoon said with a note of sadness.

"You weren't there, sir," Thomas replied. "The newspaper boys made everything worse, stamping around, mucking up crime scenes, speculating and harassing witnesses. If we tell the papers that he is back and running amok in Liverpool, we'll have a full riot on our hands."

Muldoon sucked his teeth and sighed deeply. Then he fished out his pipe from his breast pocket, packed the bowl, and lit it. A cloud of aromatic smoke engulfed his head before being whisked away by the sea breeze.

"We'll tell them she was cut up by a pimp. They'll buy that, for the moment anyway. And we'll make our enquiries discreetly."

Thomas looked down at the corpse. He felt uneasy. There was something here beyond the usual evil.

"I don't know who did this," Thomas said, "And I don't know if it's that devil back from whatever purgatory he's been in for three years. But if it isn't him, then they've done a damn good job mimicking his handiwork."

Thomas looked up at Muldoon, his forehead wrinkled.

"If it's him, sir, or someone like him, she won't be the last."

"We can't put people on their guard without raising the alarm," Muldoon said.

"We can increase the night patrols around the docks," Thomas said, "And have a talk with the lads. They know the girls around here. They can keep an eye on them for us. Quietly."

"And Polly?"

"You say she worked up at the Adelphi?"

Muldoon nodded.

"I'll go and sniff around. Maybe she found her friend for the night among the guests. Someone might have seen them leave together."

Muldoon nodded, inhaled deeply on his cigar, and pointed towards the photographer.

"Go with Mr Watson back to the station house and wait for him to develop his photographs of the girl. Bring a couple of the cleaner ones to show around the staff and guests. With a little luck, it'll turn out to be some bastard come off a mail boat, on his way to America, and we can have him in the cells before sunset and in front of the beak by the morning."

"You don't really believe that, do you, sir?" Thomas asked. Muldoon chewed the end of his cigar thoughtfully.

"No," he said. "No, I don't."

Chapter Six

It really was a busy night. But such a release that I had a hard time keeping quiet. Surrounded by the sweet scent of the tobacco, I felt her struggle under my weight as I stuck the knife in. She tensed at the pain, my gloved hand across her mouth. Then I slit her throat for good measure. Then I made a start on the arms.

But I'm not completely satisfied. I didn't have time to finish. The footsteps of the watchmen outside the gates, the flicker of their lamps, distracted me. They think I'm lying in the dark, rutting against her belly, feeling her soft naked flesh contract not with pain but with disgust. I haven't used a woman like that for many years. Why would I? There's far more pleasure in the kill than in the ecstasy of carnal desire.

I take a leisurely stroll through one of the city's more affluent neighbourhoods, enjoying the leafy shade cast by the oak and birch that line the cobbled streets. The tall and slender brick houses fronted by wrought iron fences belong to the city's mercantile classes, to retired military officers, local politicians, novelists, and poets. The sidewalks are thronged with mothers and nannies taking their children and charges to the parks. I sidestep an older woman who walks arm in arm with her daughter. The daughter catches my eye. I stare back, perhaps too intently, and her mother catches my eye and frowns. I keep walking. Not a good hunting ground. Girls from good neighbourhoods are missed too quickly.

My ebony cane clicks rhythmically against the pavement. To an observer, I appear as any other gentleman. Perhaps those who glance in my direction think me a stockbroker or financier, out to enjoy the weak October sunshine.

Perhaps out to purchase a pastry or baked potato for lunch from one of the barrowmen who stand at every street corner.

Eventually, I settle myself at a table outside a coffee house on the corner of Faulkner Square. From my vantage point, I can see everyone entering and leaving the small, well-kept park that marks the centre of the square. When the black-jacketed waiter appears at my shoulder, I order an apéritif, a glass of absinthe. Expensive stuff, perhaps, and money is tight these days. But then again, I am a man of the world after all. And would life really be worth living if one could not sit and enjoy a fresh breeze while feeling the aniseed burning in the throat?

I look around at the ladies and gentlemen. At the drovers and carters who curse and shout, bringing goods throughout the city. The barrowmen and women with their carts. The flower girls catch my eye briefly. They carry bunches of posies down the street, and when they see a young couple, they stop and proffer their wares. It would be a cold-hearted gentleman indeed who would refuse to purchase a penny posy for his sweetheart, especially when offered by a sweet young flower girl, not yet ten years of age, with the large watery eyes of a young doe. The flower girls are tempting. But too young. There's less pleasure in the young. They go into shock too quickly and die too easily.

A couple of constables stroll past my seat, their hands behind their backs. One of them glances in my direction. I nod politely, and he returns my greeting with a lazy salute to his round blue helmet. I feel like laughing. Here I am, thinking of death and mutilation. And there he is, strolling along without a care in the world.

Still. Maybe I should take the night off. I have never seen the inside of a jail cell, much less stood before a judge or jury. Not even once. And all my experiences have taught me that patience and care are far more important than satisfying a passing fancy. I'll go out for a fine meal instead. I still have a few coins left in my pocket. After they run out, well. That is a problem for the future. For now, I want to drink my absinthe in peace and sit quietly watching the world pass by while I contemplate past glories.

* * *

It was past noon when Thomas finally arrived at the Adelphi hotel. One of the hotel's uniformed porters recognised him and bowed him into the foyer. Not many years ago, any constable or detective would not even have been tolerated on the front steps of the hotel. Instead, they would have been sent firmly to the staff entrance. But these days, after the police reforms in London, Manchester, Liverpool, and other major cities across the land, the local constabularies carry a great deal more clout.

Nevertheless, Thomas was barely halfway across the crowded foyer before his worn jacket, scratched leather boots, and dirtied shirt collar was noted, and he was intercepted by the hotel's concierge. He was a tall and gangly man, his thinning grey hair slathered across his scalp with liberal helpings of pomade. He had a rather thin and weedy moustache and, along with his weak chin and pale grey eyes, it gave him a distinctly hangdog appearance.

"Good afternoon, sir," Thomas said. "I'm Detective Sergeant Thomas O'Callaghan from Rose Hill."

Thomas held up his tattered warrant card, and the man's eyes widened.

"Please," the man said, "I must insist we speak in my office. There are guests present."

He gesticulated at the crowds of well-dressed patrons. Thomas looked around. There was certainly plenty of wealth on display. Well-fed stomachs strained behind embroidered silk vests, the chains of gold and silver pocket watches glinted in the light from the crystal chandeliers that illuminated the foyer. Women in heavy crinoline dresses in bright reds, blues, and greens made their stately way across the marble-tiled floors towards one of the hotel's three tearooms.

"And I insist that we speak here, sir," Thomas said. The man's attitude irked him. It reminded him of the days when he had been a young, untried and untested constable, looked down upon and harassed by every butler, housekeeper, and upper servant he had met in the line of duty. These men and women were often the products of the same tenements and slums as Thomas himself had been, but when they gained any status at all in the world, they kicked down at those who tried to clamber after them. They protected their wealthy superiors like loyal gundogs, and often a young constable needed to argue and threaten his way past a cadre of such people before he could speak to any member of the bourgeoisie.

The man opened his mouth to protest, but Thomas forestalled him by opening a leather satchel and drawing out one of Mr Watson's photographs.

"I believe you employ this woman," he said, holding up an image that showed the murdered girl's face. Thomas held the cardboard square in such a way that the fingers of his right hand obscured the obscene cut to the girl's throat. "Her name's Polly Wilkes." The concierge glanced at the picture and paled.

"She's one of the chambermaids," he said quietly, unable to tear his eyes away from the image. "But she's not come in to work today. I was just about to send someone around her house to look for her."

"Don't bother," Thomas said. "I'm afraid I have to tell you that she was murdered during the night."

"My sweet Lord, what happened?"

"We're not certain yet, sir," Thomas said noncommittally. "But I need to speak to any guest or staff member who may have seen her leave the hotel yesterday."

The man mentally shook himself, throwing off his initial shock and bridled.

"I'm afraid I cannot let you interrogate our guests, sir," he said.

"You misunderstand me, sir. I wasn't asking your permission," Thomas said. "What floor did she work on?"

The concierge looked around the foyer as though hoping that help would magically appear. Their raised voices and the man's obvious shock had attracted the attention of several porters as well as some of the guests standing closest.

"The fifth floor," he hissed between unmoving lips. "On the east wing."

"Thank you, sir," Thomas said, making a quick note in his small leather-bound notebook and making no effort to lower his voice. "I'll begin with the guests staying there."

"Please," the man continued, grasping Thomas by the shoulder. "You can't just stomp around here and harass my guests. Please contain your investigations to those staff members who worked with the poor girl, they knew her best. There's no need to make a scene in the hotel."

Thomas stared in disbelief at the man, suppressing an urge to thump him on the side of the head.

"You do realise, sir," he said, "That this young woman was brutally murdered? I believe I made that clear to you."

"Yes, yes," the concierge replied, waving a hand. "But what's done is done, and I must consider the comfort of our customers."

Thomas sighed inwardly. Any further conversation with the jumped-up little pettifogger was evidently a waste of time. He pushed past the man, heading for the grand staircase at the other end of the foyer, while privately vowing to order half a squad of the rudest, grimiest and most tactless constables he could find to conduct interviews in all of the hotel's tearooms, restaurants and common areas as soon as he got back to the station house.

He took the stairs three at a time, the concierge having given up on any notion of accompanying him. When he reached the fifth floor, Thomas was out of breath. He leaned against the polished copper stair rail, pulled out a handkerchief, and wiped his face.

The east wing of the fifth floor comprised five doors opening into well-appointed three or four-room suites, suitable for wealthy solo-travellers and families preparing for their journey across the Atlantic to America. No one replied at the first or second doors, the patrons having left their rooms to take tea downstairs, perhaps, or to explore the city. When he knocked at the third door, he heard a faint shuffling that told him that the room was still occupied.

He expected the door to be opened a crack so the occupant could see who was knocking, but instead, he heard a confident voice from inside the room call out.

"Enter."

He squared his shoulders and pushed the door open. The tall, arched windows were the first thing to catch his eye. They offered spectacular views over the city's rooftops, and from this height, the guests could see as far as the river, even identifying individual ships as they passed by. As he looked around, Thomas found his attention drawn to the only other person in the room, a tall woman sitting in a wingback armchair, one of two standing by a roaring fire, a book on her lap.

He blinked. Her eyes were deep-set and the clearest blue he had ever seen. Her skin was pale, with faint wrinkles around the eyes and in the corners of the mouth. Her lips were thin and slightly parted in surprise at his appearance. She wore a heavy, dark blue satin dress, and her hair was simply styled into a single plait down her back. She closed her book with a snap.

"Can I help you?" she asked, her expression turning from puzzlement to annoyance. He detected the slightly dulled tones of a Nordic accent hanging on her words. Danish, perhaps, or Norwegian, but not as lilting as the Swedes and Finns he sometimes met on the docks.

"Excuse me, miss," he said, standing to attention and touching his forelock. "I'm Detective Sergeant Thomas O'Callaghan from the Rose Hill station. I'm here to ask you about your chambermaid."

The young woman's expression did not change, but after a few moments, she gestured to the chair standing next to her.

"Please take a seat, sergeant?" she asked. Thomas smiled curtly and sat down. The woman glanced across the room towards a well-appointed bar cabinet standing between the two windows.

"Can I offer you a drink?" she asked. Thinking about the no doubt fine cognacs, whiskeys, and other liquors likely to occupy the cabinet, Thomas considered her offer briefly, but then he shook his head.

"No, miss, but thank you for the offer."

"How may I assist you?" she asked.

Thomas opened his folder to retrieve one of the illustrations depicting the head of the murdered girl, but as he did so, several of the cardboard squares slid out of the folder, landing on the floor. Thomas glanced down and realised to his horror that several of the sepia photographs depicted not just the head and features of the chambermaid, but her entire mutilated corpse, as well as details of her severed arms and the wounds across her body. He nearly fell out of his chair in his hurry to grab the little cardboard squares, but the woman got there first. She picked up one of them delicately between her thumb and forefinger, gazing intently at it.

"I beg your pardon, miss," Thomas said, his face blushing crimson, expecting the woman to scream in fright, perhaps even faint at the grisly sight. But to his surprise, her face did not betray any emotion. Instead, it was strangely cool and impassive.

"Poor girl," the woman said, staring intently at the photograph which showed the chambermaid as she had been found, nearly beheaded, disemboweled, and partially dismembered.

"Please, miss," Thomas pressed, grabbing an edge of the cardboard, trying to tug it out of the woman's hand. "Please don't look at these horrid things."

"I've seen horrors before," the woman said quietly, refusing to relinquish the cardboard square. "Even worse than this. I remember this girl. She ran me a bath yesterday afternoon. I'm afraid I was very tired after my journey, and I didn't pay her as much attention as perhaps I should have."

Thomas finally succeeded in retrieving the photograph, and the woman turned her crystalline gaze upon him. For the briefest of moments, he felt as though she could look through him, as though she was not looking merely at his skin and features, but right into his thoughts and inner feelings. Then she blinked, and the moment was gone.

"My name is Miss Steenberg," she said. "Miss Sophia Steenberg." She made no motion to extend her hand for Thomas to shake.

"Did you see anyone with the maid?" he asked. "Any other guest?"
Sofie shook her head.

"I was exhausted, as I said. I fell asleep early. I haven't left my room since I arrived yesterday afternoon. She pointed at a silver tray bearing empty plates, stands of condiments, and a carefully folded napkin. "I rang for one of the porters this morning to bring me breakfast. I wanted to spend the day catching up on some reading, I'm afraid it was a rather taxing crossing from Le Havre."

Thomas glanced at the book lying in Sofie's lap.

"*Histoire de la Medicine et des Doctrines Medicales*," he said, stuttering and mangling the French words. Sophia looked away to hide a brief smile. "A book about medicine?"

"Medicine and surgery, yes," she said.

"A strange topic to read about for pleasure," Thomas said.

"I am not reading for pleasure," Sofie said, "But for professional reasons."

"Oh?" Thomas said. "And what is your profession, miss?"

"I'm an anatomist and a trained surgeon."

Thomas blinked. He threw about for a reply to this unlikely statement.

"Indeed," he said lamely, "Perhaps those horrors you alluded to were related to your practice?"

Sofie smiled faintly. She rose to her feet and replaced the book in a small leather case.

"I trained at the Royal College of Medicine in Copenhagen," she said, "But I've spent the last three months working with Mademoiselle Madeline Brès in Paris. She's perhaps the world's foremost authority on the female anatomy, on childbirth, and the diseases of children."

She turned around, her head tilted to one side, and a faint smile playing around her lips.

"Have you ever been present at a birth, detective sergeant?" she asked.

Thomas was flustered and found himself stammering his reply.

"That would hardly be proper."

"Then I take it that you have not seen what happens when a birth goes wrong. Nor the steps that a surgeon must take to save the life of mother, child, or both?"

"I can't say that I have, miss."

"If you ever do, then you will understand what I mean by horrors. I'm hardly likely to be troubled by a photograph."

Thomas stood up. The young woman's supercilious attitude was irksome. He felt in her company, like a failing student in a school room.

"If you cannot provide any further information, miss," he said coldly, getting stiffly to his feet. "Then I believe I should take my leave."

"I wish you luck with your investigation, Detective Sergeant," Sophia said. "And I'm sorry I could not be of more help. I hope, for the girl's sake, that you find other, better witnesses."

For a few moments, Thomas remained standing irresolute in the middle of the room. Then he cleared his throat and turned towards the door. When he reached it, Sophia spoke again.

"The cuts are intriguing, Sergeant O'Callaghan," she said. "The symmetry between the placement of the two initial cuts to the shoulders betrays your murderer's expertise. I highly doubt that this is the first time he has conducted such work."

Thomas frowned, his hand on the door handle.

"I shall keep that in mind," he said.

"Please do, detective sergeant. And for the sake of those who dwell in your city, I hope you find the killer quickly. I fear that you may be dealing with a very disturbed mind."

Chapter Seven

Thomas looked around the crowded laundry room in the bowels of the Adelphi. The brick-built, high-ceilinged space was paved with sandstone slabs, permanently covered in a thin film of soapy water from the enormous copper basins which stood in ranks along the walls. A network of flues directed heat from a central boiler to the washtubs. Groups of women stood on wooden stools set at intervals around the tubs, using long birch paddles to agitate the boiling water. When they were finished, they fished out steaming sheets and pillowcases, transferring the soaking laundry to baskets to drain. When most of the scalding water had drained, they transferred the laundry to the other end of the room and onto wooden mangles. The mangles squeezed out any remaining water, and the damp laundry could then be hung up to dry before being ironed, folded, and delivered back up through dumbwaiters to storage cupboards located throughout the hotel.

The small group of young girls standing nervously in front of Thomas was all dressed in identical black dresses with starched white aprons and white lace mob caps. Some of the girls, those who had been closest to Polly Wilkes, wept quietly, their shoulders shuddering. Clouds of perfumed steam rolled across the room from the wash tubs. Thomas's cotton shirt stuck to his back. He looked down at his notebook.

"Did Polly often spend time with strange men?" he asked, trying his best to formulate his question in as delicate a manner as possible. One of the girls, the most brazen by the look of her, looked him straight in the eye.

"She'd a few gentleman friends," she said. "The pay isn't good here, and she had two baby brothers."

"I'm not here to pass judgment," Thomas said "Please believe me, ladies. I'm trying to find out who might have done such horrible things and bring them to justice. We don't want any other young girls coming to harm."

He looked intently at the group of girls. A few of them noticeably blanched at his words, and he made a mental note of their faces. Those were no doubt the girls who, like Polly, earned a few extra coppers by walking the docks at night. The initial shock of Polly's death had now been replaced by a fear for their own safety.

"Lots of girls do it," one of the crying girls said through sobs. "Polly wasn't bad, sir, honestly."

"I know," Thomas said, "But I need the truth. Tell me anything you saw. Did Polly leave yesterday with a guest from the hotel?"

The brazen girl looked around at the others. Then squared her shoulders and raised her head.

"Polly didn't go with guests, sir," she said. "Sometimes one of the gentlemen tries to get fresh, but if the concierge finds out, he'll kick us out. Polly needed the extra money, sir, but she didn't want to lose her position."

"So, she never went with hotel guests?"

"No, sir."

"Or stay with them in their rooms?"

The girls shook their heads.

"Did she have any regular customers that she told you about?" Thomas asked. The girls looked nervously at each other, glancing around the room as though afraid the walls would hear their words and report them to the hotel management.

"There was a young docker," the brazen girl said, "Polly said she liked him. She said he might ask her to go steady one day. I told her she was being silly."

Thomas smiled despite the seriousness of the situation.

"Do you have a name, miss?" he said.

"Kathleen," she said, "My name's Kathleen."

"And did Polly's customer have a name, too?"

Lilly hesitated. Thomas could sense the girl's calculation. With Polly dead, her customers would be looking elsewhere to satisfy their needs. But they could not do so if locked in a police cell undergoing interrogation.

"Kathleen?" Thomas pressed, and the girl cracked.

"Evans," she blurted out. "I don't know his first name, but Polly called him Evans."

"Good," Thomas said, making a note in his journal. "Any others?"

Gradually, with much hesitation, many covert glances and discussion among the girls, a list of some half a dozen names was produced.

"And these were regular gentlemen?" Thomas asked.

The girls nodded.

"But there were others?" he asked.

"Sometimes," Kathleen said, "Some nights she couldn't get any of her regulars, so she'd hang around by the docks until she found someone."

"Was she alone on the docks yesterday?"

The question hit the girls like a physical blow, and Thomas cursed inwardly. He should have spent more time talking around the issue rather than confronting it head-on. He lowered his voice.

"Listen, ladies," he said, "I know what's going on. I may be a bizzie, but I'm not a fool. I'm certain Polly wasn't the only one of you who spent a few nights a week on the docks. And to be blunt, I don't really care about all that. No, that's the honest truth. I'm only interested in finding the man who killed your friend. So please, be honest with me."

The small group of girls huddled around. Snippets of their whispered conversation rose above the general hubbub in the laundry room, and eventually, they turned their attention back to Thomas.

"Sometimes we went with her," Kathleen said noncommittally.

"And last night?"

"I was with her for a few hours after work," Kathleen said, her hard stare seemingly daring Thomas to judge or mock her.

"And then?"

"I left for a while," she said, "And when I came back, she was gone. I thought she must have found a gentleman and taken him somewhere."

"Did she often take her gentlemen to Stanley Dock?" Thomas asked. He registered the shock flitting across Kathleen's face.

"Y-yes," she stammered. "Always. The watchmen let us in, and if someone cuts up rough, they come and help us out."

"Did that happen often?"

Kathleen looked down. Several of the girls stared intently at their feet.

"Sometimes," she said quietly. Thomas sensed a yawning chasm opening up in the conversation. The unspoken words seemed to pull at him. They made him feel quite as uncomfortable as the Danish woman he had interviewed in her suite.

"Well," he said, "Last night, they weren't there to help Polly."

"Sir," one of the girls said timidly, stepping out of the line of maids. "What'll become of her brothers?"

"Didn't she have parents?" Thomas asked.

"Her dad was lost at sea," Kathleen said, "And her mum died last winter. Consumption."

For a long moment, only the creak of the heavy mangles and the thudding splashes of the paddles stirring the wash tub could be heard. Then Thomas sighed and closed his notebook.

"I won't lie to you," he said to the huddled girls. "I don't know what'll become of them. The orphanage, maybe, or the workhouse. If they're not too old, maybe some neighbours can take them in."

"I live next to Polly, sir," Kathleen said. "I'll ask my mum for help."

Thomas nodded. He knew that the outcome was almost certainly preordained. There was great poverty in the city, and no poor household needed more mouths to feed. If their father had indeed been a sailor, then the little boys would most likely end up in the Liverpool Seaman's Orphanage in Newsham Park, a large gothic manor house set in the middle of a vast estate on the city's eastern boundary. There were worse places, Thomas knew. The orphans housed at Newsham were mostly well-cared for, and the many shipowners, captains, and merchants who relied on a steady stream of sailors to crew their vessels were often generous to the institution. The Newsham boys became a family of sorts, many of them seeking out a life at sea once they left the orphanage, following in the footsteps of their deceased fathers.

"I want to thank you, ladies," Thomas said, closing his notebook and straightening up. "Thank you for your honesty."

He turned to leave but then stopped. He thought carefully for a few moments and then turned back to the girls. When he spoke, he did so slowly, carefully, and in measured tones.

"I do not need to know who of you works as Polly did. But I want you to listen to me carefully. We do not yet know who killed her. But a killer who could do something so heinous to one girl can do it again to another. If you know any girls who make it a habit to walk the docks at night, then can I suggest you tell them how important it is not to go with men they don't know, and to stay together in groups as much as possible."

He looked intently at Kathleen. A lock of her black hair escaped from under the mob cap, and she tugged it away with an irritated gesture. He knew how feeble and hollow his warnings must sound. A girl like that could not decide her customer freely. She could only decide whether to work or not to work. And if she did not work, then she could starve. He knew that, despite his warnings, a handful of the girls would be down on the docks after nightfall, each one placing themselves in danger for the sake of bread, meat, and perhaps a pint or two of gin.

Thomas found himself growing steadily angrier as he left the laundry, walked up a narrow set of wooden stairs, and emerged into the splendour of the hotel's foyer. The gilded statues, the marble flooring, the granite pillars that supported the soaring domed glass ceiling mocked him. Such wealth and beauty, and yet down a single flight of chipped stairs were girls who were forced to debase themselves to make a decent living.

A trip by growler across the city from the Adelphi to Rose Hill had not mollified Thomas's mood. He barged into the station house, his features stony, his muscles taught as though readying himself for a fight. He took off his tatty brown Homburg hat and flung it on his desk. He looked across the crowded watch room and caught the eye of the desk sergeant.

"You look in fine spirits, sir," Sergeant Fraser said with a twisted smile.

"I'm in no mood for pleasantries, Fraser," Thomas snapped. "Where's the detective inspector?"

Fraser leaned forward, placing his elbows on the desk and looking questioningly at Thomas.

"He's down in the cells with the coroner," he said. "They brought that young piece of skirt in about an hour ago."

"Her name was Polly," Thomas said.

"As you say, sir," Fraser said. "She looked cut up pretty bad."

Fraser's eyes were narrowed as he looked at the detective sergeant. Thomas knew what he was going to ask, as if the question already hung heavy and toxic in the air between them like smog from a factory furnace.

"Is it him, sir?" Fraser asked.

Thomas looked hard at the old desk sergeant while he contemplated his reply. Then he leaned in close to Fraser's scarred cauliflower ear.

"We don't know, Fraser, and that's the honest truth. I know the lads are already gossiping, but I don't want that gossip reaching the papers. There's no need to start a panic in the city until we're certain."

"And how're you going to be certain, sir?" Fraser asked. "Wait for him to send a letter like last time?"

"If it's him, then she won't be the last," Thomas said. "We'll be certain when we find the next one."

"Well then," Fraser said, standing up straight, his large ruddy face suddenly flushed with a determined anger. "What should we do, sir?"

Thomas looked at the old custody officer. Fraser was blunt and blustering, sarcastic and at times a bully to some of the younger constables, especially those who cheeked him or tried to skive off early and head home. But he was as solid as they came, equal parts scoundrel and copper, existing in that grey zone where the best policework was done.

"Talk to the constables," Thomas said, "Tell them to keep their gossip to themselves. They need to keep sharp, and alert, and I want double patrols along the docks."

"Yessir," Fraser said, standing to attention. "I'll get out the word."

Thomas patted the officer on the shoulder.

"I'll go and see the detective inspector," he said, turning away from the front desk and making his way through the mismatched furniture littering the watch room. He sensed the constables throwing covert glances in his direction, though none of them had the courage to confront him. The room breathed a sigh of relief when the door to the cells closed behind him.

Thomas made his way down the narrow stone steps leading to a small antechamber occupied by a single desk. The constable on guard sat with his boots on the scuffed table surface, his face hidden behind a broadsheet. Thomas said nothing but pushed the man's feet off the desk as he passed. Two corridors led off from the antechamber from opposite walls. Cells, some large and some small enough to house only a single prisoner, led off from each corridor. The cells were little more than bare stone chambers with tiny window slits along the ceiling opening up to the street outside. Paillasses stuffed with mouldy straw, and cracked brass washbasins were the only furniture, and the only light came from oil lamps hanging from the corridor's ceiling.

Only half the cells along the west corridor were full. The prisoners were docile enough, influenced perhaps by the sudden pall of anxiety that had infected the station house. In the two larger cells, the prisoners sat in groups whispering together, looking up furtively as Thomas passed.

"Looks like someone cut her up good," a voice said as Thomas passed the last cell on the block. He glanced sideways and saw that the prisoner held in the cell was staring straight at him, an indolent expression in his deep-set dark eyes. Thomas thought for a moment and then plucked the man's identity from memory. The man was known only as Buttons, his Christian name most likely only found in the records of some orphanage or institution. He had earned his nickname as a boy from his first job as a buttoner, a swindler who put on rigged games of chance in the street, known as "running buttons" in the criminal underworld.

"Looks like it, Buttons," Thomas said. "Aren't you getting sick of spending so much time in my cells?"

Buttons stretched out on his paillasse, his legs crossed, looking for all the world like a well-to-do tourist enjoying the sun at a resort on the French

Riviera.

"The food could be better," he admitted. "But at least it's out of the rain, and warm enough when that lazy bugger you've got on guard duty remembers to put coal in the stove."

Thomas smiled despite himself.

"I guess you don't know anything that could help us catch whoever did this, Buttons?" he asked, knowing with certainty the reply.

"I don't know nothing," he and Buttons said at the same time, and Buttons grinned wickedly.

"That's right, detective," he said. "You're learning."

"I figured scoundrels like you out a long time ago," Thomas said, turning away from the crook and opening the heavy iron door at the end of the block.

The door led to a large, low-ceilinged room, lit by oil lamps and candles set in mismatched saucers and holders on every surface. One side of the room was hidden behind a heavy black linen curtain, and, from behind it, he could hear the photographer Mr Watson moving about, slowly and methodically developing his little rolls of cellulite. The stench of the chemicals he used hung heavily in the air, but could not entirely suppress the stench of death and decay emanating from the other half of the room. It did serve as a dead room, a place to conduct autopsies and temporarily store those unfortunates who had died in public places, until their remains could be claimed by families or by church officials.

Detective Inspector Muldoon looked up at the sound of the door. He was standing beside an elderly and finely dressed gentleman with bushy white mutton chops and a pair of gold-rimmed pince-nez balanced carefully on the tip of his rather bulbous nose.

"Thomas," Muldoon said with a mixture of irritation and relief, "You'll be pleased to know that your arrival was preceded by a messenger from the Adelphi Hotel. The hotel management wishes to make a formal complaint about your behaviour and comportment while on their premises."

Thomas tried to suppress a smirk. Muldoon's expression was serious, his face drawn, but there was a twinkle in his eyes which Thomas knew well.

"I beg your pardon, sir," he said contritely. "I must work on my manners."

"See that you do," Muldoon said, turning away from Thomas. "In the meantime, please join us."

He stepped aside, leaving a space for Thomas. Thomas took it and looked down at the corpse. The young girl had been laid out on her back on the heavy slate slab the coroner used due to its ability to hold the cold. Prior to the arrival of the body, the slab had been covered in blocks of ice purchased from a nearby icehouse, and even now, with the ice removed, the slate steamed in the warmer air.

"Please, Doctor Pettigrew," Inspector Muldoon said, nodding to the coroner. "Give us the benefit of your experience."

Emmanuel Lovell Pettigrew had worked as a coroner and surgeon in the city for close to four decades, and in this time, he had seen every depravity of the human condition, every injury that man could inflict upon man. But the partially dismembered young girl had nevertheless shocked the old sawbones to his core. He had felt unable to begin his investigation of her hardening flesh before closing her eyes, so that she could not see the indignity which he would wreak on her body with his scalpels, pliers, and forceps.

"The injuries to the body are extensive," he began, clearing his throat. "Somewhat self-evident, I know, but gentlemen, I confess myself somewhat lost for words."

"Which injury killed her?" Thomas asked. The doctor pointed a scalpel towards the throat.

"The wound to the throat is so deep that she would have bled out in a few seconds, a minute or two at most. There is also an injury to the side," he pointed again to a long, thin wound, like a tightly closed eye weeping blood, "located between the third and fourth rib. The wound punctured a lung, and I believe it was inflicted pre-mortem."

"And yet no one heard her scream," Inspector Muldoon mused.

"Ah," Doctor Pettigrew said, leaning over the girl's face. "I may be able to offer an explanation."

He reached into his black medical bag and drew out a small pair of pliers.

With one hand, he levered open the girl's mouth, gazing into it thoughtfully. Then he used the pliers to extract a small piece of black material which had been lodged on the back of one of Polly's small lower teeth. The doctor placed the material in a little tin bowl.

"I noted this during my initial examination of the body. I believe it to be a small fragment of leather," he said.

"She was gagged?" Thomas asked.

"I doubt it," the doctor replied. "There's no evidence of any contusions on the face which we would expect had she been tied or gagged."

"A glove then," Thomas said. "The killer held a gloved hand over her mouth and nose, smothering her screams. She must have tried to bite the killer's hand."

"But only managed to tear off a small piece of leather from his glove," Muldoon interjected.

"Damn risky," Thomas said. "With watchmen right outside the warehouse. What if she had managed to throw off his hand, they would have been there before he could get away."

"Your killer did not work quickly," the coroner said, pointing to the cuts which had separated the young girl's arms from her body. "The disarticulation and dismemberment would have taken time. Perhaps as much as half an hour."

"During which time the watchmen could have arrived at any moment," Thomas said, his tone almost impressed despite himself.

The coroner nodded and continued.

"In addition to the cut throat and the wound to the side, the most noticeable injuries are the dismemberments," His tone was dispassionate, but Thomas could tell that the old man was more rattled by the spectacle in front of him than he was willing to show. "The technical term is shoulder disarticulation. The murderer cut the skin, the tendons and muscles underneath, and laid bare the joints between the humerus and the scapula. Breaking the arms upwards, he then removed the humerus from its socket and cut through the last remaining skin and tendons holding them to the torso."

"Like breaking down a chicken for supper," Muldoon said, shaking his head. "I've never seen anything like it."

Thomas and Inspector Muldoon glanced at one another. The examination of the wounds had confirmed a shared suspicion. The brazenness of the act, the cruelty, and the bloodthirsty injuries were terrifyingly reminiscent of an old phantom. Both of their gazes now moved, as though controlled by an external force, to the most noticeable injury, and, in their minds, perhaps the most indicative.

"And her abdomen," Muldoon prompted. Doctor Pettigrew sucked air through his tightly clenched teeth as he rested the tip of his scalpel on the mound of grey and purple intestines which had been pulled from the girl's stomach cavity and placed between her legs.

"Quite unusual," he said. "I must admit, I've never seen anything like it. At least not in person," he clarified, his glance flickering to Thomas' impassive face. "A single cut across the stomach, long enough to allow the entrails to be pulled out in their entirety."

"And her organs?" Thomas asked. "Are any of her organs missing?"

Doctor Pettigrew froze. Then he slowly straightened up and looked straight at Thomas.

"Her kidney is still present, sergeant," he said. "If that's what you're asking."

"And the other organs?"

"All still in place."

Thomas breathed deeply.

"It doesn't prove or disprove anything, Thomas," Muldoon said quietly. "He wasn't consistent between his victims. Remember Mary Kelly."

Thomas nodded. As if he could ever forget her. She had been the reason he had sought a transfer back to the Liverpool Constabulary. Four years in the nation's capital, four years that had seen him learn more about policing than he would have learnt in a lifetime in Liverpool or Manchester. Four years, which he felt coming to an end the moment he stepped into the dinghy ground-floor room in Miller's Court and saw the grotesquely mistreated form lying on a narrow bed. Her injuries had been more extensive, more gruesome than any others inflicted by the monster which the broadsheets had referred to first as the Whitechapel Killer, then as Leather Apron, and finally as Jack the Ripper.

Thomas nodded.

"Please continue, doctor," he said. The coroner gazed at the sergeant for a long moment before continuing.

"As I said, there was no attempt made to remove the organs or even to damage them."

"Are there any other wounds?" Thomas asked, "Especially around the groin?"

Doctor Pettigrew shook his head.

"The only other wounds inflicted on the body are these."

He pointed with the tip of his scalpel to two finely incised wounds running from the top of both thighs almost parallel to the tight cluster of curls covering the girl's pudenda. Inspector Muldoon leaned closer and frowned.

"Those are not very deep," he said.

"You are quite correct, sir," the coroner said. "And I must admit that their purpose confounds me. They strike me almost as a perverse decoration."

"They must have had a purpose," Thomas said. "Even if it is not apparent to us, there must have been a purpose."

"With a madman, who can say?" Doctor Pettigrew said. He crossed to a low workbench and rinsed his hands in a copper basin. "I'm afraid that's all I can say on the matter. I can tell you how the poor girl was killed, but the 'who' and the 'why' is up to you fine gentlemen. But I will say one thing."

"Yes?"

"I do not believe that such work could have been conducted by an Englishman," Pettigrew said, his back still turned.

Thomas frowned.

"What do you base this on, doctor?" he asked.

Pettigrew turned and frowned.

"The injuries bring to mind certain rituals rumoured to still be carried out in parts of Africa and the Far East. Given that this city is home to plenty of individuals born in such places…"

"Thank you, doctor," Muldoon said with an air of finality. "We'll bear that in mind, although with thousands of foreign sailors arriving in the port every day, this may not help much to narrow down our list of suspects."

Pettigrew shrugged and crossed to a high chair where he had hung his jacket. He began to pull it on when a thought struck Thomas. He glanced towards the cuts that had severed Polly's arms.

"Before you go, Doctor," he said: "Would you indulge me."

"I am at your disposal, Sergeant," the coroner replied, turning back to the corpse.

"These wounds," Thomas pointed with his pencil to the cuts. "Would you say that they have been placed carefully?"

The coroner frowned.

"I'm afraid I don't take your meaning, sergeant?"

"I mean, do they appear symmetrical and careful in their placement?"

The coroner, with an annoyed gesture, took out a pair of callipers from his surgical kit and bent over the body. He measured the distance from both cuts to the centre of the throat, the delicate divot that denoted the meeting point of the clavicles.

"Seven and a quarter inch precisely," the doctor muttered as he straightened up. "The wounds are placed with precise symmetry. May I ask how on earth you knew that sergeant?"

Thomas frowned.

"Call it a hunch," he said. Doctor Pettigrew glanced at Muldoon, who shrugged. Then the doctor turned away, packed his surgical kit, and left the two detectives standing in the gloom of the basement, by the side of Polly Wilkes' abused corpse. As soon as the door closed behind the coroner, Muldoon turned to Thomas.

"Would you care to offer me a more fulsome explanation, Thomas?" he said, a stern note in his voice. "I've seen hunches, and good ones. This was something else."

Thomas felt nervous, for the first time in many years, in the detective inspector's company. He could not explain his hesitation, but he knew that he did not yet want Muldoon to know the entire truth. He settled instead for the well-tried method of telling his superior mostly the truth.

"I'm not certain, sir," he said. "One of the guests at the Adelphi suggested it to me. A surgeon."

Muldoon's eyes widened.

"You showed photos of the poor girl to one of the guests?!" he exploded. "No wonder the owners want your head!"

"It was an accident," Thomas said, brushing the accusation aside. "I didn't intend it. But this surgeon spotted something from a simple photograph that our coroner didn't notice until I drew his attention to it."

Muldoon was still bristling with anger, but Thomas' steady gaze gradually deflated the older man's ire.

"Well then," he said. "What do you suggest we do about it?"

"I would like to invite this surgeon to come here and take a look at the girl before she's carted off. Perhaps more can be learned, and surely two sets of trained eyes are better than one."

Muldoon sighed deeply.

"Unconventional," he said. "And Pettigrew will blow a gasket if he ever finds out. But I suppose you're right." Then he frowned again, an expression of sudden suspicion falling across his distended features.

"You say this guest is a surgeon," he said. "And do they happen to live in one of the rooms where Polly worked?"

"Yes," Thomas said, knowing instantly what direction his superior's train of thought had taken.

"Well then," Muldoon said slowly. "Perhaps you should invite this surgeon down here. Let him examine the body, by all means. But while he does, be careful to keep your eye on him."

"I certainly will, sir," Thomas said and turned away from the detective inspector to hide his smile.

Chapter Eight

Thomas strolled past the soaring neo-Classical frontage of St George's Hall with its bronze equestrian statues of Victoria and her late husband, Albert. He noted with pleasure the heavy police presence, which was already growing apparent. Pairs of constables patrolled down the broad boulevard or stood on street corners, casually observing the masses of humanity that spilled from the Lime Street Railway Station. The visitors went on foot, in carriages, or packed tightly into one of the horse-drawn trolleys running from the centre of the city all the way to the suburbs and down to the river.

A small knot of uniformed constables stood in the lee of two vast granite columns that fronted the entrance to the Lime Street terminus. Known affectionately as the Candlesticks, the columns had been added to the front of the building during a major expansion nearly four decades earlier. More track and train sheds were added every few years to accommodate the exponentially rising numbers of passenger and goods trains arriving and departing from the city.

Thomas raised his hand in a lazy salute. The men hurriedly packed away the pipes they had been stuffing and stood to attention. Thomas jogged across the street, earning a loud tirade of curses from a carter who had to pull up his span of horses to avoid running him down.

Thomas' height allowed him to see over the heads of the people thronging the sidewalks. His disfigured ear lent him a roguish appearance which more than once caused a careful mother to grab her children by the hand and steer them across the street to avoid him. He had grown used to this reaction. Rather than grow bitter or angry, he smiled or winked at the nervous mothers, who usually grew flustered and embarrassed at the attention. As he arrived at the small square which fronted the Adelphi Hotel, he spotted an old acquaintance in the crowd.

"Careful how you go, Skittles," he said loudly, stepping close behind the young boy, not yet ten years old, who still had his back turned. His attention was focused on a well-dressed gentleman dangling a silver pocket-watch from his white-gloved hand. The boy was focused as intently on the treasure as a shark making a final run at its prey. At Thomas's words, the boy jumped and turned quickly. When he recognised Thomas, his face broke into a broad grin.

"Afternoon, sergeant," he said. "How's tricks?"

"Don't give me that tosh," Thomas said, trying to suppress a grin. "I thought we'd had a talk about you and your thieving ways."

The boy's eyes widened, and he held up his hands in a gesture of supreme innocence.

"What do you mean, sir?" he asked in a hurt voice.

Thomas cuffed him around the head, carefully wiping his hand on his trousers after touching the boy's greasy, louse-infested locks.

"Come now, Skittles. Are you really telling me you weren't planning on dipping that toff's thimble?" Thomas asked, nodding in the direction of the intended mark and slipping into the patois of the city's urchins.

Skittles shook his head firmly, his locks flying about his face. Thomas knew the boy well. And knew him well enough not to trust him an inch. Skittles was one of the city's best thimble-twisters, pickpockets who specialised in unhooking pocket watches from their chains either with nimble fingers or small pliers. The lad had only been caught once, when he had tried to lift Thomas' own battered pocket watch and suddenly found himself pressed against a wall, his arm twisted around behind his back and Thomas' friendly voice telling him that if he tried that again, the price would be a finger.

"Be fair, sergeant," Skittles said with an entirely unconvincing look of wounded innocence. "I was just watching the fine ladies and gents."

"You see that you don't do anything more than watch them," Thomas said, waving a finger theatrically in front of the young boy's face.

"What're you doing down here anyway?" Skittles asked cheekily. "I thought you'd all be down by Stanley Dock, figuring out who cut up that bit of skirt."

Thomas was not surprised. Rumours travelled through the city's underworld faster than any telegraph service. Those men held overnight or for a few hours in the cells while they slept it off, or until a fine could be paid, would overhear the constables talking, and as soon as they were back on the streets, they would tell anyone who would listen their news. Thomas fished out his pocket watch and glanced at it. Not even three o'clock yet. The girl had been discovered less than eight hours ago, and the story was already making the rounds. No doubt with embellishments and speculations added at every re-telling.

"Keep it quiet, Skittles," he said. "It's not a good tale to be telling around."

Skittles looked serious for a moment, a rare feature on the boy's usually carefully crafted carefree face.

"They say it's bad," he said. "Worse'n bad."

"They're not wrong, my lad," Thomas said, fishing a penny out of his vest pocket. "Get yourself a warm bowl of scouse for dinner and don't let me catch you staring at pocket watches again."

"I must say, Sergeant O'Callaghan, you keep strange company." Thomas and Skittles looked around in unison. Sophia Steenberg was making her way towards them through the crowd, amused puzzlement on her face. Unlike many of the other women in the square, she did not carry a flimsy lace umbrella to shield herself from the sharp glare of the sinking autumn sun. She wore more muted colours than he had seen her wear earlier in the day. Her broad skirt was in a light-grey material which seemed to shimmer in the light, the dress bordered by a geometric band reminiscent of the patterns he had seen on Greek vases displayed in the city museum. She wore a tight black jacket over the dress, buttoned up to her neck, and a feathered hat, perched atop her braided blonde hair, secured with a leather strap.

"Good afternoon, miss," Thomas said, nodding formally to her. She did not reply but glanced down at Skittles. The young street urchin was grinning from ear to ear, evidently under the impression that he had interrupted Thomas on his way to a romantic rendezvous.

"Are you not going to introduce me to your friend, Sergeant?" Sophia said, arching her eyebrows. Thomas frowned.

"Miss Sophia Steenberg," he said in Skittles' general direction. "Allow me to introduce Master Skittles, an expert pickpocket of my acquaintance who will be leaving now."

He stared hard at the young boy who bowed with comical exaggeration to the new arrival. This was evidently too much for the Danish surgeon, who burst out laughing.

"A pleasure to make your acquaintance, sir," she said, curtseying to the urchin.

"Run along now, lad," Thomas growled, and Skittles, knowing when not to push his luck, vanished as if by magic into the crowd. Thomas turned to Sophia, his expression grim. The smile faded from her lips.

"I've come to ask you a favour," he said. "A favour of a rather delicate nature."

Sophia looked around surreptitiously. Their position in front of the stairs was creating a blockage of guests entering and leaving the hotel. She reached out and grabbed his arm.

"Perhaps we should take a stroll together, sergeant," she said. "And you can elaborate."

They walked arm in arm down the stairs and across the square, Thomas leading them back along the boulevard towards St George's Hall and the labyrinth of alleys that led to the Rose Hill station house.

"Earlier today, I showed you a photograph of the murdered girl, Polly Wilkes," Thomas said.

"I'm not likely to forget that photograph in a hurry," Sophia said.

"You made an observation about the cuts to the poor girl's upper body, the cuts that severed her arms."

Sophia narrowed her eyes and clicked her teeth in contemplation.

"Yes," she said finally after several moments of silence. "Yes, I remember those now. Remarkably symmetrical and carefully placed. Clearly not made by some thug with a switchblade."

"Our coroner has examined the remains of the girl, and he concurs with your assessment. They are indeed entirely symmetrically placed. To within a fraction of an inch, in fact."

Sophia did not respond, but a brief satisfied smile flittered across her face. Thomas frowned. Certainly, the young woman could not be satisfied with the gruesome death of the young girl, he thought. But perhaps her professional pride had been validated by the coroner's measurements.

"What I'm asking, miss," he continued. "Is for you to accompany me back to the Rose Hill station house and conduct a personal examination of the girl's remains."

Sophia stopped abruptly, nearly pulling Thomas about. He looked at her and saw that her eyes had widened in surprise.

"You surprise me, Sergeant. Why would you think I could contribute further information beyond what your coroner has already learned?"

Thomas spent several moments formulating his response. Even this brief conversation with the Nordic surgeon had allowed him some insight into her personality. She was undoubtedly intelligent, far more so than he himself was. And she was proud. But the pride in her skill and intellect, as with many clever and skilful people, also contained the seeds which could grow into a weakness, a point where pressure could be applied to control or persuade.

"Our coroner did not pay any particular attention to the nature of those wounds until I asked him to investigate them closely. That leads me to think that there may perhaps be other injuries, small details easily missed, which he failed to register in his examination."

"Details which you believe me capable of identifying?" Sophia asked.

"Yes," Thomas said. "I could order you to accompany me, of course. You are in my city, and I am an officer of the law. But I much prefer to be civil and ask you simply, for the sake of the poor girl, if not mine, to devote some of your time to this endeavour."

A trolleybus rumbled past, the footfalls of the shire horse pulling it thundering against the cobbles. Sophia's sudden smile was almost unnerving.

"I would be honoured to render assistance if I can," she said graciously.

"Thank you," Thomas said, for the first time smiling with genuine pleasure at his new acquaintance. Sophia noticed that when he smiled, his brown eyes twinkled warmly.

The remainder of their stroll through the centre of the city was conducted in silence as the Danish surgeon gazed around at the landmarks. The two of them looked for all the world like a married couple out to take the late afternoon air, but when they approached the Rose Hill station, Thomas felt a pang of nervous anxiety. He hoped that the detective inspector would be in his office away from the main watch room, but even in his absence, Thomas' plan required them to move quickly down to the cellars.

"Miss, I must give you some instructions before we arrive," he said as they approached the squat brick building. He pulled her into a side alley, barely wide enough for the two of them to stand across from each other. He glanced across to the station house. Stone steps led up to the door, which was kept wide open at all times to show the population that the force was always vigilant and present. A lantern hung from a rusted iron chain, its light illuminating the small crowd of constables hanging about on the stairs, smoking and chatting quietly.

"Please walk quickly," he said. "If someone asks your business, ignore them. You're my guest and do not need to explain your presence to any of the constables."

Sophia's smile was twisted, and her tone sardonic.

"How very exciting, sergeant," she said. "I feel like I'm taking part in a Penny Dreadful."

Thomas did not reply. Instead, he focused on the door. He half-guided, half-pulled her out of the alley and walked towards the station house door. He sped up as he reached the stairs, barging through the constables, Sophia behind him. He was halfway across the watch room before Sergeant Fraser looked up. The old Scot opened his mouth, but a look from Thomas made him close it again.

Thomas threw open the door to the basement, and he and Sophia rushed down the stairs, past the constable on guard in the anteroom, and down the cell block. The rustle of crinoline had an almost magnetic force on the prisoners. Their heads jerked around, and before the detective and his guest were halfway down the corridor, the jeers and catcalls started. One of the convicts reached through the bars, but a swift kick from Thomas' heavy boots forced his hand back. Thomas opened the door to the dead room, standing aside to let Sophia pass through before following her and closing the door behind him.

The stillness of the room washed over him like a cooling breeze, and he exhaled deeply. The scent of decay in the room had increased noticeably since his last visit. He tweaked aside the dark room curtain, but the space behind it was deserted. The steady drip of water running off slowly warming slate drew his eye to the corpse of the girl. Sophia had already approached. She was standing by Polly's head, a mixture of concern and fascination on her face.

"Merciful God," she said. "She looks much worse in person, doesn't she?" Thomas nodded.

"Do you need more light?" he asked. He did not wait for Sophia to reply but grabbed one of the oil lamps standing on the workbenches, which lined the room, and carried it to the slab. He put it down with a dull thud and turned up the flame. The flickering light sent strange shadows rippling across the girl's naked skin, skin that had long lost any vibrancy and life. She looked like one of the waxworks on display on Marleybone Road in the galleries of the fabled Madame Tussauds.

Thomas stepped back, giving Sophia space to walk around the corpse. She moved slowly, her face never leaving the body, her eyes barely blinking as she observed every detail.

"Scalpel," she said quietly. It took Thomas a moment to realise that she was requesting such an instrument. Flustered, he moved to the workbench and picked up one of the coroner's scalpels. She reached out a hand blindly, and he placed the knife in her hand. She gently probed the edges of the shallow cuts on the girl's thighs. Then she applied a little pressure, enough to lever the cut open by the merest fraction of an inch.

"These are guiding incisions," she said with a frown. "Preliminary cuts made at the start of a surgical procedure. Observe here," she waved Thomas closer with her left hand and pointed to the wound. "The murderer has cut through the epidermal and dermal layers but has stopped short of cutting into the fatty tissue and muscles."

"Why?" Thomas asked. "For what purpose?"

"At a guess," Sophia said. "I would say that whoever your killer is, he—or indeed she—used two blades. These cuts are made with a scalpel, similar to this one. But the cuts that severed her arms were made with a much heavier blade, something more akin to a Liston knife."

Thomas nodded.

"I think I know the type," he said. "Heavy, with a long and straight blade."

"Indeed. Ideal for removing limbs and cutting through muscles and fibres."

"Could such a knife have made this wound?" he asked, pointing to the long and narrow wound between the girl's ribs.

"Absolutely. The wound is too long for any kind of scalpel, and there are tough muscles between the ribs. Perforating them would have required a wickedly sharp blade and one long enough to reach the lungs or the heart."

Thomas looked back to the wounds on Polly's thighs.

"I still don't understand," he said. "Why make these incisions at all?"

Sophia hesitated, then cleared her throat.

"If I had to guess, sergeant, and please do realise that this is merely a guess, I would say that this poor girl was only partway through her indignities when she was discovered."

Thomas stood in stunned silence.

"You mean that the killer intended to dismember her legs as well?"

"Yes," Sophia said. "I believe that he began with the arms, you can see the traces of guiding incisions by the edge of the shoulder here," she pointed towards Polly's right shoulder. "He killed her first with the Liston knife and probably used it to cut her throat." As she spoke, Sophia moved the scalpel in her right hand from Polly's side to her neck, its sharp edge catching the light of the oil lamp and glittering malevolently. "Then he used a lighter scalpel to make the guiding incisions and to disembowel her. Then he dismembered her arms."

"At which point he was interrupted."

"Yes," Sophia said.

"She was discovered by a watchman," Thomas mused. "Perhaps the steps of the approaching guard spooked the killer." He suddenly blanched. "My God," he muttered. "He might have been gone only a few minutes when the guard found her. We might have missed him by mere moments."

Sophia looked sadly at him.

"It was too late for Polly in any case," she said in an unusually comforting tone. Thomas shook his head. If the watchmen had alerted the constables just a little sooner.

The sound of approaching footsteps from the corridor outside brought Thomas sharply back to reality. He turned around to face the door in time to see it thrown open. Detective Inspector Muldoon barged into the room, followed closely by the coroner. Thomas could not remember seeing the usually so docile detective inspector looking more outraged.

"Thomas!" he exploded. "What in the name of the Devil himself is going on?"

"Sir…" Thomas began, but Muldoon had glanced past him, spotted Sophia still holding the scalpel, watching the police officers with a detached curiosity.

"Hell's bells, Thomas," Muldoon roared. "What is this woman doing in my dead house?" Muldoon turned to Sophia, took in the quality of her fine crinoline dress, and lowered his voice. "Begging your pardon, miss," he said coldly, "I believe that my sergeant has overstepped his boundaries by a considerable margin."

"I would be grateful, madam," Doctor Pettigrew said icily. "If you could replace my scalpel on the table." Sophia's eyes narrowed. She lowered the scalpel but made no move to lay it back in its place.

"Detective inspector," Thomas said urgently. "Please listen to me. Miss Steenberg is an educated woman, a trained anatomist and surgeon. I found her insight into the case compelling; that is why I asked your permission to bring her."

Muldoon scowled, his bulbous nose vibrating as he fought to contain his temper.

"You know very well what you did, Thomas," he said quietly. "If you had told me that you were bringing some woman, a foreigner no less, into my dead house, I would never have permitted it."

"And we would have lost valuable insight," Thomas said, his own voice rising angrily. "Please, sir, just listen to what she has to say."

"Where were you trained?" Pettigrew cut in, looking hard at Sophia.

"I received my license to practice medicine from the Danish Royal College of Medicine," Sophia said stiffly. "And I was tutored in surgical techniques by Professor Christian Fenger."

Pettigrew narrowed his eyes.

"Fenger," he said. "That is surprising."

"Do you know this man?" Muldoon said, turning away from Thomas in disgust.

Pettigrew hesitated.

"Yes," he said grudgingly. "Or I should say. I know of him. He is a Danish anatomist and pathologist. I've heard that he's now one of the leading physicians in Chicago."

"He's not some fabrication, then?" Muldoon said, a note of disappointment in his voice.

"I didn't say that," Pettigrew replied peevishly, "I merely said that I am aware of Fenger and his work. I still very much doubt that this woman would have been allowed to learn under his tutorship."

Sophia's cheeks blushed crimson with anger.

"If you are accusing me of lying, sir," she said icily to Pettigrew, "I would be more than happy to provide evidence that I am not." Her voice was rising, and Thomas decided to intervene before the harsh tone developing between her and Pettigrew broke into a full-blown argument.

"I am certain that Miss Steenberg will be happy to provide documentary evidence for her training and education as required," Thomas said, raising his voice to pre-empt any protestations from the coroner. He glanced at Sophia, who nodded curtly.

"That is all well and good," Muldoon said. "But I did not give permission..."

"Begging your pardon, sir," Thomas cut in. "But you did. You gave permission for me to bring a surgeon here to consult on the case and contribute further observations to those made by our own coroner."

Muldoon opened his mouth to argue back, but then closed it again. For a long moment, he stared hard at Thomas, and the younger detective sergeant knew that there would be words between them as soon as the two civilians had departed.

"What have you learned then?" Muldoon asked coldly.

Speaking rapidly and stepping to the side of the corpse, Thomas summarised Sophia's findings while the surgeon stood mutely by his side. By the end of his brief speech, Muldoon was leaning close to the corpse, observing the thin incisions on her thighs.

"The Devil," Muldoon breathed. "He can't have had more than a couple of minutes to get out of the way before the watchmen raised the alarm."

"He must have slipped out in the confusion," Thomas said. "The backdoor was unbolted."

"And the blood?" Muldoon asked. "He would have been covered in it."

Thomas thought for a few moments.

"If he wore a dark jacket, it might not have been as readily apparent. He might have simply slipped it off and dropped it from the pier."

Muldoon, who had been writing down notes in his own small journal as Thomas spoke, tapped the end of the pencil on the slab, the clicking echoing slightly in the low-ceilinged space.

"I won't lie," he said. "This information is certainly of interest. Would you agree, Doctor Pettigrew?" he turned to find the coroner standing back, his arms folded.

"I do not agree, inspector," he said. "These assumptions are fanciful at best. And in any case, I have yet to see evidence that this woman is anything other than a fraudster who has tricked your subordinate."

Now it was Thomas' turn to blush red with anger. He turned to Muldoon but caught the older man's look and did not respond.

"Let us assume," Muldoon said quietly. "That my sergeant has not been hoodwinked and that this young woman," he nodded towards Sophia. "has indeed undertaken the surgical training that she claims. Would you not agree that her conclusions are at least useful in illuminating the methods of our killer?"

Pettigrew rolled his eyes.

"Even if they are," he said dismissively. "I hardly see how that helps you apprehend him."

"Perhaps we should just accept the learned gentleman's theory and arrest every foreign sailor in the port. There's only a few thousand suspects after all," Thomas said coldly. Pettigrew bridled.

"Young man," he began. "I do not care one bit for your tone. Your superiors may permit you a certain leeway, but I do not. I have worked as a coroner in this city for more than three decades, longer than you have been alive, and I will not have aspersions cast upon my work."

Thomas opened his mouth to argue back, but Muldoon stepped between them.

"Please calm yourself, doctor," he said. "I am certain that my subordinate spoke out of turn. Thomas," he said, turning to him. "Please apologise to our colleague."

Thomas stiffened, but Muldoon's unflinching glare made it clear that this matter would not be up for negotiation. Thomas grudgingly inclined his head.

"I apologise, doctor," he said. "I did indeed speak out of turn."

"Very well," Pettigrew said with ill grace. "I believe that we are done here, gentlemen."

He pulled on his coat and, without further acknowledging Sophia, he turned his back on the officers and left the dead room. When the heavy door closed, Muldoon turned to Thomas.

"What the hell were you thinking, Thomas?" he said, shaking his head. "Pettigrew might be a bit of an old woman, but he's the only coroner we have. If he takes against us, he could muddy up every criminal investigation and every trial on the books."

"I'm sorry, sir," Thomas said in a defiant tone in his voice. "But I've had enough of crackpot theories in London." He looked darkly at the inspector.

"If I learnt anything from the Ripper case, it was that to catch a killer like this, we need to use every resource at our disposal."

"Even so."

"While I am delighted to be of assistance," Sophia said from behind them. The two men jumped. In the heat of the moment, they had quite forgotten about her presence. "I must agree with Sergeant O'Callaghan."

"What do you mean?" Thomas replied, sidestepping the detective inspector.

"Whoever committed this crime is no ordinary killer," Sophia said. "This murder took planning and a great deal of skill. I don't doubt that the killer will strike again."

Sophia walked over to the slate slab holding the earthly remains of the young Polly. She looked intently at the corpse for several long moments, then glanced at Inspector Muldoon.

"I know that my involvement was very much against your wishes, detective inspector," she said, and for the first time, Thomas heard a softening of her tone. "And I am sorry for inserting myself into this investigation in quite such a brutish manner."

Muldoon looked flustered.

"No blame attaches to you, miss," he said. "I fear that it must be lain squarely at Sergeant O'Callaghan's door…"

"But now that I am involved," Sophia continued, talking over the inspector, "I do have another observation to make, inspector. Would you care to listen?"

Muldoon narrowed his eyes and for a long moment both time and the cool air in the dead room seemed to stand still. Then he nodded.

"Go ahead," he said.

Sophia smiled briefly. Then she ran a finger along the jagged edges where the flesh had been separated.

"The initial incisions were placed with precision," she said. "Swift, clean motions. But the actual cuts are messy, untidy even. As though the person cutting lacks the dexterity to cut clean for prolonged periods of time."

"An interesting anatomical observation," Muldoon began. "Though I am not certain of how much help it…"

"It suggests one of two scenarios to me," Sophia interrupted. "Either, your killer is in fact killers, two men, perhaps one skilled and the other one less so. Or, the killer has experience and the knowledge, enough to know where precisely to place the incisions. But he lacks the manual strength to carry them out cleanly."

"Why would that be?" Thomas asked. Sophia looked at him for a long moment before replying.

"Age," she said simply. "The older a surgeon gets, the untidier their work. As we grow older, our eyesight fails, and, as with anyone else, our hands shake. Age is the surgeon's curse."

Muldoon glanced at Thomas and inclined his head towards the curtain separating the dark room from the dead room.

"Please forgive us, miss," he said. "I must confer with my colleague."

Muldoon grabbed Thomas by the shoulder and half-guided, half-steered him through an opening in the curtain. They arrived in the cramped photographer's workspace, the smell of chemicals increasing sufficiently to overpower the stench of the decaying corpse of Polly Wilkes. Muldoon pulled the curtain closed behind them.

"Thomas," Muldoon began quietly, "I want to speak with you honestly and privately. And I demand honesty from you in return."

Thomas braced himself.

"I will do whatever I can to help in this case, inspector."

"Indeed," Muldoon said, a note of accusation in his tone. "You have already made a jolly fool out of me, and the girl's not been dead for a day yet."

"Please, sir," Thomas said, raising his hand placatingly "I did not intend any disrespect to your rank or person…"

Muldoon waved a hand dismissively.

"You may not have intended any disrespect, Thomas, and I am not so small a man as to claim that Miss Steenberg's insight has not been beneficial. I merely ask that you, in future, think more highly of my character, and I for one will work to live up to your faith in me. Had you told me your intentions, I may have objected, but I do have a great deal of faith in you as I have demonstrated before. Had you been honest with me, I believe that I would have come around to your point of view. Eventually."

Thomas looked down, a sudden shame washing over him. Muldoon had been speaking openly of retirement for nearly a year, complaining of the many ailments that plagued him, and planning his future. He intended to leave the city, Thomas knew, and move to the suburbs and buy a small cottage where he and his wife could watch their grandchildren grow up. But Muldoon had not left the force yet, and—though old and tired—was still a force to be reckoned with.

"I'm sorry, sir," Thomas said quietly. Muldoon looked at him for a long moment, then nodded decisively.

"We'll say no more about it, lad," he said. "It all worked out for the best. But now, we must speak of darker things. I do not relish dragging you back to depths you would rather not again plum. However, I fear that I may have little choice."

"I understand."

"You knew the Ripper case better than any man on this force," Muldoon said. "You know it because you lived it. I am asking you directly. Could it be him?"

Thomas glanced over his shoulder to the thick cotton curtain.

"I'm struck," Thomas said. "By Miss Steenberg's theory. She claims that whoever killed Polly had medical experience. Was that not, in effect, what Dr Bond concluded in the report he sent to the yard about the first four victims? Even his description of the knife, long, straight, and heavy, sounds like the Liston knife Miss Steenberg mentioned."

Muldoon nodded; his eyes narrowed.

"I agree," he said. "Both Anderson and Abberline suspected that the Ripper possessed detailed knowledge of human anatomy, and by the looks of things, Polly's killer did too."

"He didn't remove her organs, though," Thomas said. "And the Ripper never dismembered his victims. He nearly beheaded Kelly, but that was in a fit of rage. There was no plan to it, no logic at all."

Thomas swallowed as, for the thousandth time, the mutilated corpse of Mary Kelly lying on her narrow bed in the sparsely furnished room in Mitre

Square flowed like viscous tarmac across his mind.

Muldoon noted the far-away expression in his sergeant's eyes and cleared his throat to recall Thomas to the darkroom.

"The only question that remains to me is this. If the Ripper has indeed come to Liverpool, then where has he been? He struck five times in ten months and then nothing but silence for three years."

"He could have been arrested?" Thomas said.

"That is possible," Muldoon replied. "But how many surgeons could have been arrested in that narrow window of time? Most surgeons are unlikely to be pickpockets or housebreakers."

Thomas closed his eyes and pressed his hands to his face. When he spoke, he did so slowly and in measured tones.

"Let us assume," he said. "That Polly's murderer was also responsible for the five killings in Whitechapel three years ago. Let us also assume that he is a medical man, a surgeon, a coroner, or perhaps a pathologist."

"Yes," Muldoon said.

"The flaw in this theory is a long gap of time where the murderer, for whatever reason, was not active. This leaves two possibilities. Either he was arrested and therefore prevented from killing, but has now been released."

"Or?"

"Or he hid in plain sight, somewhere we did not expect, and has in fact been killing ever since."

"Where could such crimes be hidden?" Muldoon asked.

"That depends," Thomas said. "I've heard of other gruesome crimes committed all across the country, hundreds of them since the Ripper vanished from Whitechapel."

"You're saying," Muldoon said, his tone leaden, "that this monster could have killed for years right under our nose?"

"While we were waiting on tenterhooks for the next murder to occur in Whitechapel, yes," Thomas said.

Muldoon stood in silence for several long moments, and then his face twisted in a mask of disbelief and doubt.

"Surely", he said. "Any murder which even resembled slightly the Ripper's handiwork would have attracted the attention of the Yard."

"That leaves the first possibility," Thomas said. "He was arrested and has only very recently been released."

"But that too is difficult to believe," Muldoon said frustrated. "If, at least, we accept that the murderer was a medical man of any kind. Surely, the Yard would have suspected every single surgeon placed under arrest at the time of the killings. Certainly, they would have grown suspicious once they realised that the killings had stopped."

"But, sir," Thomas interjected. "You assume that this killer of ours was arrested in London, under the watchful eyes of the Yard. What if the killer left the capital, sought a place of less notoriety, and was arrested there? Would the constabulary in Edinburgh or Dublin or Glasgow or Leicester have connected a surgeon arrested on a completely unrelated charge to the killings of five women in Whitechapel? Would we, sir?"

Muldoon hesitated, his moustache bristling as he moved his lips from side to side, thinking deeply. "You may be right," he said. "He could have gone anywhere, even abroad to one of the colonies, and we would never have known."

"Let us begin with what we know," Thomas said. "Let me instruct a small group of our most trusted constables on what we so far suspect. They can go through the archives and records looking for any medical professional who arrived in the city around the spring of 1889 and who was arrested shortly thereafter. Any such individual could be the man we seek."

Muldoon nodded.

"Instruct your men in secret by all means, Thomas," he said. "But I doubt that we can contain this for much longer. I would be very surprised if one of the gentlemen of the press doesn't already know the whole story."

"Then it's a matter of time before the story is printed."

"And a matter of time before the city comes to us demanding answers."

"We have more, this time, sir," Thomas said, though he did not believe it. "We have, at least a lead, an idea of where to begin. Trust me, sir. I was there. I know how it feels to be fumbling around in the dark."

Muldoon smiled sadly at Thomas.

"I had hoped to spend my last few months on the force in peace, lad," he said. "I know what the press made of Abberline and Andrew and Moore. They damn near destroyed their reputations, blamed them and threw them to the crowd. That's not the way I wanted to end my career."

"Don't worry, sir," Thomas said. "Ripper or not, we'll get whoever killed Polly. We won't let him escape again."

Muldoon sighed deeply and nodded.

"Yes, Thomas," he said. "Yes, you're right. Let us get to work."

He turned to lift the heavy curtain aside and re-join Sophia, but Thomas stopped him.

"I have a favour to ask you, sir," he said. "And this time I will ask you straight and not conceal the truth from you."

Muldoon smiled.

"That would certainly make a welcome change."

"I believe that Miss Steenberg could be a useful ally in this investigation. She intends to sail for America on the *Britannic*."

"Yes," Muldoon said. "And what of it?"

"I would like to ask her to postpone her departure from this city, at least for a few weeks."

Muldoon bridled.

"We already have a coroner, Thomas, and I doubt that after today's display, he will want to cooperate with Miss Steenberg."

"I know, sir," he said. "But Pettigrew serves two other station houses and half the private hospitals in the city. We cannot rely on his undivided attention. Miss Steenberg is a visitor to the city. She has no family here and no friends."

"So, she will not be distracted," Muldoon said.

"Indeed, sir. And I saw her expression when she saw the remains, sir," he continued hurriedly, eager to press his advantage. "I believe she'll be a valuable asset."

Muldoon's small deeply set eyes narrowed as he stared at his subordinate.

"She's your responsibility, Thomas," he said. "Consult with her if you wish. But remember, she's not a member of this force and not under my protection or authority."

"I understand, sir."

Five minutes later, only the lifeless body of Polly Wilkes remained, the steady drips of water running from the slab the only thing to break the silence in the dead room.

Chapter Nine

As Thomas exited the Rose Hill watch house, he found Sophia waiting for him. Wordlessly, she took his arm as they made their way through the labyrinth of alleys and narrow cobbled streets which surrounded the station house on all sides. The weak autumn sun had set, a rosy glow above the horizon the only evidence of its presence. The coming of the night had not yet impacted the press of humanity on the streets. Rather it had increased its volume. Raucous laughter emanated from every pub, inn and gin palace mixing with the cries of the street sellers. These in particular had taken on an added urgency as they pressed hard to sell their few remaining wares.

As they crossed Williamson Square, weaving in and out between families making their way to and from the eateries that ringed the vast open space in the centre of the city, Sophia's eye was drawn to a tightly packed crowd standing in front of a large stone and brick building. The structure's edifice was impressive, inspired by Greek revival architecture with tightly set arches, each level of the building delineated by stuccoed decorations. The front doors around which the crowd milled were dominated by Corinthian columns, and two towers with bronze cupolas topped the structure. Torches burnt in brackets every few feet, and along with the warm glow from thousands of candles lit inside the building shining through every window, it gave the appearance of great warmth and welcome.

Sophia shuddered in the brisk October air and came to a stop. Thomas looked questioningly at her.

"An impressive structure," she said, her warm breath condensing in the air. The temperature had been dropping steadily since the late afternoon, and the shimmering clarity of the star-strewn heaven promised the arrival of the first frost of the year.

"The Star," Thomas said. "A music hall."

"I've heard of those," Sophia said. "I had little time for pleasure while I was in Paris, but I did get a chance to visit a few shows. We do not have such places of entertainment in Copenhagen. Only theatres, for plays, ballet, and opera."

Thomas grinned.

"You'll not find ballet or opera in The Star."

"Good!" Sophia exclaimed. "I've spent a good deal too much of my life watching fat men declaiming in Italian. Let us explore, Sergeant."

Thomas hesitated.

"I'm sorry, miss," he said. "I just wanted to make sure you got back to your hotel safe and sound. I must get back to my duty."

Sophia smiled up at him, her eyes narrowed.

"Surely a few hours make little difference, sergeant," she said. "I've noticed the constables standing on every street corner. I'm certain that you cannot move for policemen down on the docks."

Thomas frowned.

"That is certainly true, miss," he said. "But nevertheless…"

"Nevertheless, I believe that you intend to ask me to postpone my departure to America in order to aid you," Sophia said. Thomas cleared his throat awkwardly. Then Sophia's stern expression cracked, and she laughed. "Oh, Sergeant, please don't stand there looking like a turbot about to be boiled. Did you really think a piece of sail cloth could shield your conversation with the detective inspector?"

Thomas blushed out of a mixture of shame and annoyance, though it was tinged with slight amusement at the young woman's brazenness.

"Well," he said. "Since you know already, then there is hardly any reason for me to postpone asking you any longer. Will you, then, postpone your departure from my troubled city?"

Sophia looked directly up at him, and he was again struck by the sheer depth and sparkle of her eyes. She did not reply for several long moments as the noise of the street washed over them. Then she seemed to make up her mind.

"I will," she said simply.

Thomas smiled.

"Thank you, miss," he said. "I'm sure that your insight will be of great help."

"I do, however, have a price," Sophia said, raising an admonishing finger.

Thomas raised an eyebrow but did not respond. The Danish surgeon clearly came from significant wealth, but he had often had a chance to remark that the most parsimonious of people, those who most hated to give anything away for free, were those who in reality had the most to give.

"I'm frozen to the bone, sergeant," she said. "And The Star looks a welcoming sort of place. My price is a few hours of your time. It is not done for a lady to attend a theatrical performance without an escort," she added in a sardonic tone.

Thomas relented and allowed Sophia to steer him by the arm through the crowds seeking to gain admittance to the music hall. At the door, Sophia handed the red-jacketed usher a handful of coins, which purchased them two seats on the lower balcony and a fine programme printed on silk paper.

The double doors opened up to reveal a foyer so covered in gilt that it nearly blinded the eyes. Everywhere were cherubs and cornucopia overflowing with grapes, oranges, and apples. Columns of every design ringed the walls, and a glittering chandelier of glass and crystal cast radiant beams of light. Young women passed through the crowds carrying small bags of salted popcorn and sweet, juicy oranges, already cut into wedges for ease of consumption. A long bar took up one whole wall, and from it were dispensed glasses of gin and cognac, fine champagne imported from France, and mugs of good local ale.

Thomas had visited the music hall before and had marvelled at the great diversity of the crowds it attracted. There were well-dressed gentlemen in top hats and tails, beautiful ladies in silk dresses hanging on their arms. But there were also newspaper boys, sailors on shore leave, shopkeepers, and every other manner of profession. For a single penny, this great turbulence of humanity could buy one of the hard wooden seats in the stalls. Many smuggled foods with them, a piece of bread covered with a thick layer of bacon fat, or perhaps a baked potato purchased from a vendor outside. If a performance was deemed poor, if actors forgot their lines, or the musicians were too drunk to play in tune, then the smuggled food became impromptu missiles. Thomas had more than once been called to one of the city's music halls as a young constable to bring order to an auditorium when apples, pies, and potatoes flew through the air, and the actors cowered behind the scenery.

"Sergeant!" Thomas turned to see a tall, stout man making his way through the crowd. His thinning hair had been darkened with black dye and teased across his scalp with liberal helpings of grease. He sported a magnificent curled moustache, and his face was caked in the heavy makeup used by the actors to enhance their features on the stage.

"Senor Malaspina," Thomas said nodding his head in greeting. "Good to see you. It's been too long."

"And you too, sergeant," Malaspina said, an insincere smile stretching his rouged lips. His voice was unctuous and overlaid with a heavy Italian accent. Camillo Malaspina had never, to Thomas's certain knowledge, set foot anywhere in the Kingdom of Italy. Rather, he had been born in a small tenement in Gradwell Street to Mr and Mrs Billy Procter and been given the far less exotic name Frank. But young Frank had ambitions and no small talent for stagecraft. Through many trials and tribulations, he had eventually found himself a sought-after comic actor across the many music halls and backstreet theatres in Liverpool and Manchester.

"What tales will you be regaling us with tonight, Senor Malaspina?" Thomas asked. The actor pointed to the programme in Sophia's hand.

"You need only consult the programme, dear sergeant," he said and turned to Sophia, bowed deeply and kissed her hand. Sophia returned his beaming smile with a gracious gesture.

"But now, alas, I must be off," the actor said and bowed again with an exaggerated flourish. "The curtain waits for no man."

Thomas watched as the tall actor made his way gracefully through the crowd, nodding left and right, greeting familiar faces and old friends.

"How very cosmopolitan," Sophia said. "A leading man all the way from Italy."

"Well," Thomas began, but then caught the twinkle in Sophia's eye and the twitch in the side of her mouth. Sophia leaned close to Thomas.

"I've met many Italians in my life, from tailors to sailors to ambassadors," Sophia whispered. "But I must admit that none of them, whether they came from Sicily, Calabria, or Liguria, ever had an accent quite like Senor Malaspina's."

Thomas coughed to suppress his snort of laughter. Sophia squeezed his arm and, gradually, allowing themselves to be swept by the crowd of humanity like flotsam riding upon the waves, they crossed the vestibule and ascended the stairs that led to the raised circle.

The atrium itself was even more splendid than the vestibule. The seats in the circle and the boxes were upholstered in plush red velvet, so thick that Thomas almost sank backwards into the chair when he sat down. The stalls were gradually filling up, more than six hundred people packing the seats. The talking, shouting, the crying of babies, and the discordant tones of the orchestra tuning their instruments in the sheltered pit made it quite impossible to speak together. Instead, Thomas and Sophia sat in comfortable silence, Sophia eagerly looking around, staring at the people who passed by their row.

"Honourable ladies and gentlemen!" The shout from the stage cut through the hubbub. Gradually, the gas-powered lights which illuminated the gallery dimmed. A single electric spotlight flashed into life and revealed Senor Malaspina standing in the centre of the stage, one hand raised in a dramatic gesture.

"As the Bard tells us. All the world is but a stage," he declaimed turning to face the audience with a flourish. "And tonight, good people of this great city, we shall show you the world! There will be amazing acrobats from the Far East," the audience cheered. "There will be Cossack singers from the darkest Russia who will share with you the mournful tunes of their people," the cheers intensified. "There will be thrills, spectacles, and spectaculars to thrill even the most cynical and world-weary among you!"

"Then get the show going, Malaspina, you powdered prick!" someone in the crowd shouted. The audience roared with laughter and Senor Malaspina waved graciously at the wag.

"An eager audience," he roared. "What more can a poor treader of the boards and tripper of the light fantastic desire?"

He bowed deeply and retreated towards the wings. The spotlight dimmed, and for a long moment, the anticipatory susurration of the audience gradually rose. Then the spotlight flashed back into life, revealing a trio of Chinese acrobats, each dressed in differently coloured silk robes, their long beards bound into thin plaits, their bald heads gleaming.

"I take you now, to the court of the Jade Emperor..." Senor Malaspina's voice rang out through a loudspeaker set by the side of the stage. A discordant chord cashed from the orchestra pit, and the acrobats leapt in unison into the air.

Thomas allowed the music and the spectacle to sweep him away. But as he ooh'd and aah'd with the rest of the audience, a part of his mind could not dispel the image of Polly Wilkes lying dead, cold and abandoned on the slab in the dead house. Who could do such a thing to another human being? Murder was not uncommon in the city, certainly not, but most murders were understandable, even if they were bloody and horrific. When a couple of sailors got into it with each other after too much gin and one of them ended up with a knife in his throat, that killing, at least to Thomas, made sense. The world was a violent place, and mankind a violent animal. Kings and emperors threw thousands to their deaths for pride and land and riches and sheer thick-headed arrogance. Against that backdrop what was a couple of sailors and a quarrel over wages or the attentions of a girl?

But to stalk a defenceless girl, to hunt her like a deer through the forest, and then not only snuff out her life, but also abuse her earthly remains. That was different. A man who killed another man in drink was not, at heart, an evil man. He had done an evil deed. The soldier who fired his rifle at whoever his sergeant told him to shoot was not an evil man. He had done an evil deed. But Polly's killer, even though Thomas did not know who he might be, exuded such breathtaking, perverted malice that it seemed to hang upon the air.

He had felt the same way before, when he had pounded the London streets with his colleagues looking for the Ripper or for his next victim. Life was cheap in Whitechapel; Thomas had known that. A killing could be purchased for a handful of pennies and bottle of gin. But that, at least, was only good business. The Ripper had lain across the city, suffocating it, as thick and poisonous as the smock that coloured every sunset orange, pink and purple.

Thomas glanced sideways. Sophia was laughing at the antics of the acrobats, and for the first time, Thomas truly appreciated that she was a woman. Thomas had not felt any physical attraction to the Danish surgeon. Not even now that he sat so close that their shoulders rubbed together, fine crinoline against unwashed cotton. She was beautiful, of that there was no doubt. Thomas knew that she knew more and had done more in her life than he had or likely ever would. But he did not feel bitterness towards her. He sensed a pain inside her, a pain buried so deep that only faint echoes of it carried across on the words, on a glance, a brief expression.

After a heart-wrenching performance by the Russian choir, which reduced several ladies, and a few gentlemen in the audience to tears, Senor Malaspina reappeared on the stage. Aside from his black morning suit, he now also wore a silk top hat and a short opera cloak.

"Honoured guests," he began. "I must confess that a most grievous injustice has been done to you all."

He paused to wait while the audience jeered and sneered.

"At this point in the evening, it would normally be my pleasure to present that timeless classic, that most divine of comedies, *The Tale of Romulus and Remus*. However, tonight, I can do no such thing."

More jeers. Some of the newsboys sitting in the front row of the stalls picked up their discarded apple cores and orange peels, ready to hurl them at the stage to show their displeasure.

"But fear not!" Senor Malaspina continued quickly, a sharp eye on the would-be hecklers in the front row. "For news has reached this company, rumours of the most dark and bloody. We hear that a poor girl was murdered only yesterday by a stranger in the night!"

Thomas's faint smile froze on his lips. There was a strange ringing in his ears.

"And in honour of that poor murdered girl," Senor Malaspina continued. "We would like to perform for you discerning people tonight. *The Ballad of Spring-Heel Jack!*"

A roar of applause greeted this news. Thomas cursed under his breath. *The Ballad of Spring-Heel Jack* had first seen the light of day mere weeks after the first of the Ripper killings in Whitechapel in the form of a gaudy penny dreadful. But soon, every music hall in London had performed the thinly veiled tale of Jack the Ripper to audiences of thousands. In the tale, the murderer appeared as an avenging angel, seeking vengeance upon a decadent city. A cunning killer pursued by a bumbling and useless constabulary.

"And why should we care for Spring-Heel Jack, you may ask," Senor Malaspina roared. "For, he has not lifted a blade for nigh on three years. But if the rumours are to be believed, and believe them we must, then Spring-Heel Jack may be loose in our own fair city!"

The roar of the audience grew as people argued, shouted, laughed and boo'd and applauded in equal measure. Senor Malaspina raised both hands.

"Or perhaps we are wrong," he said. "Perhaps, our streets are safe, and our bonny girls can walk the docks and piers unafraid of strangers in the dark."

Catcalls and wolf-whistles greeted this thinly veiled reference to the whores working the docks.

"After all," Senor Malaspina continued. "Even our brave and diligent detectives have found the time to view our humble performance. And in the company of a beautiful lady, no less!"

Thomas jumped as he felt one of the electric spotlights fall upon him. His mutilated ear made him an easily recognisable figure, and those in the audience who knew him soon whispered about him to those who did not. He felt the mood of the audience turn sour. Felt their judging glares.

"I hope you enjoy the play, detective sergeant," the actor said with a broad smile. "Perhaps it can teach you how to catch a killer."

"Shall we leave?" Sophia asked quietly.

"No," Thomas said through pursed lips. He forced himself to smile coldly and inclined his head towards the actor.

"Let us begin then," Malaspina roared. "It is a cold and frosty night in our nation's capital, and the bells of St Mary's have tolled the midnight hour…"

Chapter Ten

Sefton Park was once upon a time a reserve for royal prey under the administration of Lord Sefton. However, some thirty years previously, the city of Liverpool had purchased the vast green space for a vast sum of more than a quarter of a million pounds. The space had been converted, gradually, from a veritable wilderness to manicured park——land bisected by dozens of well-kept gravel paths connecting small plazas and bandstands. Its crowning glory was an artificial lake, kept stocked with carp and trout, despite the best efforts of Liverpool's hungrier citizens, and a small island only reachable by boats which could be rented on warm summer days by a small pier. Large mansions and manors lay along the park's southern edge, separated from it by pleasantly shady tree-lined boulevards. The wealthiest of the city's merchant families had purchased homes there when the parkland had first passed into public ownership, and to this day, they helped pay for the park's maintenance.

At night, Sefton Park lay quiet. Flocks of ducks and Canada geese rested on the lake banks. The bandstands were closed and locked, and the ice cream vendors had long gone home to rest. Only an experienced observer would note the occasional muted giggle from the bushes, which showed that the ladies of the night had long since claimed the park's abandoned spaces in the hours of darkness.

Tonight, with the murder of Polly Wilkes so fresh in the mind, patrols of constables along the circumference of the park were more frequent than would otherwise be the case.

Occasionally, one of the patrols would cross the park itself, their swinging lanterns the only source of light in the stygian gloom. But the majority of the constabulary were down on the docks, walking back and forth like Buckingham Palace guards, stopping every passer-by, questioning every suspicious character—of which there were plenty—and encouraging any lady of the night they met to go home and take the night off.

Even the most experienced and acute observer would only with difficulty have noticed the slightly deeper pool of darkness behind a stand of willow trees. Only long, unbroken observation would show that the shadow occasionally moved unnaturally.

I nearly giggle when I think about the hundreds of constables standing around by the dock gates, waving their truncheons and lanterns about, inflated with self-importance. I'm finished with the docks. For now, I keep to my private pool of obscurity between the willows. It isn't comfortable, but a regrettable part of the business. Not every prey animal presents itself as willingly and trustingly as little Polly had done. With the whores and the police on the watch, the game has changed. It now requires patience. A few of the whores has passed close by me, but always in groups or with a customer. And though I can strike quickly, why should I take the chance of a customer getting away and raising all hell? Far better to wait. Perhaps my prey will come tonight. Perhaps tomorrow or the next night. I can afford to wait. The anticipation fills me as I feel the reassuring weight of the perfectly balanced Liston knife in my belt. Soon I'll need it. It's only a matter of time.

* * *

The persistent hammering on his door echoed the pain in the back of Thomas' head as he was roughly ripped from sleep. He bolted upright, waving his arms about, his thin blanket falling to the floor. He stared wildly around and half-staggered, half-fell off his bed. He stepped on an empty gin bottle, its cylinder shape skittering away into a corner of his room and sending him sprawling to the floor. He got back to his feet and in the gloom of his musty room, he stared down, realised that he was naked and quickly pulled on a selection of the garments lying in a pile on the floor where he had dropped them the previous night. Someone was knocking on his door so heavily that it was nearly pushed out of its frame.

When he was dressed, Thomas grabbed his heavy rosewood truncheon, stepped to the door, and tore it open. His action nearly catapulted an out-of-breath and distinctly dishevelled inspector Muldoon into Thomas' room. Thomas dropped his truncheon and steadied the old man.

"Bloody hell, Thomas," Muldoon gasped. "Not only did I have to get up three damn flights of stairs, then you also keep me waiting at the door."

"Sorry, sir," Thomas mumbled, his mouth gummed up with sleep and the residual effects of the gin. He turned his face from Muldoon, but the stench of gin in the room and on Thomas' breath was undeniable.

"What's wrong with you, man?" Muldoon snapped. "You're as drunk as a lord!"

"I was," Thomas murmured, crossing to his wash basin, scooping up handfuls of water and letting the cool liquid run down his face, feeling it rejuvenate him and chase away the mist of sleep and inebriation. He grabbed a stained cloth and dried the sleep from the corners of his eyes.

"Well, you'd better sober up, Thomas, and sober up quick," Muldoon said. For the first time, Thomas appreciated the older man's urgent tone.

"There's been another murder," Thomas said, standing up straight, his hands balling into fists.

"No, thank God," Muldoon said. "But it's bad, Thomas. It's your friend, that foreign woman."

"What's happened?" Thomas's tone was suddenly sharp and clear.

"The boys from Seel Street arrested her just before dawn. I only just found out from Sergeant Fraser."

"What?" Thomas gaped. "What on earth for?"

"They're holding her on suspicion of murder," Muldoon said gravely.

"That's..." Thomas began, casting about for a descriptor robust enough to convey his strength of feeling. "That's absurd."

"I agree," Muldoon said.

"She's barely been in the city for a day, who on earth would she have had time to murder?"

"Polly Wilkes," Muldoon said.

Thomas stood in shocked silence.

"They can't be serious," he said. "Sergeant Fraser must have misunderstood a message. Maybe they simply enquired about why she was helping us out on the investigation."

"Helping *you* out, Thomas," Muldoon said, raising a finger. Thomas brushed the intervention aside with a wave of his hand.

"What reasons have they given? What evidence do they have?"

"I don't know," Muldoon said. "But we need to get to Seel Street in a hurry and sort this out."

"You don't believe them, sir, surely?" Thomas asked aghast. Muldoon stared at his subordinate for a long moment.

"No," he said. "No, I don't. But given that you want the woman to postpone her journey to America and remain here to help us freely, then might I suggest that having her hauled out of bed and thrown into a dark cell in Seel Street does not exactly show off our city's fabled hospitality from its best angle."

The growler which had brought Muldoon from Rose Hill to Thomas' abode was still waiting outside, its driver looking around suspiciously at the gang of kids who were eying up his wagon. Kids hitching rides on the back of growlers had led to a permanent state of war between the street urchins and the drivers and had even caused a few deaths when a child was knocked off the jolting vehicle going at speed.

The sun was only just up, and the traffic through the city was not yet congested. Within twenty minutes, the two officers arrived outside Seel Street. Thomas had spent the journey trying to brush dust and dirt off his jacket and hat, to limited effect, while Muldoon had sat in antsy anticipation, checking his pocket watch every few minutes.

The Seel Street station house looked so similar to Rose Hill that the two buildings could have been twins of one another. The constables and detectives based at Seel Street were also part of the Liverpool Constabulary, but their remit was the south of the city, the parks and suburbs, whereas the north and the docks were under the auspices of Rose Hill. The two stations maintained a mostly cordial relationship, though it was one occasionally strained by a competitive streak among the constables, sergeants, and inspectors based at the respective stations.

The desk sergeant at Seel Street was a skinny man with a thatch of blonde hair and pair of wire-rimmed spectacles balanced on a long, pointed nose. He looked up with an irritated expression when Thomas and Muldoon barged into the room, then adjusted his expression when he recognised Muldoon as a superior officer.

"Good morning, detective inspector Muldoon," he said with a hastily adapted smile. "What brings you by?"

"You can skip the pleasantries, Fawcett," Muldoon snapped, his tone brisk. "Where's Detective Inspector Cooper?"

"In the cells," Fawcett replied, his nose wrinkling with barely suppressed annoyance at Muldoon's curt tone. "He's interrogating that bit of skirt they brought in this morning."

Thomas glared hard at the desk sergeant but remained silent. He rushed across the half-empty watch room, closely followed by Muldoon. He opened the door to the cells, and the two of them made their way down a set of narrow stone steps.

As soon as he opened the door, he could hear raised voices.

"You're telling me you don't have an alibi then?" That was the gravelly tones of Detective Inspector Cooper.

"I didn't know I needed one!" the higher-pitched voice of Sophia. Thomas could not hear any fear in her words, only a good measure of anger.

Thomas and Muldoon ignored the constable on guard who stood up to greet them and, still going at a trot, they set off down the block until they reached the last cell. Its door was ajar, the heavy iron keys still hanging in the lock.

Sophia was inside, sitting on a rickety three-legged stool. She wore only a thin cotton chiffon, her arms cuffed behind her back. Thomas felt a small charge of fury detonate in his chest. They had not even given her a chance to get dressed.

Two men were towering over Sophia. One was the coroner, Dr Pettigrew.

Pettigrew looked up at Thomas but gave no sign of recognition. The other man had a wide, ruddy face with a domed forehead that overhung his features slightly, like a ledge balancing precariously on the side of a mountain.

"Inspector Cooper," Muldoon said loudly. "Perhaps you could enlighten me as to why I find this lady in your custody?"

Cooper turned his head slowly, glaring angrily at Muldoon and Thomas. He drew out a handkerchief and wiped it across his forehead.

"I don't recall sending out for reinforcements, inspector," he said. "Please be certain that should I ever need assistance, you Rose Hill boys will be first up on my list."

"Cut the crap, Cooper," Thomas snarled. "For what reason did you detain Miss Steenberg?"

"Watch your tone, lad," Cooper said. "Muldoon may tolerate your insubordination, but I see no reason to."

Thomas crossed to Sophia, pulled off his jacket, and laid it across her shoulders. She did not acknowledge his presence. Instead, she held her gaze fixed on Detective Inspector Cooper.

"Well?" Muldoon said. "I asked you a question, Cooper. What's the nature of your evidence against Miss Steenberg?"

"That would be mine," Dr Pettigrew said smoothly. "As you may recall, the wounds which severed the Wilkes girl's arms from her torso were rather distinctive. Knowledgably placed, but carelessly carried out."

"Yes," Muldoon agreed. "We have theorised that the killer may be a medical man of some advanced age…"

"Or" Cooper interrupted. "A female doctor whose skills are blighted by the limitations of her sex."

Thomas opened his mouth but caught the eye of Inspector Muldoon. The older man shook his head jerkily, silencing Thomas.

"There ain't many woman doctors in the city," Cooper continued. "In fact, there isn't a single one. The murder occurs the night after this lady arrived, and she evidently has the medical knowledge to perform the mutilations done to the girl. At least that's what Dr Pettigrew tells me. Personally, I very much doubt she has any practical medical experience."

"I've explained to you the reason for my presence in the city, and I have given you a full account of my movements prior to arriving here?" Sophia snarled, rising out of her seat, but Cooper shoved her roughly back down. "Are you calling me a liar, sir?"

Cooper glared at her.

"Yes," he said simply. "I am."

"A woman may study medical books," Dr Pettigrew said loftily. "But what sort of patients would voluntarily allow themselves to be administered to by a woman?"

"You searched my room," Sophia said angrily shifting her glare from the inspector to the coroner. "You must have found my medical certificate. You will also find correspondence with several notable European doctors and surgeons."

"We did," Cooper said. "And we are having the letters translated as we speak. But they do not in any way clear you of suspicion."

"Nor do they serve to place her under it," Muldoon interjected. "What is your evidence, Cooper, beyond the hunch of a coroner?" For the first time, the older detective inspector looked at Dr Pettigrew, and his normally placid gaze was so full of hard anger that the man took an involuntary step back.

"We found a surgeon's kit with knives that fit the shape of the wounds," Cooper said.

"Of course!" Thomas exploded, unable to keep his tongue. "And I daresay you could find a hundred identical kits in this city! Including one in Dr Pettigrew's possession."

"Are you accusing…" Dr Pettigrew began, his voice rising as he drew himself to his full height.

"Of course, I'm not," Thomas said. "That would be madness. But so is this."

"The lady has no alibi for the night of the murder."

"I told you; I was asleep…"

"That's highly convenient."

"For Gods, sake, man," Muldoon shouted. "Go and ask the hotel's night porter if the lady left the hotel during the hours of darkness. Or are you suggesting that she climbed down a five-storey wall to murder a prostitute in a city where she'd only just arrived?"

Cooper glanced at Dr Pettigrew, and the truth dawned on Thomas. The instigator of Sophia's arrest had not been the detective inspector, but rather the coroner, and now, confronted by irate colleagues, Cooper was looking to Pettigrew for instructions.

Muldoon noted the glance, too.

"I can understand how a private citizen such as Dr Pettigrew, eager to help the investigation, may have advised a rash and unsubstantiated course of action," carefully extending a linguistic olive branch to his fellow detective inspector.

"Well…" Cooper began.

"But" Muldoon interrupted. "Let me tell you this, Cooper. Detective inspector you may be, but I remember when you were still a constable and wet behind the ears. And I am telling you this as someone who has known you for a long time. I am going to unshackle this lady and bring her back to her hotel. You will call off your constables and return her room to the order in which you found it."

Cooper opened his mouth to argue, but Muldoon raised his hand.

"And if you try to stop me, Cooper, then the next person you'll hear from is the superintendent of police. And he's known me for a damn sight longer than he's known you. Is that clear?"

Cooper looked for a moment as if he intended to argue. But then he caught Thomas' steely glare and deflated.

"Very well," he said. "I'll take your word for her innocence. But this city and its people demand justice, Muldoon. Or haven't you had time to see the papers yet?"

Muldoon smiled sardonically.

"I was planning on reading them at my leisure when I retire, Cooper," he said. "Now, please, unlock this woman's cuffs."

"This is outrageous," Dr Pettigrew began, stepping between inspector Cooper and his prisoner. "The woman is a clear suspect!"

"Who is or isn't a suspect is not up to a coroner to decide," Thomas snapped.

"You're far out of bounds, doctor."

"Out of bounds, am I?" roared Pettigrew. "I rather suspect it is you who is out of bounds, detective sergeant. Since when was it standard police procedure to seek advice from an untrained and potentially dangerous woman ahead of a respected coroner?"

"I'll seek the advice of anyone who can help me solve this murder," Thomas answered. "And in the last twelve hours, you have suggested two suspects with no shred of evidence."

"I merely opined that the killer was unlikely to be an Englishman," Pettigrew said, his nostrils flaring. "That opinion does not exclude your female companion from suspicion, sergeant!"

"That's enough, both of you," Thomas was surprised to see detective inspector Cooper stare angrily at Dr Pettigrew. "If you two fine gentlemen want to carry on like this, then you can do so outside of my station house."

Pettigrew glared back for a long moment. Then he blinked.

"Very well, inspector," he said. "You know my opinion on this matter. I have other duties to attend to."

With ill grace, he picked up his black medical bag, threw his overcoat over his arm, and pushed through Muldoon and Thomas to get out of the cell. Cooper was breathing heavily like a boxer winded after a fight. He tossed the keys to Sophia's shackles to Thomas with a disgusted expression.

"Get her out of my cells," he said before following after the coroner.

Within five minutes, Muldoon and Thomas had unshackled Sophia and led her from the cells and back into the waiting growler. The Danish surgeon was shaking, not with cold, but with suppressed anger. As soon as the door of the growler closed, she burst into a tirade in her native language. Neither Thomas nor Muldoon understood the words, but the tone and inflection made their meaning clear. The two detectives glanced at each other, neither daring to interrupt her. Eventually, as the growler bounced and trembled along the cobbles towards the Adelphi, Sophia took a deep, shuddering breath with her eyes pressed closed. Then she opened them and looked squarely at detective inspector Muldoon.

"Thank you, sir," she said her voice still shaking. "I know the cost of going against one's own allies and colleagues. I appreciate your faith in me."

Muldoon contemplated her for a long moment.

"I am not certain whether I have any faith in you, miss," he said. "But I have faith in my sergeant and that's enough for now." Sophia nodded, detecting the silent message that passed from the detective inspector. Muldoon might not think her a killer, but he was also not yet ready to allow himself to fully be convinced of her usefulness to their investigation.

The roads were beginning to fill with growlers, carts, and hordes of workers going on foot to factories, shops, and down to the docks. The growler was eventually forced to slow to a crawl, the driver arguing loudly with pedestrians, the horses neighing and stamping their hooves impatiently.

"I fear we have made an enemy of the coroner," Thomas said to Muldoon. Muldoon nodded heavily.

"I've known him for a long time," he said. "He was a coroner back when I worked my very first cases. He's always been stubborn and prone to jumping to conclusions, but he's not a stupid man."

Thomas did not reply. Pettigrew was a well-educated man, but as with many men of great knowledge, he also believed that others should simply believe his assertions and theories without recourse to evidence. Thomas wondered how many murders had been declared solved as a result of one of the coroner's hunches. And how many innocent men those hunches had seen locked up or sent to the gallows at Kirkdale.

"I spent some time last night thinking about the case," Sophia said, interrupting his train of thought. "I must admit, I found it difficult to sleep after our experience in the music hall."

Muldoon looked questioningly at Thomas, who quickly explained their experiences in The Star and the reactions of the crowd to news of the killing.

"I can't say I'm surprised," Muldoon said, passing a newspaper across to Thomas. In between tightly packed advertisements for Sunlight Soap, a carpet shop, and a newly opened apothecary, the headline was clearly visible. *The Ripper Strikes Again.* Thomas read the short piece with an increasing sense of doom. The writer had had few facts available, so had instead filled in the blanks with wild speculations. The wounds to the girl's abdomen proved it, according to the reporter. The police might not want to admit it, but it was clear that the man who had so terrorised Whitechapel had now arrived in Liverpool to repeat his feat.

"This is going to get bad," Thomas said, passing the paper to Sophia. She scanned the article, an eyebrow raised.

"Rather sensationalist," she said coldly when she had finished, placing the paper on one of the growler's empty seats.

"Sensationalist or not," Muldoon said. "People will listen. Some perverse part of their nature wants it to be real."

"They can't genuinely want the Ripper to return," Sophia said, shocked. The two seasoned policemen looked at each other for a long moment before Thomas said, with hesitation in his voice.

"In some ways they do, and in some ways they don't," he said. "The Ripper has become a figure of legend. Something out of a fairy story. The way he struck out of nowhere and successfully evaded the largest manhunt ever conducted on these islands. People found it exciting. And if this is the next chapter in the Ripper's story…"

He trailed off. Sophia nodded slowly.

"Do you still believe it likely, then, that this murder was the work of the Ripper?"

Thomas thought for a moment and then nodded.

"There are differences in the methods, true," he said. "But also similarities."

"But how does that help us?" Muldoon asked, staring gloomily out of the window at the passing pedestrians. Even as they slowly made their way down the street, he saw several of them carrying copies of the same paper that lay by his side.

"It doesn't," Thomas said, rubbing his forehead. "It merely complicates our investigation."

"Then the way forward seems clear," Sophia said. She was looking directly at Thomas, a strangely warm expression in her blue eyes. Almost like pity.

"I'm glad you see a clear path ahead," Muldoon said. "I fear that I don't."

"It seems to me that if your killer is indeed the Ripper, then that provides you with a great deal of potential evidence," Sophia said. "For a start, it will allow you to know for certain where your killer was three years ago."

"And if we know where he was three years ago," Thomas said. "That at least gives us a starting point."

"Precisely," Sophia said. "And if he is not the Ripper, then that too is important information. If it can be proven that this is a different killer, it will stop you wasting resources and time, and perhaps even calm down the population of the city."

"But how can we prove this?" Muldoon cut in. "It's a fine theory. But as Thomas said, some elements of Polly's murder suggest the shadow of the Ripper. And some do not."

Sophia bit her lip. She seemed to be steeling herself to say something.

"I think the time for hesitation has passed," Thomas urged her. "Please speak your mind."

Sophia glanced at him and smiled briefly. Then she leaned forward her folded arms resting on her knees.

"More than eight hundred years ago, there was a gifted surgeon by the name of Song Ci. He lived within the domain of the Chinese Emperor and was called upon to investigate the murder of a farmer who had been disembowelled. Song Ci carefully examined the wound and, by conducting experiments on dead pigs with various types of blades, he proved that the murder had been committed using a sickle."

"A fascinating tale," Muldoon interrupted. "But I hardly see the relevance… "

Sophia held up a hand.

"Patience, please, inspector," she said. "Song Ci's work was developed further by other surgeons, including a Frenchman by the name of Ambroise Paré, who worked on battlefields creating a catalogue of different types of wounds inflicted by different types of blades, and of course by different people using those blades in a variety of different manners."

Thomas narrowed his eyes. He had realised what the young Danish surgeon was describing.

"You want to compare the wounds inflicted by the Ripper on his victims in Whitechapel to those on Polly Wilkes," he said.

"Precisely," Sophia said. "Following the examples of Song Ci and Paré. Different killers, like different soldiers, use their weapons in distinct manners. If the type of wounds inflicted by the Ripper in London matches those on Polly, then I believe we can safely assume the killer to be the same individual."

"What would you need to conduct this analysis?" Muldoon asked, his tone now eager. Sophia hesitated for a moment as she thought.

"I would need to access any records or archives, letters or correspondence you possess which relate to the Ripper murders as well as the original photographs and sketches produced at the scenes of the murders in London."

Muldoon sucked air between his teeth and shook his head.

"You won't find that up here," he said.

"There's only one place you're going to find that," Thomas said, looking at Muldoon. "At Scotland Yard."

Sophia nodded curtly.

"Very well," she said. "I've never visited London. I believe there is a regular train between Liverpool and the capital."

"Hang on, miss," Muldoon interrupted throwing up his hands. "You can't just go to London and barge in on the Yard. They'd throw you out on your ear."

"Not if I go with her," Thomas said quietly.

Muldoon leaned back in his creaking seat. His hands were folded over the knob of the ebony cane he had taken to wearing after his left knee began to send spasms of pain through his entire leg on cold days.

"I know you have friends in the Yard, Thomas," he said. "But this is a big favour to ask of them."

"Not if there's a chance at nabbing the Ripper," Thomas said. "You know how much Abberline wants him, even now. He never got over the Ripper slipping between his fingers."

"And if it turns out that Polly's murder has nothing to do with the Ripper, then you'll have burnt every bridge you had in London."

"It's worth it, isn't it, sir," Thomas said. "What other leads do we have?"

Muldoon sighed deeply.

"Not a shadow of one, Thomas," he said. "I won't deny that Miss Steenberg's deductions were illuminating," he said, inclining his head to Sophia. "But they have not yielded anything so far."

"Well then," Thomas pressed his advantage. "The noon train to London arrives in Piccadilly Circus at six o'clock tonight. We would not need to be away from the city for more than a few days."

"I'll have to discuss this with the superintendent," Muldoon began.

"Why?" Sophia interrupted.

"Expenses," Muldoon said. "I can't just go around sending my detectives all over the country without seeking the leave and permission of my superiors."

"Please inspector," Sophia said. "I would be more than delighted to pay for our transportation and accommodation, given that Thomas is merely going as my escort."

"I can't ask that of you, miss," Muldoon protested.

"Consider it a repayment, inspector," Sophia interrupted. "A thank you for, what is the common phrase you use," she mouthed silently for a moment and then her face broke into a mischievous grin. "Ah yes," she said. "A thank you for springing me from the cells."

Thomas burst out laughing, and even the corner of Muldoon's mouth twitched under the cover of his walrus moustache.

"You're persuasive, miss, I'll give you that," Muldoon said, a note of grudging admiration in his voice. "Let us say, Thomas, that I am giving you a few days of leave. Go to London, talk to your contacts at the Yard, and get Miss Steenberg access to the material she requires. And as soon as you know one way or another, send me a telegram. I'll try to keep the situation under control up here in the meantime."

"Thank you, sir," Thomas said.

"And Thomas," Muldoon continued, his expression inscrutable. "If you're going to represent my station at the Yard, might I suggest a change of shirt and jacket?"

Chapter Eleven

The first intercity train, some sixty years previously, had departed Liverpool's Lime Street Station bound for Manchester. In those days, even that relatively short journey took more than six hours, the train chugging along at a snail's pace with carriages open to the sun and rain. But despite its slowness, the train was still more efficient and faster than going the same distance by coach and horses, and this proof of concept had ignited a war as railway lines and companies fought each other like wild animals to be the first to connect Britain's cities with each other.

Land was purchased, houses and farms cleared if they were in the way, stations established, and new villages and towns sprang up around them. Eventually, a line all the way to London was completed. It meant that a traveller arriving in Liverpool from anywhere in the world could avail themselves of the five daily departures to the nation's capital from the central train station. Goods of all sorts could be offloaded on the Liverpool docks and piers, brought by trolley and rail to the goods yards and shipped onwards to London, Newcastle, Edinburgh, Hull, and wherever else it was needed. A cargo of valuable porcelain sailed by steamer from Shanghai could be offloaded in the Canada Dock in Liverpool in the morning, and by the late afternoon, those same plates, bowls, and saucers could be placed on the tables of a high-end restaurant in Westminster or Kensington.

Thomas found himself relegated to a supporting role the moment he and Sophia set foot on the platform. The pair of first-class tickets purchased by Sophia saw them greeted by a uniformed porter who took hold of their meagre luggage and directed them to their private compartment, leading them through a luxuriously appointed dining car on the way. With their luggage settled, the whistle blew and gradually, stutteringly, the massive cast-iron boiler built up a head of steam, and the heavy locomotive began moving forward. With a series of juddering thuds, it took up the load of its carriages and, in a stately fashion, steam and smoke billowing around the crowds on the platform, the train left the station. It followed the rails through a deep cut in the natural sandstone upon which the city had been built, a culvert which provided not only a passage for trains to and from the station but also a home for hundreds of souls too poor even for the tenements.

Thomas felt a stab of guilt as he settled himself in the dining car. Sophia picked up a menu printed on fine white cardstock and glanced at the curly, gilded words that covered it. Without consulting Thomas, she turned to the waiter who had appeared at her elbow.

"The mock turtle soup, I think," she said. "To start at least. And perhaps a pair of Cornish game hens for our main, would you agree, sergeant?"

Thomas, who had never eaten game hens, from Cornwall or anywhere else, stuttered an affirmative, and the waiter, throwing the detective sergeant a somewhat pitying look, nodded curtly and bustled off. Glancing up at the young surgeon, Thomas suddenly realised that she was, in fact, enjoying his discomfort. She might have forgiven the Liverpool constabulary for the indignities of the morning, but she nevertheless needed to reassert herself, and his befuddlement provided a welcome avenue for that task.

"Why did you transfer from Scotland Yard, Sergeant O'Callaghan?" Sophia asked suddenly, and Thomas started. Then he thought for a moment, taking a sip of water from the cut crystal tumbler which the waiter had placed at his elbow.

"Thomas, please," he said. "Let's not stand on formalities. The Yard has some of the best detectives and coppers in the world. Better even than that private outfit in America that the newspapers are so fond of, the Pinkertons."

"I've heard of them," Sophia said. "I must admit I always thought they sounded very similar in manner and comportment to the villains they hunt."

Thomas laughed.

"Well," he said. "A good bizzie has to have a little scoundrel in him, deep down. The trick is not to have too much."

"A good doctor," Sophia mused. "Is one who empathises with their patient. A good bizzie," she tasted the unfamiliar slang term and looked pleased with it. "A good bizzie then is someone with the ability to think like a criminal, but not sympathise with him."

"Sometimes it's difficult not to," Thomas said. "When the criminal is a young boy who picks pockets to eat. Or a widow who steals bread to live."

"In those cases, a good policeman is perhaps someone who knows how to turn his head and look away?" Sophia asked, her eyes not leaving Thomas' face. He squirmed under their unflinching glare.

"Your words, miss," he said noncommittally "Not mine."

She nodded, apparently satisfied with the reply.

"I left Liverpool because I didn't see a future in the city," Thomas said. He touched his right ear gently. "You've never asked how I got this," he said. "Most people ask me as soon as they meet me."

Sophia glanced at the wound, but her gaze was disinterested.

"It's a wound," she said simply. "I've seen many. It looks like it was cut off with a sharp blade."

Thomas smiled.

"Very good," he said. "A souvenir from one of the first bar brawls I tried to break up. Before I learned how to approach the job more carefully."

"And you left for London after that experience?" Sophia asked.

Thomas looked shocked.

"God, no," he said. "I spent five more years on the Liverpool constabulary. Five years of breaking up street fights and bar brawls, and scuffling with dockers and stevedores."

"And that became too much?"

Thomas leaned back to allow the returning waiter to place two deep bowls of brown mock-turtle soup. Small forcemeat dumplings floated on the surface, and the waiter also poured two glasses of rich red Madeira port to accompany the soup.

"I didn't want to spend my life getting beaten up in the street," Thomas said. "I wanted more. Detective Inspector Muldoon recommended me to the Yard. He told me to go and get some of my edges knocked off in London and come back when I felt ready to be a detective."

Sophia lifted her spoon and blew gently on it to cool the scalding soup.

"And so, you spent some time in London at Scotland Yard."

"Nearly three years," Thomas confirmed. "Until December of 1888."

Sophia sipped the soup and glanced up at him.

"After the autumn of the Ripper killings."

Thomas nodded. The conversation was making him uncomfortable. He felt on the precipice of baring his soul to this woman who had been a complete stranger only days before. He decided to play her at her own game.

"New York is a long way from Copenhagen," he said. "I noted that when you agreed to stay on in Liverpool, you did not ask me to take you to the telegraph office so you could notify your family back home. Would they not like to know that you've been delayed on your way across the Atlantic?"

Sophia avoided his eye, staring fixedly at her soup and covering her embarrassment by taking a sip of her port.

"Be fair now," he said. "I answered you readily enough."

Sophia cleared her throat, a mixture of discomfort and annoyance on her finely carved features.

"There's no one in Copenhagen who would care if I was in Liverpool or in New York, or indeed at the bottom of the North Atlantic."

Thomas looked shocked.

"I'm certain that's not true," he began but Sophia interrupted him.

"I do not make a habit of embellishing, sergeant," she said, and her tone cracked like the snap of a drover's whip. "Copenhagen is in my past."

For several minutes, there was no sound aside from the clinking of their silver spoons on the soup bowls and the steady chuffing of the train, the rhythmic and perfectly timed clunks as the steel wheel hit the rail spikes set into the track every few feet.

"Would you care to elaborate?" Thomas asked. "Curiosity is somewhat of an occupational hazard for us coppers."

Sophia smiled despite herself and laid down her spoon.

"Are you familiar with the Nordic Telegraph Service?" Sophia asked. Thomas shook his head.

"Not from personal experience," he said. "Though I can imagine what it is."

"It is, as you would imagine, the largest telegraph company in Scandinavia."

"Yes?"

"My father owns it," Sophia said matter-of-factly. "Or, I should say that he owns a controlling share of the company."

Thomas mirrored his companion, placing down his spoon and leaning back in the seat. For a long moment, he simply stared at her in bemusement.

"I'm not certain what to say," he began.

"Then say nothing," Sophia said. "Let me tell you instead a story which may explain why you find me here in Liverpool on my way across the Atlantic."

She took another sip of port, as if to fortify herself.

"I'm the oldest of three girls," she said. "My two younger sisters made good matches to two of my father's business partners. But I must admit that domestic bliss never attracted me much as a career opportunity. My grandfather was a battlefield surgeon, a proper old-fashioned sawbones, during the war between Denmark and Prussia in 1864. It was a horrid war. The Danish army was utterly destroyed by the Prussians. Grandfather told me of bodies so crushed and mangled by cannon fire and stampeding horses that nothing remained to identify them. Humans reduced to quivering lumps of flesh and pain."

Thomas coughed and pushed away his soup.

"It sounds like he was trying to scare you," he said. Sophia laughed.

"That was undoubtedly his plan. But little by little, he realised that I enjoyed learning about medicine and anatomy and surgery. He began to tutor me, much to my father's chagrin."

"I'm surprised your father allowed it," Thomas said. Sophia looked at him, almost pityingly.

"My father always had more control over me in his head than in reality," she said with a hint of bitterness in her voice. "My grandfather pressured him to allow me to study medicine. Then he reached out to his old friends and comrades, some of whom had become coroners, surgeons, and doctors in Copenhagen and elsewhere in the country. Eventually, they accepted me at the University and allowed me to read medicine."

"That can't have been easy," Thomas said quietly. Sophia looked up, stared hard at him for a moment, and then her features seemed to soften.

"No," she said in a monotone voice. "It wasn't."

"But you succeeded," Thomas said, trying to steer the conversation away from the chasm that had opened in front of it. "You became a surgeon."

"I did," Sophia said. "And with my father's monetary help, I set up a clinic in the centre of Copenhagen. It went well for several years."

"And then?"

Sophia sighed, waved at the waiter, and asked him to remove the soup. Soon, the white cotton tablecloth was empty, awaiting the arrival of the Cornish game hens.

"Most of my patients were women and children," Sophia said. "My father used to tell me that a man would have to be so ill before volunteering to see a female surgeon that he'd die on the way to the clinic."

Thomas coughed embarrassedly. Until he had met Sophia, he would in all likelihood have reacted in precisely such a manner confronted with the choice of either continuing to suffer pain on the one hand, or on the other, allowing a female surgeon to minister to him. As he looked at Sophia, the expression in her eyes told him as clearly as though she had used words, that she knew precisely what he had thought.

"In any case," Sophia continued, covering up the moment of awkwardness between them. "I didn't complain. There were plenty of women and children ill and in need of help. But then one day the women and children stopped coming too."

Thomas narrowed his eyes.

"Why?" he asked.

"I wondered that for weeks," Sophia said. "Eventually, I reached out to a regular patient, and she confessed the truth to me."

She reached out and emptied her port with an angry jerky move.

"Agents of my father had sought out my patients and paid them considerable sums to seek out the ministrations of other doctors and surgeons."

Thomas frowned.

"A low trick," he said.

"Yes," Sophia replied. "My father had grown tired of waiting for me to settle down, and so had decided to take matters into his own hands."

"And after that, you left your home?" Thomas asked.

"No," Sophia said. "I went home to my room in my father's townhouse. And while he was out on business, I took every dress he had ever bought me, every gold ring, every diamond necklace and tiara, every pearl earring, he had given me so I could glitter and gleam and charm those he wanted me to charm and marry. And believe me, Sergeant, there were many. And I took it all from my wardrobes and chests, and I brought it to the jewellers and the tailors, and I sold the lot. By the evening, I was on a coach to Hamburg and from there I went to Paris. In Paris, I bought new clothes, clothes that I chose for myself."

Thomas fought hard to contain a smile. He could imagine, though he had no idea what the man looked like, the lanky figure of Sophia's father, well-dressed, running through his sprawling townhouse, gradually realising that he had lost his oldest daughter. Thomas almost felt sorry for the man. Almost.

"Madame Brès in Paris agreed to tutor me on the diseases of children," Sophia continued. "It was a hard life. The Madame has a puritanical bent of mind. Her hospital is rather spartan, but her results speak for themselves. After spending several months with Madame, I was accepted as a junior staff member at The Hôtel des Invalides, ministering to veterans from the Franco-Prussian War. Old men with injuries that had never truly healed."

Thomas felt an uncommon sense of admiration. After so many years with the constabulary, there were few things that could stir him. But the Danish woman's determination had impressed him.

"A rewarding experience, I'm sure," he said.

"Yes," Sophia agreed. "But I do not work well as a subordinate. I wanted to run my own practice, so I reached out to a relative of my mother in New

York. My plan was to set up my practice there with the remainder of the capital I had raised."

"A big risk to take," Thomas said. "Why America? Why not Paris or London?"

Sophia thought for a long time before answering.

"I grew up with tales of America," she said. "More than a third of the families in Denmark left for America during the last fifty years. Did you know that?"

Thomas shook his head.

"Our land is not always fertile, our customs not always fair. For many, it was the only way out of abject poverty. I will not be so arrogant as to compare my own life with that of tenant farmers and day labourers, but I grew used to thinking of America as a place of opportunity. A land where anyone can be anything."

"Perhaps," Thomas said. "I would not presume to know."

"Well," Sophia said, clapping her hands together. "Now that you have satisfied your policeman's curiosity, you could perhaps tell me why you left the Yard?"

"Because Liverpool is my home," Thomas tried but Sophia scoffed.

"You're a poor liar, Thomas," she said. "For a bizzie, I mean."

Thomas squirmed uncomfortably in his well-upholstered seat. Sophia's questions had brought to the surface those memories that only rested temporarily in shallow graves. Mary Ann Nichols being brought into the Yard, her throat opened, and her bowels laid bare, with a series of jagged cuts. Annie Chapman and Elizabeth Stride, he had only seen them after their autopsy, as sad shapes lying lonely and abandoned in a corner of the dead house under bloody sheets. But he had been among the first to respond to the fourth of the Ripper's kills. The image of Constable Watkins' face, white as a sheet, sheer terror and panic washing off him in waves that had infected the entire squad, floated across his mind. Then Catherine Eddowes was lying like discarded garbage in a corner of Mitre Square, her intestines hanging from her disembowelled abdomen. And finally, the worst. The stench of blood and death in the little room in Miller's Court.

Thomas swallowed and pushed his plate to one side. Sophia's eyes had not left his face.

"If you cannot tell me…" she began.

"No," Thomas said resignedly. "No, you were honest with me. I'll return the favour."

He stared out of the window as he thought. Steam and smoke drifted along the length of the train as it gathered speed. They had exited the suburbs and were fast approaching the county of Staffordshire, where the train would pause to take on water and coal.

"I have never worked harder than during the autumn of 1888," Thomas began. "I can't remember sleeping at all, though I must have done. I was one of dozens of constables working with Detective Inspector Fred Abberline and Sergeant William Thick."

"An unfortunate name given the accusations against the police in certain quarters of the press, I'm sure," Sophia interjected. Thomas nodded.

"Oh yes," he said. "We had no good leads, every witness, every piece of evidence just led us around in circles. And everywhere we went, the gentlemen of the press were there first, hounding our every step. People wanted answers, and we couldn't provide any."

"So, you left and went back to Liverpool?" Sophia asked, and Thomas sensed a slight note of accusation in her tone.

"No," he said. "I stayed until the death of Mary Kelly, the last of his victims. I was one of the constables who found her lying on her bed in her lodgings. The Ripper had not just killed her. He had destroyed her. She was no longer human. With the others, at least you could list the injuries inflicted upon them, and determine the one that likely killed them. But with Mary, she was more gaping wound than person. He must have worked on her for hours."

"They even wrote about her murder in the newspapers in Denmark," Sophia said. "In gruesome detail, I seem to recall. Certain elements of the press and population seemed to almost relish the killings."

Thomas snorted derisively.

"Yes," he said. "I never could understand it. People were screaming at us to catch the killer and bring him to justice, but at the same time, those very same people went to music halls to watch plays about the cunning Ripper and read penny dreadfuls about his deeds. They feared him and hated him, but some perverted part of their minds also hungered for more blood, more outrageous tales."

"*Panem et circenses*," Sophia said sadly. Thomas looked at her, confused. "It is a line from a poem by a Roman author named Juvenal. It means 'bread and circus', the two things valued above all others by the mob. cheap food and bloody entertainment. We no longer force slaves to fight each other to the death for the amusement of the masses, nor send unarmed Christians to be devoured by lions. But we are no different in reality to those who did such things thousands of years ago."

Sophia looked around the carriage. It was filled with couples and families enjoying their lunch and excitedly discussing plans for their stay in the capital.

"We think we're so civilised," Sophia said quietly. "We are masters of the land and the sea, masters of electricity now as well, and steam and so many other primeval forces. But we can never escape our craving for something darker, something much simpler."

"Bread and circus," Thomas said.

"Yes."

Sophia took a shuddering breath and seemed to reawaken from a trance.

"So, you returned after the death of Mary Kelly?" she asked. Thomas nodded.

"I helped as much as I could, but when it became clear that her death would not help us catch the Ripper any more than any of the others had, I telegraphed Detective Inspector Muldoon and told him I was ready to come home. He rewarded me with a promotion to detective sergeant on account of my new experiences, and I've worked as his assistant ever since."

"He's a funny sort of man, isn't he?" Sophia said with a strange half-smile. "He looks harmless, even a bit bumbling. But I sense that that is a mere veneer."

Thomas smiled.

"Then you're more observant than half the constables on the force, miss," he said. "There's a value in appearing simpler than one really is. And inspector Muldoon is a master of that game."

"Will you take his place when he retires?" Sophia asked casually and Thomas frowned. The thought had occurred to him, but he was not yet ready to face the reality of a constabulary without Inspector Muldoon on it. The old man had been a staple in the Rose Hill station house ever since Thomas had joined the force as a fresh-faced seventeen-year-old. To come to work without seeing Muldoon sitting in his office by his scuffed and scratched desk or, even more unthinkable, to sit himself at that desk, was not something Thomas cared to contemplate.

"That decision lies with the superintendent," he answered non-committedly, and Sophia fell silent, aware that she had been rebuffed.

After refuelling at Stafford, the train continued south-east, skirting the great city of Birmingham, its presence marked by plumes of acrid smoke and smog from its many factories and workshops. After another brief stop at Watford, the train began its final ascent into the bowels of the metropolis.

For more than 75 years, London had been the largest city on the face of the planet. Housing well over five million people, its population had grown exponentially over the past two decades, leading to a wild, untamed spread of urban occupation. Tenements, slums, even tents and lean-tos were employed to house the multitudes who came to the city from the countryside seeking employment and a better life for themselves and their families. Most of them, Thomas knew, found neither. Instead, the city swallowed them up and spat them out as beggars, pickpockets, day-labourers, whores or thieves.

Thomas hailed one of the growlers parked rank upon rank in front of the cavernous station hall. As he held the door open for Sophia to enter, she turned to the coach driver.

"Please take us to the Savoy Hotel," she said curtly as she brushed past Thomas, the scent of her perfume lingering on the early evening air and, for a brief moment, disguising the stench of the capital, the mixture of smog, unwashed bodies, and horse urine.

Thomas scrambled in after her and was almost thrown back into his seat as the driver cracked his whip and pulled into the traffic-laden roads.

"The Savoy," he said, a note of accusation in his voice "I don't remember agreeing to such accommodations."

Sophia waved a hand dismissively.

"I've never been to London before," she said. "But even in Copenhagen and Paris, I heard about the luxury of the Savoy. Apparently, the owners insist upon only hiring French chefs."

Thomas nodded gloomily. The Savoy Hotel had opened some five years previously, while Thomas was stationed with the Yard. The hotel was fitted with electric elevators and was the first hotel in the world to utilise only electricity for lighting. The hotel's chef, Auguste Escoffier, was a celebrated gourmand and culinary innovator from Nice in southern France who had entirely redesigned the Savoy's menu. The sumptuous dining experience attracted only the best clientele and even members of the royal family were known to dine at the hotel. Despite having changed into a newly washed and starched white shirt and a coat which had at least at some point in its long history been of a rich blue colour, Thomas felt distinctly aware of his unshaven face, his mutilated ear and the myriad other little clues which would reveal to a member of the upper classes that he had no place at such an exclusive venue.

He glanced moodily out of the window as they wound their way towards the Strand, through the bustling crowds. As a young constable, Thomas had read a book about the people of the capital written nearly thirty years before by the famous social justice campaigner and politician Henry Mayhew. Mayhew had, with utter fearlessness and a jangling pouch of small change, moved throughout the capital's seediest districts. He had interviewed everyone, high-born and low, and recorded their jobs, their experiences, their earnings, as well as their hopes and dreams. He had collated these tales from the gutter into two heavy volumes which could be borrowed from the Liverpool Lyceum, a subscription library to which Inspector Muldoon maintained a membership which allowed him to bring any constable who wished to further educate himself through the medium of the printed word.

The London Labour and the London Poor had opened Thomas' eyes to the state of the nation's capital, its extreme poverty, but also its industry and the sheer diversity of its life. It had helped fire the young man's imagination and had inspired him in no small measure to leave his home city for London's bustle.

The book was dedicated simply. "Those that will work. Those that cannot work, and those that will not work." All these classes of people were to be found between the book's leatherbound covers. And as Thomas stared out at the street, he saw these classes reflected among the commotion. There were oyster girls, pushing heavy barrows they had dragged and pulled all the way from the banks of the Thames. The oysters were eaten raw, perhaps soured slightly with a small glug of vinegar.

There were men selling baked potatoes directly from small grills, known as potato cans, balancing precariously on thin wooden legs. These men were often accompanied by their wives and children, who helped dole out the steaming spuds to the customers. There were street-sweepers and rubbish carters, scavengers, violinists from the east of Europe, bone-grubbers and mudlarks of all kinds coming back from the banks of the Thames after a long hard day of scrabbling about in the mud and middens of the city for any scrap of value to be found. old cloth, animal bones for fertiliser, dog shit and lost pennies.

Thomas' practiced detective's eye also spotted the men and women whom Mayhew had defined as those who would not work, even if they could. He spotted cardsharps and gamblers, sitting up against barrels and walls, throwing loaded dice and playing poker with marked cards against anyone naïve enough to engage with them. There were groups of prostitutes, too, some well-dressed seeking only high-class gentlemen for the night. Others were older and more haggard, seeking anyone who would pay them in a good measure of gin. Young boys and girls, unwashed, skinny, and quick and darting as sparrows, moved in and out between the crowds, and more than once, Thomas caught the flash of a small hand dipping into the pocket of a passing gentleman heading down the Strand towards Westminster.

Eventually, after much swearing and shouting by the driver, the growler arrived at the imposing box-like building which housed The Savoy Hotel. Most of the larger buildings in the capital were built from sand- and limestone, but the Savoy's outer walls were covered in glazed tiles which served the dual purpose of setting it apart visually from its nearby competitors and secondly, to prevent the filth and smog which clogged the capital's air from discolouring the edifice. Union Jack flags hung like bunting above its arched entrance, and two of the largest flags Thomas had ever seen cracked merrily in the evening breeze from two flagpoles mounted on the hotel's slate roof.

As soon as the growler had come to a stop, a hotel porter bustled up to open the door. The heavyset man was dressed impeccably in a double-breasted tailcoat with shining brass buttons, pressed burgundy trousers, and a dark bowtie, so tightly bound that Thomas wondered how he could breathe. Sophia smiled at the porter, who bowed her graciously out of the grocer's. As soon as he saw Thomas, his eyes darted to the small stain on Thomas's collar, to the tattered lining of his jacket, and the dust on his dark-brown homburg. His lip curled, and he looked about to speak when Sophia reached out, grabbed Thomas' arm, and steered him up the hotel's marble front stairs and through the gilded glass doors, which were held open for them by another pair of porters.

Sophia and Thomas crossed the hotel's foyer, not dissimilar in appearance and architecture to the Adelphi in Liverpool, though much grander and more sumptuously appointed. The maître d'hôtel's evident displeasure at Thomas's appearance vanished as soon as Sophia pulled out a purse and handed over a stack of notes, which Thomas estimated to be valued at considerably more than his monthly salary. He remained a step behind Sophia, his hands clasped behind his back. He noted two porters whispering together and throwing him covert glances. He reached up to scratch his chin, drawing attention to the missing part of his ear, and the two stopped their chatters and broke apart.

"Miss Steenberg," the maître d'hôtel concluded with an insincere smile. "It will be our pleasure to have you stay with us. Please allow one of the bellboys to take you to your rooms. Your luggage will be brought up shortly."

A porter materialised by Thomas' shoulder and attempted to take the detective's small brown leather satchel from him, but Thomas held on and, after a brief struggle, the porter gave up and devoted himself instead to

Sophia's scant luggage.

They crossed the foyer, following a young bell-boy who led them to one of the two electric lifts set into the marble cladding at the back of the space. When the elevator arrived with a crisp ping from an unseen bell, Thomas glanced nervously at Sophia. He did not want to admit to her that he had never before set foot in such a contraption, but nor did he have any desire to step into the small brass box.

However, seeing Sophia step smartly after the bell-boy, Thomas realised that he could not remain behind. Taking a breath to steady his nerves, he entered the elevator, and the bellboy reached across to close the sliding door with its intricate ironwork. Thomas suppressed the urge to throw the doors open and run for his life. When the lift began to rise, he experienced the uncomfortable feeling that he had left a part of his stomach behind on the ground floor, but with another steadying breath, he managed to bring his fear under control.

Arriving in a long and lushly carpeted corridor, the bellboy led them to two heavy and highly polished oak wood doors. He opened the first and led Sophia inside. Thomas remained in the hallway, glancing at the gilt-framed mirrors and paintings hung every few feet, and the electric lightbulbs with their red silk covers, which illuminated the space in a soft and yielding light. Soon, the bellboy reappeared, tucking a coin into his pocket and nodding at Thomas before leading him to the second door.

When the door opened, Thomas had to fight hard to contain a small gasp. The room was large and high-ceilinged. It was dominated by an enormous four-poster bed with red damask hangings and an intricately carved headboard. Leading Thomas into the room, the bellboy pointed out the *en suite* bathroom, every surface except the ceiling covered in marble tiles. Thomas guessed that the bathroom itself was larger than his room in Liverpool. Comfortable armchairs and a small couch upholstered in green velvet stood grouped around a circular card table in one end of the room, opposite the four-poster bed, and two glass doors could be thrown open to gain access to a narrow balcony which overlooked the Strand.

"Sir," the bellboy said politely. "I would advise you that any firearm you carry can be stored safely in the hotel's armoury. It is against hotel policy to keep firearms in the room."

"What?" Thomas looked confused at the young man, but then something clicked into place, and he had to suppress an urge to laugh. The hotel staff, in the dark about why the evidently wealthy and elegant young lady was to be found in the company of a rogue such as himself, had assumed that he was her bodyguard.

"I don't need a firearm to do my job," Thomas said to the bellboy, winking in a not-entirely friendly manner. The young man gulped and moved towards the door at some speed. As he turned to close it, Thomas fished a penny out of his pocket and threw it to the boy, who caught it in a white-gloved hand.

When the door closed, Thomas remained standing for a long moment in the centre of the room. Then he slowly moved to the bed. Tentatively, as though expecting at any moment to be told off, he tested the soft, yielding goose feather mattress with a hand. Walking into the bathroom, he noted the ceramic toilet and tested the flush by pulling the chain hanging from the reservoir. Then he knelt by the large oval bathtub and opened the two taps. He laughed as he felt the temperature of the right tap gradually increase. He opened small glass bottles of perfumed soap and pomades, intended for the bath water. There were also larger glass vials of bath salts with scents Thomas could not name.

When he closed the taps, he heard an insistent knocking on the door, which the rushing water had drowned out. He dried his hands on a soft cotton towel, left the bathroom, and opened the door to the suite. Sophia, hand raised to knock again smiled warmly at him.

"Will you join me for dinner, Sergeant?" she asked.

Thomas hesitated. He had not liked the looks thrown at him by the porters and the maître d'hôtel. He could not imagine that the white-jacketed waiters or the other guests would look any more favourably upon him in the dining room.

"I don't think so, miss," he said apologetically. "It's been a long day, and I need to rest."

"Are you certain?" Sophia said, looking hurt. Thomas nearly buckled but remained resolute.

"Yes," he said. "It is a kind offer, but…"

He left the word hanging in the air. Sophia nodded, her expression hardening. Then she nodded to him and retreated to her room. Thomas closed his door, and five minutes later, he heard her step back into the corridor, her footsteps gradually vanishing in the direction of the elevator. Thomas sighed deeply and allowed himself to fall backwards onto the bed, upsetting the multitude of soft silk pillows which had been laid artfully across it.

He had not been entirely truthful to his host. He did not feel like resting. On the contrary, his mind was racing with new impressions and experiences. A jolt of pain in his stomach brought to his attention the six hours which had passed since his last meal.

He stood up with a resolute expression, picked up his homburg, and rammed it on his head. Then he checked the contents of his pockets, counting out a few handfuls of pennies. Easily enough for a square meal from one of the street sellers, and perhaps a few drinks in one of the local alehouses. He slung his jacket over one shoulder and left the room, securely locking it behind him as he went.

Chapter Twelve

The bells of St Margaret woke Thomas shortly after dawn. He fought for a moment to surface from under the heavy eiderdown, then he reached for the girl who had fallen asleep beside him. He felt nothing, and by the coolness of the sheets, he realised that she must have awoken earlier and left. His eyes still gummed up with sleep, he rolled out of bed and made his way to the bathroom. The girl's cheap scent had overpowered the sweeter and milder scents of the soaps and perfumes provided by the hotel. She had been so excited to see the large bathtub with warm running water that Thomas had not had the heart to dissuade her from using it to bathe her lithe body.

He ran a bath and sank gently into its warm embrace, feeling the usual background aches and pains of his hard-worn body wash away. When the water began to cool, he got up, dried himself off, and dressed. He grabbed his leather satchel and left the room, throwing an envious look back at the comfortable bed. He grinned at the thought of bringing it with him back to Liverpool, tying it to the roof of the train, but then realised that if placed inside his flat, there would hardly be room to move around it.

He waited for Sophia by the hotel's highly polished mahogany reception desk. The night porter threw him an accusatory look. When Thomas had arrived back at the hotel, arm-in-arm with a lady friend and reeking of cheap whiskey, the man's patience had been tested to the limit. But, knowing that Thomas travelled in the company of a very wealthy guest, the night porter held his tongue and bit back his reprimand. It was, though, with clear relief, that he noticed Sophia emerging from the elevator in the company of the bellboy.

"I hope you had a restful night, dear lady?" he said, a forced and entirely fraudulent smile on his lips. Sophia nodded.

"I did," she said. She glanced at Thomas, who noted hostility in her look. "Though I must say that the walls of the suites are rather thin."

Thomas blushed at her words and stepped clumsily out of the way as she swept out of the foyer. Sophia was a tall woman, and Thomas had to jog to keep up with her as she descended the front steps, stepping out into a true London autumn day, cold and with a fine mist of rain hanging in the air.

"Miss Steenberg," he began. "I feel I must apologise…"

"No apology needed, sergeant," she said in clipped tones as she waited for a porter to open the door to a waiting growler. "We all have our vices. You do not need to explain yours."

She entered the growler without another word, leaving Thomas to give instructions to the driver to bring them to the new Scotland Yard building on Victoria Embankment. The journey was a short one, but conducted in complete and uncomfortable silence. Thomas did not know what to say, and Sophia evidently had no desire to speak at all.

Thomas had never set foot in this larger and better-positioned station house, the move to it having been affected the year after he returned to Liverpool. From the outside the red brick building with its bands of Portland limestone and round towers set in each corner gave the fleeting impression of an impregnable Crusader castle. The iron bars which blocked the windows at street level and on the lower floors added to this effect, as did the placement of the building, directly against the banks of the Thames, which appeared almost to be a moat to this fortress of policing.

The growler rumbled under a limestone arch leading to an inner courtyard. Groups of constables readying themselves to go out on parade and then take up their beats around the city were milling about aimlessly, awaiting the arrival of the duty sergeant. Their uniforms looked similar to those worn by the Liverpool constabulary – dark blue great coats, round helmets, and light-blue short capes to keep out the wind. What set the Metropolitan police force apart were their buttons. They were cast in gilded brass, embossed with a crown by contrast to all other constabularies in the country, where silver buttons were worn. Without thinking, Thomas pressed a hand to his chest, feeling the round shape of the gold button he wore on a leather string around his neck. He had cut it from his uniform jacket on his last day in London, and it had never left his presence since then.

Though Thomas recognised several faces among the crowd, he did not wish to answer questions or hang about. As soon as the growler stopped, he grabbed Sophia by the arm and quickly steered her through a pair of tall wooden gates. They led to a spacious stable where the Yard kept its horses and to a narrow door that led to a flight of stone steps. At the top of the steps, Thomas and Sophia passed through another door, emerging in a large watch room, almost empty now that all the constables were mustering outside. Thomas looked around. Small wooden desks were set in rows where constables could sit when not walking the beat, and a series of wooden doors with large windows set along one wall led to offices belonging to the assistant and deputy police commissioners when they were present, as well as to the inspectors who commanded the Yard's detectives.

Sophia jumped involuntarily at the loud crash of one of the doors being thrown open. She and Thomas both looked around to see a tall man with bushy, light brown sideburns merging together with a scruffy moustache. Both sideburns and moustache were streaked liberally with grey. The new arrival was wearing a tweed jacket and a dark red bowtie, a tan bowler clutched in one hand.

"O'Callaghan!" he roared. "What in the name of all the devils in hell are you doing here?"

Thomas' face split into a grin of genuine pleasure.

"Inspector Abberline," he said, stepping forward and reaching out a hand. "It's been too long."

"It has, my boy, it has," Abberline replied, shaking Thomas' hand with both of his own.

Frederick Abberline had started out his career as a clockmaker, but this had ill-suited his temperament. Leaving his native Dorset and moving to London, the young Abberline had enlisted in the Metropolitan Police and so impressed his superiors that he had been promoted to a detective inspector in less than five years. From plainclothes infiltration of Irish rebel groups operating in the capital, to catching rum smugglers and gun runners along the Thames harbour front, Abberline had been involved in every facet of police work before he found himself assigned to solve a brutal murder of a young woman in Whitechapel. The case had propelled him first to international fame, and then to notoriety as the man who had let the Ripper slip through his fingers. Thomas noted the grey of his beard as well as the wrinkles, heavier and more prominent now than when he had last seen him three years previously.

"I hear you're a detective sergeant now," Abberline said warmly. "A well-deserved promotion. And are those scousers keeping you on your toes?"

"Oh yes," Thomas said with a broad smile. "There's always something going on."

"I bet there is," Abberline said, roaring with laughter.

He glanced over Thomas' shoulder and saw Sophia standing in the middle of the empty watch room, glancing around with an air of nervousness that Thomas could not recall seeing before.

"And who is this charming creature?" Abberline said jovially. "Don't tell me you've married, Thomas?"

Thomas blushed and stepped aside, extending an arm and beckoning Sophia forward.

"This is Miss Sophia Steenberg, a visitor from the Kingdom of Denmark who is staying temporarily in Liverpool. She is consulting with the Liverpool Constabulary on a case."

Abberline's eyebrows rose so far as to nearly mould together with his receding hairline.

"A pleasure to make your acquaintance, miss," he said, bowing stiffly to Sophia. Then he turned to Thomas. "Consulting on a case, eh? This sounds like a story worth hearing. Please join me in my office."

He led the way into a small, cramped office. Every wall was covered with shelves and every shelf was loaded down with papers, books, case files, photographic plates, and drawings from various crime scenes. Thomas had never understood how Abberline could ever find anything in the perineal mess of his office, but the inspector's memory for the location of every sheet of paper was photographic. Abberline waved at two rickety wooden chairs standing in front of his desk. Then he took out a pipe, packed it carefully, and—lighting a taper from a candle on his desk—lit it. Soon, the fragrant scent of tobacco filled the room.

"So, Thomas," he began. "Tell me why you're here."

Thomas hesitated, but he could see no way to trick or bamboozle the inspector. He decided that straight-forward honesty would be the best policy.

"I've come to ask your assistance, Fred," he said. "We've got a nasty murder up north. A very nasty murder."

Abberline grunted but said nothing.

"A young girl, a prostitute, by the name of Polly Wilkes. We found her in a warehouse on Stanley Dock. Someone had opened up her stomach and pulled out her guts. They had also slit her throat and dismembered both her arms."

Abberline's expression did not change. His eyes were locked on Thomas, his hand carefully moving the pipe to his mouth. He inhaled deeply.

"Did you say her throat and belly?"

Thomas nodded. Abberline leaned back in his chair, his face wreathed in smoke.

"This sounds like a story I've heard before, Thomas," he said. "It didn't have a happy ending."

"I remember," Thomas said gravely.

Abberline narrowed his eyes.

"Do you think..."

Thomas nodded.

"But how? We haven't seen hide nor hair of that bastard for nigh on three years. Why would he resurface now? Why there and not here?"

Thomas shrugged.

"If I knew that, I would already have caught him," he said.

Abberline puffed on his pipe for a long moment. Then he knocked out the remaining sparks and ash from the pipe into a tin spittoon standing by the side of his desk.

"Well then," he said. "That explains this pleasant visit."

"I wish I was here under better circumstances," Thomas said. Abberline nodded slowly.

"What do you need?" he asked.

"Access," Thomas replied. He turned to Sophia. "Miss Steenberg is a trained surgeon. She made a number of observations about our victim, including deducing that the murderer had likely not finished his mutilations when he was scared away from the corpse."

The brief smile Abberline bestowed upon Sophia was friendly enough, but it did not reach his eyes, and Thomas sensed that, like Muldoon, Abberline was humouring Thomas.

"These are modern times, they tell me," Abberline said. "I must admit, I've never before come across a woman doctor."

Sophia returned his insincere smile with a cold one of her own. Thomas decided to intervene while the tone was still friendly.

"Fred," he said. "You know I wouldn't ask this of you if I didn't need to. We've got nothing, and that's the honest truth. We don't have any witnesses or any real evidence. All we have right now is Miss Steenberg and her theories."

"And you're asking me to give you both access to our archives?"

"Yes," Thomas said. "We need to determine whether the killer we're hunting really is the same man who played us for fools back in '88."

Abberline frowned. The Ripper case still made newspaper headlines, and he, as the lead investigator who had failed to catch the killer, was rarely portrayed in a flattering manner.

"Very well," Abberline said. "But keep it to yourself while you're here, Thomas. It's probably best the boys don't find out about Miss Steenberg or her role. And the same goes for the superintendent. I'm not in his good books as it is and this," he hesitated. "this irregularity," he glanced briefly at Sophia. "would not stand me in good stead."

"I understand," Thomas said, not daring to look in Sophia's direction.

Abberline stood up and led them out of his office, through the still-empty watch room, and down a narrow corridor lined with doors bearing little brass plaques identifying their occupants. There were the offices of the superintendent and deputy superintendent. There were offices of the resident coroner and the law offices of those barristers who worked with the Yard to bring the criminals brought into the station house to justice.

At the end of the corridor was a door leading to the archive room. The room was lit by electricity, and when Abberline flicked a switch by the door, lamps hanging from the ceiling burst into light. They revealed a long, high-ceilinged room filled with rows of shelves. A table and four chairs stood by the door, and the thin layer of dust on the floor showed how rarely the old records and archives were consulted.

"You'll find everything we have on the Ripper here," Abberline said leading them down the rows and pointing to a whole shelf filled with wooden crates and heavy ledgers. "Be warned though," he continued, speaking directly to Sophia. "There are some truly godawful photographs in these folders. What they show you may never be able to unsee again."

Sophia looked at the detective inspector with an annoyed expression.

"Please don't concern yourself with me, inspector," she said in clipped tones. She reached past him and pulled out one of the wooden crates, carrying it to the table. Soon she was engrossed in one of the leatherbound notebooks stored inside. Abberline stood for a moment irresolute, then he cleared his throat loudly and bustled from the room.

"A little more civility would be helpful," Thomas said quietly when the door had closed behind the inspector. The moment he had spoken the sentence, Thomas regretted it. Sophia looked at him, her blue eyes blazing with anger.

"Please do not presume to lecture me on civility, sergeant," she said. "I have spent less than four days in your country and in that time, I have witnessed the truly brutal murder of a young woman, no doubt by a man who saw her as nothing more than a piece of flesh – in much the same way as I am sure you did with the girl you purchased last night like a plantation owner at the block. I have been patronised by every man I've met, and as a crowning glory, I have been awoken by a horde of constables, locked in a cell, and accused of murder. Have I left anything out, detective sergeant?"

Thomas swayed backwards under the force of her words. From outside the room, there was a muted rumble of heavy footfalls and mutterings as the constables on duty at the station housed filed back in, taking up their seats and waiting for those members of the public, criminals and victims alike, who would be brought into the station house throughout the day.

Thomas opened his mouth, then closed it again. Sophia did not lower her glare but stared him down. Eventually, he averted his eyes and reached for one of the notebooks, almost at random. He opened it and glanced through it. It contained some of the witness statements relating to the murder of Elizabeth Stride. He closed it and replaced it on the desk. He could sense Sophia's eyes upon him.

Suddenly, he found himself remembering sitting, many decades before, in the small schoolroom on Dover Street. His teacher, Miss Flaherty, had been an elderly spinster, known and feared among her students for her acid tongue, her ability to hear even preliminary attempts at mischief clear across the room, and, despite her age, the strength with which she could wield a birch cane. He was again sitting in the front row, his head lowered in shame, trying to avoid Miss Flaherty's stare. She had asked him to solve a simple piece of calculus, but he knew that he couldn't do it. She knew that he couldn't do it. The silence stretched on for what seemed like hours. Then he felt the cane across his hand outstretched on the slanted tabletop.

"You're a stupid boy, Thomas," the older woman had snarled. "Stand up."

The humiliation of being caned in front of a school room full of friends and neighbours never quite stopped stinging. Sophia's words had made him feel that old sense of humiliation, even though Miss Flaherty was long ago laid in the ground.

Meeting Sophia's diamond-hard glare was one of the hardest acts Thomas had ever done. But when he did, his throat finally opened, and he felt able to speak to her.

"I'm sorry," he said. Sophia blinked. Her anger was still there, he could see it in her eyes and in her flaring nostrils, her tightly pursed lips. But his admission seemed to thaw the atmosphere in the room.

"I know you're trying your best," she said, still a little stiffly. "For Polly. It does you credit. And for that I am grateful."

Thomas mumbled a reply, which the Danish surgeon did not seem to hear. She had turned away and begun sorting through the many hundreds of photographs contained in the box, some on cardboard and some on square glass negatives. She cleared an area of the desk and began to lay them out in orderly piles as Thomas picked up folder after folder, not knowing truly what he was looking for, but knowing that he might perhaps learn what it was when he saw it mentioned.

After she had divided the photographs into piles, Sophia began sorting through each pile in sequence. She picked up every photograph and, using a small jeweller's eye lens, she examined the gruesome images minutely. Thomas averted his eyes from the images. He had seen the woman dead in the flesh and had no desire to relive those injuries, preserved for eternity on paper or glass.

Chapter Thirteen

The Ten Bells was among the busiest public houses in Whitechapel. Lying in the very centre of the busy Spitalfields weaving district, the brightly lit establishment attracted hundreds of weavers as they went home to their tenement houses from the spinneries and workshops that lined every street in the neighbourhood. The walls of the pub were covered entirely with blue, white, and green glazed tiles,l and lighting was provided both by two glass chandeliers hanging from the ceiling and enumerable gas-powered sconces along the walls. A drinker arriving at the Ten Bells would be confronted first by the landlord, Mr Oliver, standing in a small wood, brass and glass cage by the entrance. There he exchanged coins and notes for tin tokens which could then be taken to the bar and paid for good measures of drink, porter, rum, beer or whatever else took the customer's fancy. The little booth, known as a gin cage, were popular additions to alehouses, gin palaces, and public houses throughout the city as they removed from the bar staff any temptation to skim off the nightly takings.

It had been a long day spent in almost total silence in the dusty archives. Rather than return directly to the Savoy, Thomas had suggested that they should instead take the opportunity to properly experience life in London. Sophia had agreed with good grace, and they had made their way on foot down the Strand and through Whitechapel. Eager to repay the Danish surgeon for her generosity, Thomas had insisted on buying them dinner. two piping hot steak and kidney pies which had to be eaten with extreme care to prevent the liquid hot fat and oil dripping from them ruining Sophia's dress and Thomas' shirt.

After another pleasant stroll during which Sophia had gazed around the busy street life of the city with rapt attention, they had arrived at the Ten Bells. A couple of coins became two tokens, and Thomas used these to purchase two glasses of oily yet fragrant London gin. They found a small table in a corner of the bar which allowed them to see its patrons while remaining sufficiently far away from a large table of muckrackers whose stench was palpable.

Sophia sniffed the half-pint glass of gin and took a measured sip. She wrinkled her nose as the fiery liquid hit the back of her throat.

"I must admit that I prefer absinthe in Paris to gin in London," she said, speaking loudly to be heard over the raucous laughter and drunken singing that filled the bar. Thomas grinned.

"You get used to it," he said.

"Why are the English so obsessed with gin?" Sophia asked, looking around and noting that most patrons were drinking gin not by the half-pint but by the pint or the bottle.

"Tax reasons, mostly," Thomas said. Sophia raised an eyebrow and Thomas explained. "We originally bought gin from the Netherlands, but then people started making it themselves around here. It's easy enough if you know what you're doing, though the distilleries did cause a few fires now and then. Because the gin is made right here, there are no import licenses or taxes placed on it, so it's far cheaper than rum or other liquors imported from abroad."

"Sounds like a recipe for disaster," Sophia said with a concerned expression. "As a physician, I can't condone extreme consumption of alcohol."

"As a bizzie, neither can I," Thomas said. "The gin causes a lot of crime. But whenever the government have tried to limit its spread by imposing taxes it leads to riots."

"So, they've given up?" Sophia said with a crooked smile.

"You could say that" Thomas said. "As long as no one bothers the people living in the better neighbourhoods I don't think they care much about what happens here in Whitechapel."

Sophia took another sip of gin, shuddering at the taste.

"It's the same all over," she said. "Copenhagen, Paris or London."

Thomas nodded.

"It's the same the whole world over," he recited. "It's the poor that gets the blame. It's the rich that get the pleasure, ain't it all a bleedin' shame."

Sophia blinked and then laughed.

"What on earth was that sergeant?" she said, still giggling.

"A music hall ballad," Thomas said with a shy grin. "Quite a popular one."

"Well, it certainly rings true," Sophia said. "Although," she added. "Although, as one of the rich of this world, I don't complain about getting at least some of the pleasure."

Thomas looked intently at Sophia for a long moment. Then he smiled.

"We can't none of us help how we're born," he said. "I won't hold it against you."

Their conversation was interrupted by a loud crashing sound from the bar. They turned to see two young men, one dressed in a butcher's apron, the other in one of the stained and dirty smocks worn by the weavers, squaring off against each other. A broken glass dripping with the remnants of one of their drinks was lying on the floor. The surrounding patrons were quickly grabbing their own drinks and moving out of the way before any more alcohol was wasted on the sticky wooden floorboards.

"Enough of that, you two," the landlord roared as he emerged from his booth, brandishing a long and heavy cherrywood cudgel. "You know the rules in here. One punch and you're out on your ear!"

The two young men ignored him. The butcher's apprentice feinted left and then swiftly moved direction, catching his opponent off guard with a vicious uppercut. The young weaver fell backwards but managed to steady himself against the bar. As his opponent charged forward, he sidestepped him and stuck out his leg, tripping him up. The charging turned into a tumble as the butcher's apprentice went face-first, arms windmilling wildly to the ground.

"Cut it out!" the landlord roared as he joined in the fray, aiming his cudgel at the weaver. He hit him on the shoulder, and the man roared in pain. Sophia looked sideways as the landlord raised his cudgel again. Thomas had vanished. She looked back to the fight in time to see the detective pushing through the row of spectators. He reached out and grabbed the landlord's cudgel, effortlessly pulling the weapon from his fingers. As the landlord turned, his teeth bared, Thomas held up his warrant card without a word. The landlord visibly deflated as Thomas threw the cudgel to the floor. He gently pushed the landlord out of the way and grabbed the weaver by the arm, steering him relentlessly towards the door. Two patrons held the door open as Thomas propelled the man through it into the street.

The butcher's apprentice had gotten shakily to his feet, but when he saw both Thomas and the landlord ranged against him, he shrugged, spat on the floor, and quietly followed his erstwhile opponent out of the Ten Bells.

Thomas nodded to the landlord, who returned the gesture with a scowl. The patrons around the bar had fallen quiet. Sophia guessed that the revelation that they were sharing the establishment with a plainclothes police officer did not sit well with many of them. Even as she looked on, a few small groups of men quietly finished their drinks and vanished into the night, leaving the bar considerably less full than it had been only moments before.

The babble of conversation gradually rose in volume as Thomas retook his seat.

"Young fools," he said, swirling the few mouthfuls of gin left in the bottom of his glass. "Beating each other senseless over spilt beer."

Sophia narrowed her eyes. She felt that she had gotten to know the detective sergeant well in these last few days spent together. He intrigued her. He was rough around the edges and bore none of the marks of any higher education. But he had a genuine interest in people, and a sense for how to approach them. He had the rare gift of being able to make himself utterly at home in any given situation. He was certainly not wise by the standards with which she had been used to judge wisdom. But he wore the streets, both in London and in Liverpool, as a coat. As someone who had always felt that her predetermined destiny was wrong, she envied him that ability. The ability to fit in.

"I think you've been a little unfair to me, Thomas," she said, and he looked up at her, frowning. "I mean, I told you about my family on the train. But you have never mentioned anything about yours. Do you have siblings? Parents?"

Thomas looked away, averting his gaze from hers. After an awkward silence, long and deep, he finished his gin and cleared his throat.

"Not much to tell, to be honest," he said. "I was born in Liverpool, in Dover Street. My dad was a sailor, and my mum took in laundry to make ends meet."

"You didn't see your father much, I assume," Sophia said. Thomas shook his head, his features becoming tense and drawn.

"I hated it when he came home," he said vehemently. "He'd get drunk and beat up my mum. Sometimes my brothers or me tried to intervene. Then he'd beat us, too. Samuel Wilson was his name. A real nasty piece of work, he was."

Sophia frowned.

"Wilson," she said. "But your surname is O'Callaghan."

"I took my mother's name after dad died," Thomas said. "I wasn't going to carry that bastard's name for the rest of my life."

Sophia sat silently for a while, uncertain of how to continue. Thomas solved her dilemma by breaking the silence himself.

"Mum died a few years ago. Consumption got her in the end. She'd been struggling with it for years."

"I'm sorry," Sophia said, and she meant it. Thomas shrugged.

"At least she's not suffering anymore," he said.

"And what about your brothers?" Sophia asked. Thomas grinned quietly.

"I'm the oldest of three," Thomas said. "And probably the brightest of the bunch, even if I do say so myself."

Sophia smiled.

"Are they with the constabulary as well?"

"God no," Thomas said, and his grin widened. "Royston's a sailor like Dad. Haven't seen him in more than a year, and I've got no idea when he's coming back home."

"And your other brother?"

"Patrick became a whaler. He met a girl up in Aberdeen and moved up there. I get a letter from him sometimes, when he remembers to write."

"Don't you miss them?"

Thomas looked at the patrons standing around the bar. In the corner, a small group had brought out instruments, a guitar, a fiddle, a harmonica, and a pair of bone spoons, striking up a fast jig.

"They're my brothers," Thomas said. "But we didn't have the best of homes growing up. Sometimes when we see each other, it just brings back bad memories."

And so, you made your own family, Sophia thought. Muldoon and the boisterous Scottish desk sergeant and the constables. Even Detective Inspector Abberline here in London. She forced herself to finish the last of her gin. She was beginning to feel the effects of the drink. Colours seemed clearer, sounds somehow sharper and more muted at the same time. She turned to Thomas.

"It's been a long day," she said. "And there's still work to do."

Thomas had not spoken about the case to the Danish surgeon during their time in the archives. He had sensed that she needed time and space to make her deductions, so he had let her work in silence, looking through hundreds of photographs and sketches, making copious notes in a small leather-bound journal similar to his own.

"What do you think?" he asked now. "Do you think the Ripper killed Polly?"

Sophia did not reply. She took a deep breath as if to steady her nerve and then looked him directly in the eyes.

"I'm still not sure, Thomas," she said. "I know that's not what you want to hear, but I don't want to jump to any conclusions until I'm absolutely certain that nothing's been overlooked."

Thomas nodded.

"I understand," he said. "I wish more detectives thought like you do. We'd get a good deal fewer cases thrown out at trial if they did."

Sophia smiled and, prompted by his words and by the gin coursing through her blood, she reached out and placed her hand on his. He did not pull back.

They sat like that for a long moment. Then Sophia broke the spell, got to her feet and, with only a few stumbles on the rain-drenched cobbles, the two made their way back towards the Savoy.

Chapter Fourteen

Miss Victoria Watson was born as the fifth of seven children, all girls, daughters of a Liverpool coal trader. Victoria's mother had taken in clothing to mend and wash, at least until her eyesight began to fail her. While Victoria's older sisters had found quick employment in one of the many factories around the city, working with textiles, ceramics, and glass, as soon as their mandatory schooling was over, Victoria had expressed an interest in learning. Supported by her school mistress, who recognised the young girl's talent for reading and mathematics, Victoria had persuaded her reluctant parents. With much complaining, they had stumped up the moneys required to buy her a modest, serviceable dress and to pay for an additional two years of schooling until she had turned sixteen. With her diploma in hand, Victoria had been hired, as a school teacher herself, at a small dame school not far from her home. To save her meager salary, she remained with her parents, paying whatever she could towards the upkeep of her younger siblings.

Money was tight, and when Victoria's mother could no longer do her seamstress work, Victoria had trudged for days through the affluent neighbourhoods in Liverpool, looking for any household, who might require a private tutor. On the third day, she had struck lucky. In a well-appointed mansion, right across the road from Sefton Park, she had been introduced to the Robinsons, a well-to-do family whose patriarch had built his wealth in the cotton trade. The young Master Robinson was, however, much to his father's chagrin, a dreamer with little interest in ledgers, mathematics, and accounting. Victoria had been hired on the spot to remedy the situation.

Three nights a week, she made her way from the schoolhouse to the Robinson's manor and spent four hours tutoring the young man, trying her best to break through his shell of dreamy contemplation. Privately, she doubted whether he would ever be a titan of industry. Perhaps a novelist or a poet, though. He had the temperament and imagination for it, certainly, though she doubted that Mr Robinson would ever allow his son to venture into such an uncertain profession.

As usual on a Wednesday night, Victoria had left the Robinson's house via the servant's door on the back of the property. On the way, Mrs Gifford, the cook, had pressed a tightly wrapped oiled paper package containing a few pork cutlets into the young teacher's hand.

"You need feedin' up, my girl," the old woman had said, pressing a pudgy finger to her lips and glancing towards the stairs leading to the family's quarters.

Victoria stuffed the package into her heavy leather satchel containing her books and papers as she crossed the road towards the park. The park might be dark at night, but it was the shortest distance between the Robinson's house and her family's own apartment, consisting of only two rooms over a tannery. The constant stench of the urine and excrement used by the tanners had been such a big part of Victoria's childhood that she did not even notice it anymore.

At the entrance to the park, she nodded politely to two young constables standing either side of the gate. Only one of them returned her salute, the other, too busy watching a group of rowdy young women who were making their way down the pavement, well-lubricated, by the sound of their coarse laughter, and clearly looking for a customer with whom to spend a few hours.

A light breeze rustled through the elm and ash trees planted at intervals along the gravel path that led through the park. She could sense more than hear or see the large artificial lake to the right of the road, its surface only occasionally reflecting a single bright white flash from the moon as it passed between heavy clouds.

She could smell the coming rain and sped up, eager not to be caught outside in the deluge. Her polished high-heeled leather boots crunched on the gravel.

Something had moved in a clump of trees up ahead. Victoria stopped, staring ahead. A small stand of willows had been planted by the bank of the lake. She could have sworn that she had glimpsed, in the brief moonlight, a human face. She took an involuntary step back. Then she looked around and listened. After several long moments, she cautiously stepped forward again, having heard nothing to further alarm her. But she did not want to cross by the stand of willows.

Instead, she took a side path which wound down by the side of the lake, under a small sandstone aqueduct leading to a small plaza before it again joined the main path.

But as she walked, she could now hear that her footsteps were not the only ones on the path. As though echoing her own footfalls, crunching sounds came from behind her, getting closer.

She grasped her bag closer, trying to think, but feeling a rising sense of dread wash over her. She blinked to clear tears from her eyes as she sped up, running now, more than walking.

The footsteps matched her speed.

Victoria abandoned any pretence, turned, and threw her heavy bag at a dark figure who had appeared on the path behind her. The bag hit the figure with a heavy thud and the figure bent double. As it did, a flash of light glinted off a long blade. A knife.

Victoria screamed. Screamed, turned, and ran. She ran for her life, determinately and in total silence, sacrificing her screams for extra breath to run.

The footfalls behind her were getting fainter. Whoever was chasing her could not keep up with the lithe nineteen-year-old even with her heavy boots and long dress. Christina barrelled under the aqueduct and crossed the plaza.

It had been dropped earlier in the day by a small boy, the little wooden toy soldier. It was only as long as a grown man's thumb and so chipped and chewed by new teeth and roughly handled by chubby hands that it was worn into an almost smooth cylinder with only traces of paint. Once it had been a proud Guardsman with black trousers and a rose-red jacket.

Victoria felt the object as her right foot landed on it. The little wooden cylinder slipped away, unbalancing her. She felt her ankle twist and, almost in a dreamlike detached state, she sensed the gravel rising out of the dark to meet her.

She did not have time to throw up her hands to protect her face. Her head slammed into the ground, sending a spasm of pain radiating from her forehead and her broken nose. She was dazed, unable to tell what was up and what was down. Her ears were ringing, drowning out the approaching footsteps.

Victoria did not really sense the weight of a human body pressing her down in the gravel. The point of the Liston knife was so sharp that it cut through both her dress and the tough muscles between her ribs as though they were nothing more than thin rice paper. When the point of the blade reached her heart, severing her superior vena cava and sending oxygen-depleted blood pouring into her chest cavity, the school teacher's body stiffened and went into shock.

Victoria lay with her cheek pressed against the cool gravel, seeing the world as though it, not her, had fallen over. She blinked, her mouth opening and closing, a fish out of water desperately trying to breathe one last mouthful of life-sustaining water through its gills.

As the world faded away into darkness, Victoria felt her body lift. Her last thought was of choirs of angles, gently carrying her home.

It was more than three hours after dawn before a passing nanny, taking her charges for a morning stroll in the park, noticed Victoria's remains. Her screams of horror brought constables running. They slowed down as they approached what had once been Miss Victoria Watson. They paled. Then they sent runners for Detective Inspector Muldoon.

Chapter Fifteen

Thomas accepted the tightly rolled cigarillo proffered by Detective Inspector Abberline. The two were sitting alone in the inspector's chaotic office, the only light coming from a single electric desk lamp and the greyish light of an overcast day filtering in through the window. Thomas and Sophia had spent the morning in the archives, but after a few hours, Thomas had decided to leave the Danish surgeon to her notetaking and stretch his legs. Abberline's open door had invited him inside, and the two had spent a pleasant hour conversing about everything and nothing, about the good old days in London and Thomas's own plans for his future.

Thomas exhaled a cloud of fragrant tobacco smoke and sighed contentedly.

"What about you, sir?" he asked. "When are we going to see Superintendent Frederik Abberline?"

Abberline sneered.

"On a cold day in hell, my boy," he said. "On a very cold day in hell. They won't make the man who let the Ripper get away superintendent. The public won't stand for it, and neither will Whitehall."

"They can't still be holding that against you," Thomas said. "You weren't the only detective on that case."

"No," Abberline said. "But it's easier to go after a single target than many. And in any case, I don't know how much longer I'll be at the Yard."

Thomas looked at the older man, his lined face framed by bushy mutton-chops and wild, untamed eyebrows.

"What do you mean?" Thomas asked quietly. Abberline looked out of the window, a scowl on his face.

"Did you hear about the bust we did on Cleveland Street?" Abberline asked. "A couple of years back."

Thomas frowned as he tried to think back.

"I think I read something about it," he said. "I'd only just gotten settled back in Liverpool, I can't say I was paying much attention to what was going on here."

"Probably for the best," Abberline said, his expression still drawn and angry. "We collared a young telegraph boy, a fifteen-year-old lad. He had pockets jingling with coins, so first we thought he'd been thieving, of course. When we questioned him, he told us that he'd earned the money in a brothel on Cleveland Street."

Thomas nodded. It was an open secret that several of the brothels in the capital catered to those men who preferred the company of other men. Others still catered specifically to those who preferred the company of children of either sex.

"We raided it," Abberline said. "The place was full of young boys, mostly boys working as runners for the telegraph, earning some extra coin."

"And their clients?" Thomas asked.

"Oh, we arrested enough to fill all our cells to breaking point," Abberline said with a grim smile. "And the boys sang like canaries, too, naming dozens of other clients who hadn't been present during the raid. But then the trouble began."

"What do you mean?"

Abberline squashed his cigarillo into a ceramic ashtray with excessive force.

"Turns out that some of the clients named weren't just your run-of-the-mill street trash," he said. "There were army officers, a few members of the nobility, and even a sitting member of Parliament."

"No," Thomas said, shocked, leaning forward in his rickety wooden chair.

"Oh yes," Abberline said. "And suddenly, the investigation wasn't a priority anymore. When we finally managed to get a few of the bastards hauled up in front of a judge, the cases got thrown out as soon as they were called."

Thomas shook his head, extinguishing his own cigarillo after savouring a final drag.

"Can't say I'm surprised," he said. Abberline looked around surreptitiously as though making sure that no spies or informers were hiding in the corner of the room.

"I continued the investigation despite warnings from the superintendent," he said quietly. "But a name kept coming up when I interviewed the boys, and when the superintendent found out, he told me outright that if I didn't drop it, I'd be drummed out of the force on the spot."

"What name?" Thomas said in a whisper, leaning closer. Abberline looked around the room again.

"The Prince of Wales," he said.

"The Queen's grandson?" Thomas said, forgetting to keep his voice down. Abberline waved his hands frantically and hushed him.

"Be quiet, boy," he snapped. "You'll land us both in the cells."

Thomas let out a low whistle, leaned back and interlaced his fingers behind his head.

"I can see why you stopped the investigation," he said.

Abberline nodded.

"No point in continuing," he said. "No one was going to let me get anywhere as soon as that name started getting thrown around."

"But they didn't kick you out," Thomas said. "So why are you thinking of leaving?"

Abberline sighed.

"I'm tired, Thomas," he said. "First the Ripper and then Cleveland Street. It's all gotten too political. Can't do honest policework with the superintendent breathing down my neck. I'll stay to see my successor nominated, and then I'll bow out gracefully. The wife wants to move down to the coast. Bournemouth perhaps."

"And what will you do there?" Thomas asked with a grin. "I can't see you as a fisherman or whelk seller."

Abberline laughed.

"Oh, I have options," he said. He reached into his desk drawer, pulled out a typed letter, and passed it across to Thomas. Thomas noted the letterhead, a single open eye surmounted by the words Pinkerton National Detective Agency.

"The Pinkertons," he said, surprised.

"They've been trying to recruit me for years," Abberline said. "When I'm done with the Yard, I think I'll let them. I can put in a good word for you if you'd like."

"I don't think inspector Muldoon would like that one bit," Thomas said with a smile. "I can't see him sharing his patch with a Pinkerton man."

"Perhaps not," Abberline said, taking back the letter and replacing it in his drawer.

The two men were interrupted by a soft knock on Abberline's door. It opened and Sophia stepped into the room. Thomas could see from her tight-lipped expression and stiff bearing that the surgeon was anxious. Abberline gestured to the empty chair in front of his desk.

"Our expert," he said. "And have you finished your investigations in our archives?"

Sophia sat down gingerly, and without looking directly at Abberline, she opened her notebook.

"I have," she said. "And I don't think either of you are to be very pleased."

She took out several cardboard photographs which had been stuffed between the leaves of the notebook and laid them out on Abberline's desk. The two detectives leaned forward.

"What am I looking at?" Abberline asked.

Sophia glanced furtively up at him. She bit her lower lip, her shoulders hunched.

"I don't think whoever killed Polly killed these five women," she said finally. Thomas felt a leaden weight sink into his stomach. If they could not connect Polly's murder to the Ripper killings, then they had nothing, no evidence, not even a theory to work from. Then they were truly groping in the dark.

Sophia pointed down at one of the images. It showed a woman lying on her back. Even with the distance of several years, Thomas clearly recalled the figure. Annie Chapman. The second of the Ripper's victims. Annie had been found in a back yard on Hanbury Street.

"It turns out," Sophia said. "That the disembowelments were the key."

She picked up the photograph and pointed to a clearly visible wound on the left side of the victim's lower abdomen.

"Annie Chapman's intestines were accessed by a jagged incision on the left side of her body. Her intestines were removed, as with Polly, but laid on her shoulder, not covering her womanhood," Sophia said. Then she picked up a second photograph and pointed again. "The first victim, Mary Ann Nichols," she said. "Another jagged cut on the left side of her abdomen, though her intestines were not removed or laid bare."

She laid the images down and picked up another photograph. The black-and-white image showed the crumbled body of a tall woman with a long, straight nose and bulging eyes.

"The third victim," Sophia said. "Elizabeth Long. She had her throat cut, but there were few other injuries on her body, and nothing was done to her abdomen."

"We believe the killer may have been disturbed during this kill," Abberline supplied quietly as he gazed fixedly at the photograph. Sophia nodded.

"I would concur," she said. "But then look at the fourth victim. Catherine Eddows."

She reached for another photograph. Thomas remembered Catherine Eddowes' corpse well enough. He did not need to consult a photograph or a drawing. All he needed to do to recall the injuries which had been inflicted upon her in gruesome detail was to close his eyes. Sophia hesitated, noting his discomfort, but she continued nevertheless.

"Catherine Eddowes. The fourth and penultimate victim. Her abdomen was laid bare, with a long vertical cut running from her sternum to her pudenda. The wound is jagged, the skin almost sawed and torn in places rather than cut. No surgeon's scalpel or Liston knife inflicted that wound."

She picked up a final photograph.

"And finally," she swallowed. "The fifth victim, Mary Kelly." She stopped for a long moment, seemingly to find the right words. "The killer, I suspect, would have enjoyed this murder the most. The privacy of her small room gave him license to experiment with every grotesque perversion he could have dreamed of. Her injuries are extensive, and the abdomen was not so much cut as removed."

Thomas nodded, smelling for a moment on the air the musty scent of blood and bile that had lingered in Mary Kelly's room.

"What does this mean?" he asked. "And how does it prove that the same killer did not murder Polly Wilkes?"

Sophia folded her hands under her chin, staring at the peeling paint on the ceiling for a long moment.

"Surgical incisions are an art form," she said. "There are dozens of incision types for each kind of surgery. Surgeons practice these incision types again and again and again until they become second nature. The Ripper opened the abdomen of his victims in three different ways at least, and none of these conform to any known surgical technique."

Abberline leaned forward, resting his elbows on his knees. He looked at Sophia with a steely gaze.

"You don't think that the Ripper was a surgeon?" he asked.

"No," Sophia replied. "These cuts are crude. They reveal someone, perhaps with a passing knowledge of anatomy, but with no appreciable surgical skills. If I had to guess, I would say that they suggest a butcher, perhaps. Someone used to gutting and skinning carcasses of animals rather than humans."

"We suspected a butcher at one point," Thomas mused, looking at Abberline. "But we had no evidence to tie him to the murders."

"But now look at this," Sophia continued. She took out one of the squares of pasteboard which he had accidentally spilled across her hotel room floor during their first meeting in the Adelphi. It showed the wound which had been opened to remove Polly Wilkes' intestines and lay them out for display.

"This wound is quite elegant," Sophia said ignoring Abberline's snort of derision at her choice of words. "It is horizontal, rather than vertical, and the blade used is most certainly a surgeon's scalpel. The incision is clean. And there's something else. There are five main types of incisions used to open the abdomen during surgeries. The type used on Polly is known as a Maylard incision, developed only recently by a very learned Scottish surgeon. It is based on an older German technique and has only been in common usage among medical professionals for two or three years."

Thomas frowned.

"So, whoever murdered Polly…" he said.

"Whoever murdered Polly is not just any sawbones and certainly no butcher. He is well-versed in the most recent medical literature and trained in the latest techniques. A far cry from whatever rank amateur mutilated these five poor women in Whitechapel."

Thomas covered his mouth with a hand, rubbing his unshaven chin. He glanced at Abberline, knowing that the detective inspector had long maintained that the Ripper had been a medical man, or at least a man with medical training.

"Inspector…" he began, uncertain what to say. Abberline interrupted him with a look.

"Your case is compelling, young woman," he said to Sophia, his tone brusque. "But you have only examined these documents for a few days. I've lived with this case for years."

Sophia opened her mouth to argue, but Thomas reached out and pressed her arm gently. She closed her mouth again.

"You may be right that the Ripper did not kill your scouse girl," Abberline said. "Your reasoning there, is I think, sound."

"But that leaves us back where we started," Thomas said in frustration. He tried hard not to infuse his words with any blame towards Sophia. She was merely the bringer of bad news, not their cause.

Sophia looked at him, a pitying expression on her face.

"A negative result is still a result, Thomas," she said.

"I'm not sure Muldoon will see it that way," he replied. "We left Liverpool with little, and we're returning with nothing at all."

The atmosphere in the detective inspector's office had markedly changed. With no cause to return to the archives, Thomas and Sophia said their goodbyes. As Thomas grasped the hand of Frederik Abberline, he tried to place in the handshake both a wish to see the older man happy again with his lot in life and an apology for bringing up bad memories of his most notorious case. Abberline bowed stiffly to Sophia and saw them out of the watch room.

He led them down the stairs to the inner courtyard of the fortress-like station house, but as he raised his hand in a final gesture of farewell, they were interrupted by the arrival of a young constable. He came running into the courtyard, a slip of paper clutched in his hand. He came to a stop in front of Abberline, who wordlessly accepted the paper. Thomas recognised it as one of the flimsy pieces of yellow paper given out with messages from the telegraph service. Abberline scanned the document. His expression was unreadable as he handed it to Thomas.

The message only contained five words. It needed no more.

Another one. Come home. Muldoon.

Chapter Sixteen

ophia and Thomas only just caught the afternoon train towards Liverpool, boarding as the stationmaster blew his whistle and the engine began to build up steam. The journey was conducted in silence. Thomas refused Sophia's offer of lunch, sitting hunched over on his seat, leaning against the windows, his arms tightly folded. Sophia did not want to disturb him. She saw the pain and anger on his face and knew how he must feel. Despite what she had said, he felt that their journey to London had been a failure. It had not led them closer to Polly's killer, merely excluded their only real lead, and now another young girl was dead.

When the train pulled into Liverpool in the late afternoon, Sophia did not know whether to accompany Thomas to Rose Hill or return to her hotel. But the decision was made for her by Inspector Muldoon. The rotund officer was waiting for them on the platform, his expression thunderous. As they stepped from the carriage, leaving their luggage in the care of one of the porters, Muldoon advanced on them.

"Well?" he demanded.

Thomas cast down his gaze. Sophia glanced at him and then answered, trying to draw Muldoon's ire and anger onto herself rather than on Thomas' already overloaded back. He blamed himself enough. He did not need any extra helpings of blame from Muldoon.

"It's not the Ripper," she said. "The wounds to the abdomen of his victims are not just differently placed, they are also cut with no surgical expertise and even with a different type of blade."

Muldoon did not, to both Thomas' and Sophia's surprise, riposte with an angry tirade. Instead, he held Sophia's eye for a long moment and then nodded slowly.

"I know," he said. "I've known for a few hours now that it isn't the Ripper."

Thomas looked up in surprise.

"How?" he asked.

"Our second victim," Muldoon said. "The Ripper, whatever he was, never did anything like this. Not even to Mary Kelly."

Muldoon did not speak another word but turned around and led them to a waiting growler. They boarded it and rushed through the city. Maybe it was Sophia's imagination, but the people in the street seemed more worried, anxious, and suspicious than they had a few days before. Word had gotten out, perhaps. Everyone seemed to move in groups. She could not see a single pedestrian walking alone. Any young woman, whether whore, nurse, factory worker or lady of independent means, seemed to be escorted by at least one man.

"Who was she?" Thomas asked, but Muldoon held up a hand.

"I don't want to discuss anything until you've seen her yourself, Thomas," he said. "I've drawn my conclusions, and I want to know if they will be in agreement with those you and Miss Steenberg will arrive at."

A crowd had gathered outside Rose Hill station, filling the narrow street entirely. The growler was forced to stop at the entrance to the street leaving Muldoon, Thomas and Sophia to make their way on foot. As soon as the two easily recognisable officers appeared, the demeanour of the crowd changed. Before they had been milling about aimlessly, not knowing what to do. Now, they had a target.

"Inspector Muldoon," a young man in an ill-fitting dark suit and a too-large bowler hat shouted, pushing his way towards the officers. "Would you care to give a statement to the *Liverpool Advertiser*?"

Muldoon ignored him.

"Inspector," another reporter shouted. "Why have you not yet caught the killer?"

"Inspector, is it the Ripper back again?"

"Inspector, what are you doing to protect the citizens of Liverpool?"

Muldoon stared angrily ahead, saying nothing and refusing to meet the eyes of the crowd. The shouts had brought a group of constables from the station house. They saw their superiors struggling to get through the crowd, drew their truncheons, and began to push their way towards Muldoon and Thomas, creating a path to the door.

Thomas had grabbed Sophia tightly by the arm the moment the crowd converged on them.

"Keep close," he whispered out of the corner of his mouth. "Don't answer anyone."

"Why aren't our police doing anything to prevent these murders?" a voice in the crowd shouted.

"Disgraceful!" another chimed in. The murmurs rose to shouts as the crowd began to push and shove, trying to get closer to the detectives.

Their shouts were answered by the line of constables.

"Back! Back!"

Truncheons were lifted threateningly. Thomas knew it was moments before the first brick or cobble was thrown. Both he and Muldoon, knowing how to read the mood of a crowd from long experience, sped up. Thomas was practically dragging Sophia behind him as they arrived behind the line of constables. Sergeant Fraser loomed large; the first time Thomas had seen the Scot out from behind his desk for months.

"Give the order, sir," he said to Muldoon. "And we'll charge them."

"Do nothing, sergeant," Thomas cut in. "As soon as we're through the door, withdraw your men. Close the door and lock it, close the window shutters. We're closed for business tonight."

"What if they throw stones, sir?" Fraser asked.

"Let them," Thomas snarled pushing past the desk sergeant. "Stones can't hurt you inside the station house."

A half-brick sailed through the air and impacted against the side of the building as Muldoon, Thomas, and Sophia rushed up the stairs, the cheap building material splintering into dozens of fragments.

"Oy!" Fraser roared, stepping towards the young lad who had thrown the stone. As soon as he left the line of constables, another brick, thrown at close range, hit him in the head, glancing off his helmet with an audible thud.

"Fraser!" Thomas yelled, turning on the stairs and reaching for his own truncheon. "Pull your damn men back, now!"

Fraser dazed by the blow, grabbed one of his constables for support, raising his truncheon to Thomas in a half salute.

"You heard him, ladies," he roared. "Back inside!"

The watch room was tightly packed with constables. Some stood nervously by the door, ready for any order to launch themselves against the mob. Others sat by their desks, trying to read or write arrest reports, their eyes and hands not moving across the page betraying their inattention. In one corner, Thomas saw a young constable sitting with two mates at his side, bandaging a bloody wound on his forehead. Thomas tried to recall the lad's name.

"Roper, what's happened?" Thomas asked, making his way towards them.

"Couple of thugs jumped me down by Myrtle Street, sir," the constable said sheepishly.

"They were shouting about the murders, sir," one of his friends explained. Thomas swore.

"And they think that beating up my constables will help us find the killer any quicker?" he said. The constables shrugged.

"Dunno, sir," the wounded man said. "But it's been getting worse and worse all afternoon."

"Thomas!" Muldoon's voice cut through the clamour of the constables. Thomas jumped and quickly made his way across the room, joining the inspector and Sophia by the door leading to the cells.

The dead house was deserted, as was the darkroom. The shouts of the crowd from outside carried clearly into the basement through the narrow slitted windows leading to lightwells around the station house.

Thomas did not want to look at the slab, but kept his eyes fixed firmly in front of his feet as he followed Muldoon and Sophia. He heard Sophia gasp. Then she grabbed his arm, and he felt her shaking.

"My God," she muttered. "Dear sweet God..."

For the first time since Thomas had met her the usually self-assured and cool surgeon sounded lost. It was this more than anything that forced Thomas to take a step forward and raise his gaze.

Victoria Watson was lying on the slab. Her arms had been severed like Polly's. But her legs, too, had been amputated at the top of the thighs. Her abdomen had been opened, her purple and grey guts pulled out, covering her womanhood like the fig leaf shielding a statue. But there was more. Shallow wounds covered her torso, and as Thomas looked down, he realised that something had been done to both her feet.

"She's been flayed," Sophia said in a whisper. "Look at the soles of her feet."

Thomas moved around and saw that the layers of skin covering the soles of Victoria's feet had been meticulously peeled away, leaving only two open gaping wounds showing the muscles and sinews of each foot.

"He must have spent hours working on her," Muldoon said. "This is no doubt what he intended for Polly Wilkes."

"I've never seen or heard of anything like this," Sophia said stunned. "This is beyond mere perversion. This is…" she looked around the dingy cellar as though looking for a word to describe what lay before her. "It's almost art," she said finally. Thomas and Muldoon looked at her.

"Art?" Muldoon said. "Perhaps it is because English is not your native tongue, miss, but I would not choose such a term to describe this mess."

"You misunderstand, inspector," Sophia said, her eye not leaving the mutilated figure of the school teacher. "All art is not beautiful. Art can be horrible, and art can be ugly. And art can come from dark places. Art is neither good nor bad. Art is a masterpiece, and this, this is a masterpiece."

Muldoon looked at Thomas seeking an explanation, but Thomas merely shrugged.

"Whoever your killer is," Sophia said. "He considers himself an artist of death. The detail of the wounds, the meticulous nature. Do you have any idea, inspector, how difficult it is to skin a human being?"

"I cherish my ignorance on the topic, miss," Muldoon said coldly.

"Well, I know," she said. "The skin belongs on the body, removing it like this without damaging the muscles and flesh underneath requires real knowledge, real talent. It's like the cut to her abdomen. Whoever this killer is, they are an experienced and highly trained surgeon."

"What about the amputations," Thomas asked. "Do they show the same lack of physical strength as those found on Polly?"

Sophia bent closer to the body, examining all four cuts that had severed the girl's extremities. Then she nodded.

"Yes," she said. "Expertly placed, expertly planned. But even with a sharp knife, your killer struggled with the cuts, especially on the thighs."

Muldoon diverted his eyes from the girl's naked lower body.

"The thighs are thicker and more muscled than the arms," Sophia said. "Look here." She pointed to the cut surface of Victoria's right thigh. Long straight cuts, overlapping each other, striated the muscles and flesh. "The killer had to pause many times, maybe to catch his breath. A good ship's surgeon, used to amputating limbs, can take a man's leg off with a knife and saw in a matter of seconds. This took a great deal longer."

"Did the killer use a bone saw?" Thomas asked.

Sophia shook her head.

"No," she said. "And that is odd enough. The killer could have cut away the flesh with a Liston knife and worked through the femur with the saw. It would have been a great deal faster. But these mutilations are true dismemberments."

"What do you mean?"

"As with Polly, he has unseated both femurs as well as the right and left humeri from their housing, cutting them free at the joints."

"Why?" Muldoon asked. Sophia shook her head sadly.

"I cannot answer that, sir," she said. "Perhaps carrying a bone saw as well as a Liston knife and a scalpel was too much."

Thomas narrowed his eyes. This explanation sounded feeble to him.

"This killer," he said. "You say he sees himself perhaps as an artist?"

"Yes," Sophia said.

"Then he meant to do these things. These are not acts of convenience; they mean something to him. If he wanted to kill, then why not just slit the girls' throat and be done with it."

"How did she die?" Muldoon asked. Sophia examined the body for a several minutes, moving one of the smoky gas lamps around the corpse, looking at it from every angle.

"I cannot be certain," she said. "But I believe this is the wound that killed her." She pointed to a thing incision between the girl's ribs. "He also slashed her throat for good measure."

"Same type of wound as the wound that killed Polly," Muldoon said. "I'm glad we agree."

"Was it inflicted before the torture began?" Thomas asked. Sophia frowned.

"That is more difficult to determine," she said.

"She was killed first," Muldoon cut in, and Thomas turned to him in surprise.

"How can you be certain?"

"Because of where she was found," Muldoon said darkly.

"She was not found on the docks like Polly?"

Muldoon shook his head.

"She was found on the east side of Sefton Park, in a shrubbery across the road from a row of houses. Some of the houses are still occupied. There were people sleeping less than fifty feet from where he worked her over."

"Are you certain she was not just dumped there?" Thomas asked.

"We found her dress, cut and torn to pieces, there as well as her shoes. And the ground was soaked in blood. There is a small blood trail that leads into the park, to one of the small squares. He overpowered her there and dragged her to the place where she was found."

Thomas' eyes widened in something approaching admiration.

"The risk..." he said.

"Maybe not as great as it could have been," Muldoon said. "Many of the manors and houses on that side of the park are abandoned or rundown. And most of our constables were down on the docks. Those around Sefton were focused on the south side of the park."

Thomas swore quietly. The south side housed the most affluent houses.

The constables had, of course, taken up station there.

"We can't guard every dark place in the city at night," he said simply. "If the killer can strike anywhere, then how can we prevent another murder?"

"We can't," Muldoon said through gritted teeth.

Thomas had once read a news story about the discovery of the bones of ancient beasts in a tar pit in California. The animals, mastodons and sabre-tooth tigers, had fallen into the sticky, scalding liquid and been preserved for eternity, unable to pull themselves out. He felt now like he, too, was caught in a tar pit. No matter how he struggled, punched, and kicked he could not move forward. He could not see a way to protect those in his care. The pain of his impotence rose in his throat like acid bile.

"Then what the hell do we do?" he asked.

Muldoon sighed and sat down on one of the rickety high chairs used by the coroner.

"Send more men on the street, increase patrols. I've already cancelled all leave but if this continues, we'll have to ask other constabularies for help. Maybe Manchester or Chester can spare some men to help patrol the streets."

Thomas knew what it cost the proud old detective to talk about asking other cities for help to solve his problem.

The creak of the door to the dead house opening made Thomas and Muldoon look around. Framed in the doorway, his face pale and drawn, was Detective Inspector Cooper from Seel Street. He entered the room hesitantly, throwing a nervous glance at the corpse.

"Cooper," Muldoon said, using his cane to lever himself to his feet. "What are you doing here?"

"I..." Cooper began. Then he caught Thomas' steely glare and fell silent.

"I hope you haven't come to arrest Miss Steenberg," Thomas said. "I assure you that I can provide an excellent alibi for her."

Cooper shook his head. Then the large man squared his shoulders and seemed to steel himself as though preparing to go into battle. He crossed the room and stood to attention in front of Sophia who turned away from the corpse to face him.

"Please accept my apologies, miss," he murmured. He opened his mouth as if to continue, but then closed it, shaking his head. Sophia looked at him for a long, drawn-out moment. Then she nodded.

"We'll say no more of it, inspector," she said.

Thomas and Muldoon had exchanged a surprised look. They knew Cooper to be a hard-headed man, not unintelligent, but stubborn, and perhaps too set in his ways.

"I appreciate you joining us, Cooper," Muldoon said, eager to further foster the growth of the newly extended olive branch.

"Of course," Cooper rumbled. "We're all in this together, Muldoon. Please know that me and my boys are with you on this. This poor girl was found on our doorstep after all."

Muldoon nodded. Under normal circumstances, the imaginary line that divided the city between the two station houses ran right through Sefton Park. Victoria had been found so close to the line that, had the murder of Polly Wilkes not already occurred, then the task of solving her murder could have gone to either station house.

"I appreciate that," Muldoon said, genuine warmth in his voice. "What I need most is help to keep the peace."

Cooper nodded.

"I brought some lads with me," he said. "We'll get them lined up outside when the mob has dispersed. They'll be gone soon enough. It's too cold to riot."

"These wounds are true wounds," Sophia's soft voice made the three men turn around. She had returned to her examination of the corpse after accepting Cooper's apology. Now she stood by Victoria's head, one hand resting on the slab, the other tracing the cut edge of the girl's shoulder.

"I'm afraid I don't follow," Muldoon said.

"These wounds," Sophia pointed to the severed arms and legs, the cut abdomen and the skinned feet of the girl. "These wounds are all survivable," she said.

Thomas frowned.

"Then explain why we are looking at a corpse," he said, his tone slightly curt. Sophia ignored him.

"Amputations are commonplace enough. A human can live without an arm or a leg. It is a survivable surgical procedure."

"I've not seen many men with both legs and both arms amputated," Muldoon said, but Sophia continued.

"A man or woman can also survive for hours with their intestines removed from the purse that is the abdomen. As long as the intestines are not punctured. And while you cannot walk or run on a pair of flayed feet, it would not in itself kill you instantly."

Thomas walked to her side and pointed to the wounds that covered Victoria's torso.

"And these?"

"All too shallow to be killing blows," Sophia said.

"What does this mean?"

Sophia hesitated, biting her lower lip.

"I'm not certain," she said. "But whoever your killer is, he has experience in keeping people alive. Not keeping them free of pain, perhaps. Maybe not even keeping them alive for very long. But it is experience nevertheless."

"What sort of surgeon works to keep people alive but not cure them?" Muldoon asked. "Surely, the point of any surgery is to make people healthy, not torture them."

"I cannot say," Sophia said. "This is beyond my knowledge, I'm afraid."

"This is where surgical knowledge ends and policing takes over," Thomas said resolutely. "This girl's death is horrific, but in her death, she has given us a gift."

"Difficult to see things that way right now," Cooper said.

"We now know," Thomas continued, ignoring the inspector. "That this killer has a method, a preference in both target and execution."

Muldoon grunted in ascent, knowing what Thomas was suggesting.

"You want to contact other constabularies," he said.

"Yes. Any murder case going back, say, five or ten years. Any case that involves dismemberments, disembowelments, and in particular the flaying of the feet."

"Hang on," Cooper interrupted. "The first girl didn't have her feet flayed."

"But her shoes were removed," Thomas interrupted him. "The murderer did not have time to finish his." Thomas glanced at Sophia. "His masterpiece as Miss Steenberg calls it. But he evidently intended to."

"I'll send runners to the telegraph office right away," Muldoon said.

"Start with the constabulary in Manchester," Thomas suggested. "Then Glasgow, Edinburgh, Dublin, and down south, Birmingham and Leicester."

"And the Yard," Muldoon said, looking questioningly at Thomas.

"The Yard, too," Thomas said firmly.

Chapter Seventeen

Thomas left the station house in the direction of the telegraph office as soon as the crowd outside began to disperse, carrying with him a slip of paper with a brief message to all major constabularies throughout the United Kingdom. It contained a short description of the injuries to look out for, and a request for any pertinent information to be wired immediately back to Liverpool. Sophia remained for only long enough to write up the findings of her examination of Victoria Watson in a succinct report, before leaving the station house via a back door, escorted back to her hotel by two constables.

Muldoon chatted aimlessly with Inspector Cooper for a few moments, but their conversation was stilted and superficial. Both men had deeper thoughts to think, and both desired to do so in private. Eventually, Cooper left, leaving behind a squadron of his men to reinforce the Rose Hill station house throughout the night.

Muldoon retreated to his office, slammed the door behind him, making the glass window rattle, and half-sank, half-fell into his worn office chair. He took out a tin of snuff, cut off enough to cover a fingernail, and inserted it into his gums. The nicotine and aniseed jolted him awake, and he began to peruse the witness statements and reports which the officers who had discovered Victoria Watson had prepared for him.

As he read, his mind began to wander. His own granddaughter was only just twelve years old. She, too, wanted to grow up to be a schoolmistress. When Muldoon and his wife visited, the little girl loved to read to her grandfather snippets from whatever book she had persuaded and pleaded with her father to buy her. She read the stories dramatically, altering her voice, tone and accent and Muldoon was obliged to shudder at the grovels of Long John Silver as he explained his mutiny to Jim Hawkins, and laugh at the Mad Hatter, stuttering and stumbling over his words. "One to be a murderer, the other to be martyred. One to be a monarch, the other to go mad."

One to be a murderer, the other to be martyred. Who knew what paths in life people would take, and why they took them. Were they driven by compulsion or a genuine undefined evil. Were the priests right? Did the Devil whisper in the ears of good men and corrupt them to do evil deeds.

Perhaps it was time to call it a day, Muldoon thought. It was not healthy for a copper to think too deeply. It was something Thomas had never understood, though he would need to square with it one day. Empathy and intelligence were all well and good and had their place. But think too deep about why people did what they did, try to look too hard for patterns and logic, and you would drive yourself mad. If you spent your life staring obsessively at evil, one day evil would turn around and stare right back at you.

But then Muldoon thought again about his granddaughter. Did he want a world where she might end up like Polly or Victoria, lying on a slab in his dead house. The thought made him irrationally angry, and he threw the report he had been reading on the table. There was a soft knock on his door.

"What?" he snarled.

Sergeant Fraser entered, nervous in the face of his superior's anger. He brandished a copy of newsprint. He had a distinctly sheepish look. Muldoon adjusted his face and smiled briefly at the desk sergeant.

"What is it, Fraser?"

"You're not going to like this, sir," Fraser said, placing the sheet on Muldoon's desk. "The evening edition of the *Liverpool Advertiser*. I just got it off one of the news boys outside. Just off the press, but it's already spreading all over the city."

Muldoon picked it up. It was only two pages, a special edition, of the sort the newspapers ran quickly when they felt the need to spread something they considered truly newsworthy. Or perhaps, Muldoon thought sourly, when they had something, they thought people might pay a couple of pennies for.

A name on the front page of the folded pamphlet caught his eye. His face darkened as he read. When he reached the bottom of the page, he took a long, steadying breath.

"Would you mind, sergeant Fraser," he said, his voice shaking. "sending out a runner to Dr Pettigrew's house and bring him here. Immediately."

"Yessir," Fraser stood to nervous attention, then turned around and almost ran out of Muldoon's office.

Night had truly fallen by the time Dr Joseph Pettigrew was brought into the station house in the company of a young constable. The coroner's expression was inscrutable, but when he saw the newssheet lying on Muldoon's desk and caught the detective inspector's eye, he squared his shoulders, ready for a fight.

"What is this?" Muldoon asked in clipped tones as soon as the constable had closed his office door behind the coroner. He picked up the newssheet and flung it at Pettigrew, who caught the paper and glanced at it.

"The people needed to know," he began. "My examinations and conclusions were clearly being ignored by the constabulary so..."

"So, you thought you would give them to some damn reporter?" Muldoon interrupted. "*No Englishman could have committed such murders. The mutilations are reminiscent of rites and rituals conducted in the darkest heart of Africa and in particular in the Orient.* Bloody hell, Joseph, do you have any idea what people are going to make of that?"

"The truth, I would hope," Pettigrew said obstinately. "I gave you perfectly reasonable conclusions..."

"You gave me guesswork," Muldoon shouted. "You gave me guesswork, sir, and suppositions!"

Pettigrew looked stung.

"I have been a coroner for nearly three decades," he said. "And yet, I found my long experience set aside in favour of Sergeant Thomas' woman. What would you have me do?"

"I would have you trust me," Muldoon said. "I would have you trust me as the old friends we are. I didn't want to set your opinion aside, but that is all it was, an opinion. What would you have me do with it? Arrest every foreigner in the port?"

"I have at least narrowed down your pool of potential suspects," Pettigrew said. Muldoon looked at his old friend as though he had never seen him before.

"You have now levelled accusations against a reputable surgeon," Pettigrew scoffed but Muldoon continued unabashed. "And thousands of entirely blameless people, some visitors and some citizens of this city. And you have the gall to stand before me and claim that you have helped!"

Muldoon moved around his desk and grabbed Pettigrew hard by the shoulder, dragging him across the room to the window.

"Look outside," he snarled. "Look at the people out there." While the mob outside the station house had dispersed, there were still groups of young men standing on the pavement, some talking quietly, others simply observing the station house with narrowed eyes.

"They're scared, Joseph," Muldoon said. "They're scared and they're angry, and now you have given them a target for that anger. Do you know what the people of the West End did to the Jews when the Yard started talking to the papers about how the Ripper might be a Jew? They didn't wait for evidence or confirmation, because that's not how the mob thinks. They just found any Jew they could and beat the devil out of them!"

"I maintain that these murders do not bear the hallmarks of civilised men," Pettigrew said stubbornly. Muldoon let him go and fell back into his chair.

"Then you and I have very different ideas of what good Englishmen are capable of," he said.

"Was there anything else, inspector, or did you merely wish to berate me?" Pettigrew said stiffly. Muldoon stared at him for a long while.

"I will be making a recommendation to the superintendent in the morning that you be removed as the official police coroner," Muldoon said. "It's time we give one of the new bloods from the School of Medicine a chance."

Pettigrew blanched.

"You can't be serious…"

"We all have a time, Joseph," Muldoon said quietly. "I can feel my own drawing closer, trust me. But your time has come today."

"I'll appeal to the superintendent."

"And that is your right," Muldoon said coldly. "But I will not be told by anyone, not the superintendent, nor the mayor, not even the damn Prime Minister, who I work with in my own station house."

Pettigrew's nostrils were dilated, his breathing heavy.

"You'll regret this, Muldoon," he said.

Muldoon rubbed his eyes.

"There are few things in my life I don't regret, Joseph," he said.

As the two men faced each other, Pettigrew unwilling to depart and Muldoon unwilling to continue their conversation, the inspector heard a scuffle from the direction of the watch room. He stood up, grabbed his cane, and crossed the room, flinging open his door.

Sergeant Fraser was holding a young boy off the floor. The boy was struggling, trying to kick and punch the burly desk sergeant. He had long matted brown hair and his face was caked in dirt, his clothes little more than rags, so darned and patched that there was little original fabric left.

"What's going on here, Sergeant?" Muldoon shouted over the boy's protestations.

"I want to see Thomas!" the boy shouted, struggling in the sergeant's hand.

"Put him down, sergeant," Muldoon commanded. Fraser dropped the lad with an annoyed look.

"Begging your pardon, sir," he said. "But he came barging in here screaming like a banshee…"

"I want to see Thomas!" the boy repeated, scrambling to his feet and looking around the watch room in a panic.

"Thomas isn't here, lad," Muldoon said as kindly as he could. "Why do you need to see him?"

The boy looked at Muldoon, and Muldoon could see a flash of recognition in the young boy's eyes.

"You're Thomas' guvnor?" he asked. Muldoon suppressed a smile.

"Aye," he said. "I am sergeant O'Callaghan's, er, guvnor."

"Well, then I guess I can tell you" the lad said his face cracking into a wide grin. "Mind you, Thomas normally pays me a few pennies for good information."

Muldoon narrowed his eyes, thinking back to a remark Thomas had made several months before.

"You're Skittles, aren't you?" he asked. "The lad who tried to lift Thomas's pocket watch."

"I never did!" Skittles protested, raising both hands.

"Never mind that now," Muldoon said. "What information have you got?"

"It's kicking off, sir," he said. "Down Nelson Street."

Muldoon blanched. For more than sixty years, the port of Liverpool had been increasing its trade links with Chinese ports in Shanghai and Hong Kong. So many Chinese sailors arrived in Liverpool these days that some had settled permanently on Nelson Street, opening shops and eateries catering to their compatriots who visited the port.

"What's going on?"

"There's a bunch of lads there," Skittles said urgently. "Brawlers and drunks mostly. They say they're gonna burn out the Chinese, until they find whoever killed those girls."

Muldoon swore loudly.

"Damnit, Joseph!" he said turning to the coroner. "Now, do you see?"

Pettigrew's face remained impassive, but his eyes flickered nervously towards the door of the station house.

"I should throw you in the damn cells for disrupting the peace," Muldoon roared. Then he turned to Fraser.

"How many men can we spare?" he asked.

Fraser looked around the watch room.

"A few dozen at most," he said.

"Get them ready," Muldoon said. "And send a runner to Seel Street. We need whoever they can spare."

He walked back towards his office but hesitated at the door. Then he turned around to face Fraser, a grim expression on his face.

"And sergeant," he said. "You have my permission to unlock the armoury and distribute sidearms."

A murmur ran through the constables. The constabularies across the United Kingdom had always despised firearms, preferring to defend themselves with their rosewood truncheons. Pistols and rifles were only used in such places where law enforcement was conducted with fatal violence, like those towns in the American West that the constables read about in penny dreadfuls and saw play-acted in the music halls. A real officer of the law did not need a pistol. That had been the prevailing belief until, some ten years previously, the fatality rate among constables had grown unacceptably high. Criminals had no qualms about carrying firearms, and constables armed only with truncheons were easy targets. The Metropolitan Police had purchased thousands of Webley MK-1 pistols in response and distributed them among the constabularies in the major cities across the country.

But still, the pistols were considered largely unnecessary weapons, and most of the Webleys owned by the Liverpool constabulary were kept locked in armouries in Rose Hill and Seel Street and rarely used.

"Are you certain, sir?" Fraser said hesitantly.

Muldoon thought for a long moment.

"Better to have them and not need them, than need them and not have them, sergeant," he said. "One pistol each to your five most reliable constables, one for yourself, and one for me."

Fraser looked at his superior in surprise.

"You're joining us, sir?" he asked.

"Yes," Muldoon said. He turned to Dr Pettigrew.

"Would you like to assist us as well, doctor?" he asked sardonically. "I'm certain we'll need the skills of a medical man before the night's out."

Pettigrew looked down and shook his head. Muldoon snorted derisively and turned towards his office. Then he paused.

"And someone give that lad a penny," Muldoon roared over his shoulder. Then he stomped into his office and slammed the door.

Chapter Eighteen

I decided to treat myself tonight. These last few days, I've been having my meals in whatever chop house was closest, but scummy stew and mouldy bread are not a sustainable diet, even if it does help me preserve my savings. But tonight, I felt like celebrating. I felt satisfied, for the first time in many months. The young school teacher had been perfect. Far better than some gutter whore or street rat. A refined woman with unblemished pale skin. I still shudder when I think about the audible pops when I unseated her humerus and femurs. The sound had brought back old memories, sharp and red and deep. The moisture, the heat. The smell of unwashed bodies and smoke from the cookhouses. The screams and pleading. And the fear. Everywhere the sound, smell, and taste of fear.

I settled myself in a small restaurant on Upper Duke Street, offering a table d'hôte. I shelled out a whole three pence for a delectable meal of hare soup, steamed turbot in a lobster bisque, and a fat pork cutlet. As I devoured a water ice flavoured with rose water and finished my bottle of claret, I glanced out of the window to the street outside. People were afraid. Even in the restaurant, I sensed the oppressive atmosphere. They were all wondering who might be next.

The crowds in the street had begun to coalesce. No doubt heading down to the Chinese shops and houses to take out their frustration on the Orientals. I suppressed a smirk. A killing no Englishman could have done, eh? The bizzies lived up to their name. Busy, busy bees, buzzing about always in the wrong direction, always one step behind.

It struck me that the constables would be stretched tonight trying to stop the citizenry from ripping each other to shreds. Perhaps I could complete my triumvirate. But no, too risky, too risky. Even with the constables distracted, this final act would require a great deal more planning than the first and second. She is too clever to wander unprotected through a park, nor could I lure her to an abandoned dock with the promise of some pennies and a bottle of gin. She would require a more careful approach.

The sooner I can complete my task, I can leave this stinking city. Once I have delivered my message to them all, once the triumvirate is complete, I can leave it again as I did so many years ago.

That first exile still rankles, even four decades later. Who were they to banish me? What crime, truly, had I committed to warrant it? Not for me a glittering life of luxury and fame. Instead, I was sent to live among savages and live with their stench and pain and disease. But there again. If I had not left, I might never have discovered my true calling.

The family sitting at the table next to mine are whispering together. I catch a few disjointed phrases of their conversation.

"I heard…"

"Yes, the Ripper…"

The Ripper. I frown as I drain my glass. How can they be so blind? Can they not tell the difference between a labourer and an artist? I am to the Ripper what Bernini was to some peasant whose job it was to quarry square blocks of marble from the unyielding bedrock. I am to him like Caravaggio is to a child daubing watercolours.

Perhaps I, too, should send a poorly written letter to one of the newspapers. No, I'm not like him. Whoever he was. He was sloppy. He escaped the noose not through brilliance, but through luck and the incompetence of the constabulary. And they only need to get lucky once. I scratch the side of my neck. I prefer mine unbroken and unstretched. Through these years, no lawman, sheriff or constable or gendarme or Pinkerton, has ever come close to me. And I don't intend to allow that to change now.

The waiter comes to remove my plates. I smile warmly to him, thank him and ask him to bring my compliments to the chef. Then I gather up my things and, nodding to the family sitting by the next table, I venture outside.

Overlaid on the usual bustle of the city, even this late in the evening, I can hear shouts and a commotion from Nelson Street and the surrounding alleys. It sounds like the fun has already begun. I step aside as a squadron of constables rushes down the street, heading towards the disturbance. They are led by an officer wearing civilian clothing. As he passes me, I recognise him by his mutilated ear. My gaze follows him down the street. To get to her, I may need to deal with him first. But I can't do it myself. He's young and too strong. And no doubt made paranoid by a life rubbing shoulders with the city's riff-raff.

I keep thinking about this problem as I walk down the street, away from the commotion. I rub the coins in my pocket, mentally adding them together. There is enough, perhaps, to allow me to make Detective Sergeant O'Callaghan someone else's problem. Yes. That's the safest way, and if I'm careful, they won't be able to name me even if they should survive. I don't like leaving loose ends, but sometimes there's no other way.

I duck into the nearest gin palace and take a seat in the darkest corner in a winged armchair with a seat so worn and frayed that I nearly vanish into the pool of shadow cast by the chairback. I look around. Before midnight, I've identified my new friends.

* * *

Thomas arrived on Nelson Street at a run. He had returned from the Telegraph Office to find Rose Hill nearly deserted. The few remaining constables had informed him about the smouldering riot and, pausing only to arm himself with one of the spare Webley revolvers, Thomas had left to assist Inspector Muldoon. At the top of Duke Street, he had rallied a small group of constables milling about, uncertain what to do. The police officers had dodged and weaved between the street sellers, revellers, and diners exiting eateries and flop houses that clogged Duke Street until the small hours. A loud crash and the sound of breaking glass welcomed them to the top of Nelson Street. The street was narrow and cobbled with a tightly packed mixture of shop fronts and tenement flats. Many of the chipped wooden store signs were covered in cramped Chinese characters in riotous colours, marking out their owners.

Muldoon and his men, between four and five dozen, had taken up position in the middle of the street. They stood, shoulder to shoulder, truncheons drawn, facing off against a far larger mob of furious citizens advancing up the street to the south. Thomas saw frightened and panicking shopkeepers feverishly putting up wooden shutters to protect their windows. Others had abandoned their shops altogether and sought refuge behind the line of constables.

"Reinforce the flanks," Thomas shouted to his men. He looked around, spotting the inspector standing in the middle of the line, behind the looming figure of Sergeant Fraser.

"Inspector!" Thomas shouted, and Muldoon turned. As he turned, the first bricks and cobbles began to fly through the air. Most flew harmlessly over the heads of the constables, crashing against the street on the other side of the line. Others were impacted, and Thomas saw several constables knocked off their feet. Sergeant Fraser had thrown up an arm to protect his face. Thomas sprinted down the street, joining the inspector.

"Hell of a business, Thomas," Muldoon panted, turning back to look at the approaching crowd. Thomas scanned the mass of people. They were mostly men, and he could readily see that the majority of them were men already known to the constabulary.

"Bloody troublemakers," he said, raising his voice to be heard over the drunken shouts and catcalls of the mob.

"To hell with that coroner," Muldoon said angrily. "The only upside to this debacle is that when I go to the superintendent tomorrow and argue for his dismissal, I'll have good cause."

Thomas nodded. Another barrage of missiles forced both men to duck.

"We can't just stand here," Thomas said "They'll walk right over us."

"We can charge them down, sir," Fraser roared, his back still turned to his superiors, his eyes not leaving the front ranks of the crowds. "That'll buy us a bit of time."

"Are there reinforcements coming?"

Muldoon nodded.

"The Seel Street boys are on their way. They're bringing their sweatbox to use as a makeshift barricade."

The sweatbox was a heavily armoured coach used to transport prisoners to and from the station houses and gaols. Able to hold up to twelve men at the same time behind heavy iron bars, the cart could at least provide cover for any wounded constables and members of the public before they could be evacuated back to the station house.

"Very well," Muldoon said. "Sergeant Fraser, in your own time, please."

Fraser opened his mouth and inhaled a deep lung full of air.

"First rank," he roared. "Charge!"

The constables standing closest to the approaching mob rushed forward, their truncheons raised. The approaching rioters had not expected this, and many of them halted. Before they could turn, the constables were on them, hitting out with truncheons and heavy boots, forcing the mob back. Many of the rioters had joined not out of any great desire to see some warped justice done for the murder of the two girls, but rather because the gin had told them to. These reluctant rioters had no desire to stand in a fight against the better-equipped and armed constabulary. They broke ranks and ran, barging into others behind them. Some of the men were hurled to the ground or pushed into the brick and timber walls that lined the street.

But others remained. A hard knot of rioters organised and fought back. Clubs and cobbles were hefted and flung and hit against the wall of uniforms. Thomas had joined the rush forward, his rosewood truncheon in one hand and a small set of brass knuckles adorning the other.

A large bald man with small piggy eyes and cauliflower ears loomed up in front of him. The man was clutching a chair leg, still with nails embedded in it. Thomas ducked as the man swung it and jabbed out with the butt end of his truncheon catching the men in his ample belly. The man bent double, expelling his breath in a foul-smelling gust of tooth decay and cheap gin. Thomas caught him on the side of the head with his brass knuckles and the man keeled over sideways, falling heavily onto the cobbles and remaining motionless.

Thomas looked around for his next opponent. He did not spot the rioter who was taking a temporary breather in the lee of a doorway. A ringing thud rang through Thomas' skull as the man rushed forward and punched him. Thomas staggered sideways, swinging his truncheon drunkenly in front of him, trying to ward off another attack. He blinked furiously to clear his vision, which had exploded into a hundred pinpricks of starlight. He saw a shadow loom towards him and swung his truncheon again, this time hitting the man on the shoulder and diverting his attack. The man had come with such speed that he stumbled and fell headfirst into a crowd of fighting rioters and constables.

"Come away, Thomas, come away!"

Thomas turned at the cry and saw Muldoon beckoning from behind the line of constables. More men reinforced it. The boys from Seel Street had arrived, and Thomas recognised Inspector Cooper in the crowd. The detective was red in the face, shouting himself hoarse at his men as they slowly guided the heavy sweatbox into position. With the heavy cart blocking the street, the constables slowly retreated behind it. Thomas grabbed a wounded constable who was struggling to get off the ground and dragged him behind the barricade. The mob rushed forward, reclaiming the territory they had lost.

"We can't keep this up all night," Thomas panted, bending double, resting his hands on his knees. The constable he had saved had been carried away by his friends, blood running from both his nose and mouth.

"If these bastards get past us, they'll torch half the street," Muldoon said grim-faced. "We don't have a choice."

Cobbles, bits of furniture, bricks, and even shoes and fragments of broken shop windows rained ineffectually against the sides of the sweat box.

"At least we've got cover here for now," Muldoon said.

"Until it occurs to someone to tip the wagon over," Inspector Cooper said. He was still red in the face, and he was bleeding from a cut to his forehead. He noticed Thomas glance at the wound.

"Just a half-brick that didn't agree with me," he said with a grin. "Luckily, I've got a hard head."

"Your rank forbids me to comment, sir," Thomas replied, and Cooper roared with laughter, punching Thomas on the shoulder.

"So, Muldoon," he said. "What the Devil do we do now?"

Muldoon glanced out between the bars of the sweat box. For now, the mob were content to smash up the shops in the part of the street which lay within their control and throw missiles at the constables.

"We'll let them make the next move," Muldoon said. "If they try to tip over the cart, we'll push back."

Thomas and Cooper nodded.

"Come on, boys! Don't just throw stones at 'em. We need to get past!" Thomas spotted the man shouting in the crowd. He was a small, ferret-faced man, runty by comparison to many of the burly rioters who were clearly experienced street fighters. But he had a mean expression on his face.

"Remember this is about our girls!" he shouted, trying to cajole the mob. "First, the bizzies can't catch the killer, and now they're protecting the killer and hurting honest citizens trying to bring him to justice."

Thomas sneered. He had never met the man before but knew his type well. He was the sort of man who shouted the loudest in any street fight or bar brawl. A big mouth, but never seemed to be where the fighting was thickest. Far more content to let others fight on his behalf.

His coaxing was working. The mob was slowly turning their attention from wanton destruction back to the line of police standing between them and the cowering occupants and shop owners of Nelson Street.

"Let's turn over that bloody cart!" the ferret-faced man shouted. Some of the rioters ran forward and put their shoulders against the side of the sweatbox.

"They're trying to overturn it," Fraser shouted. "Push back, lads!"

The constables on the other side of the cart pressed up against it as the riot descended into a contest of pure strength, the mob pressing forward, the constables pressing back. Thomas found himself caught between a group of constables trying to steady the cart and the iron bars of the cart's side. He struggled to draw breath, feeling himself forced harder and harder against the bars. The constables rushing forward to help added to the pressure.

Thomas tried to inhale, and with a flutter of panic, he realised that he could not. He tried to move his arms and legs, but he was pinned in place by the press of bodies. He could reach neither his truncheon nor his pistol, and he did not have the breath to utter a cry for help.

A shot echoed between the boarded-up shop fronts. The press of men eased, and Thomas felt Muldoon's hand reach in and heave him away from the sweat box. Thomas's shoulder and chest stung with pain as he drew a deep breath, immediately breaking out into a coughing fit.

"There, there, lad," Muldoon said, an uncharacteristically gentle tone in his voice. "Get your breath back."

"Should we chase 'em, sir?" Sergeant Fraser had bounded up to Muldoon, standing rigidly to attention. Muldoon's shot, fired to attract the attention of the constables crushing Thomas, had had a marked effect on the mob. At the sound, all but the most fervent–or most inebriated–of them had come to the conclusion that they were better off spending the night in any nearby pub or gin palace, rather than lying shot through in one of the city's dead houses. Seeing the mob crumble, even the ferret-faced instigator had given up, picking up and throwing a final half-brick in the direction of the constables behind the sweatbox before he too turned and followed his compatriots down the street.

"What's the point," Muldoon said, a tired note in his voice. "In five minutes they'll be back in the pub, swearing on the very life of their ugly-as-sin mothers that they never even left their seats."

Thomas staggered to the side of the sweatbox and gazed over the battlefield. Several dark shapes were lying on the cobbles, most stirring feebly.

"There's wounded men out there," he said.

"See if any of them are seriously hurt. Send for a doctor and leave them to him," Muldoon said to sergeant Fraser. "You can put the rest in the sweatbox and take them back to Rose Hill."

Fraser saluted and bustled off to organise some of the milling constables.

"A lucky break," Thomas said quietly to Muldoon. "That could have been worse."

"Tomorrow night it may be," Muldoon said darkly.

Thomas spat on the ground. A single foolish statement in a newssheet and half a street was demolished. It was the Ripper all over again. They might be dealing with a different killer, but the behaviour of the mob never varied. They wanted blood. They wanted someone to drag to the gallows, guilty or not. They wanted a scapegoat. And if the constabulary could not provide one, then the constables themselves became the target of the population's ire. Thomas understood the anger. The city was rich, one of the richest in the world, he had heard. So much wealth passed through it every single day, offloaded by the barrel down at the docks. But how much of that glittering wealth went to those scraping a living in the tenements?

He had known poverty himself growing up. He had seen his mother's shame and frustration when she couldn't scrape enough together each week to buy enough food for her boys. She had been a proud woman, and to see her go to their landlord and plead for mercy when a rent payment could not be met…. Well. It had broken something in Thomas to see his mother like that. And it had broken something in his mother, too.

Thomas, lost in thoughts and gloom, jumped when he felt a hesitant hand on his shoulder. He turned around, his hand flying to his truncheon. An older Chinese man jumped back, startled. Thomas lowered his hand quickly, and the man shuffled forward, his eyes downcast. Speaking to Thomas' shoes he muttered something Thomas could not understand.

"I'm sorry?" Thomas said. The man cleared his throat and looked up.

"Are we safe now?" he asked in heavily accented English. Thomas glanced behind the old man and saw a crowd of Chinese men and women, some holding crying babies, awoken by the cold night air. Others clutched the hands of older children, shivering in the gathering mists.

"I…" Thomas began, but then closed his mouth and looked to Muldoon for help. The old inspector looked hard at the crowd of Chinese shopkeepers and then sighed.

"Best keep indoors for now," he said. "We'll send constables to stand watch in the street after nightfall. If they come back, so will I. You have my word on that."

After the briefest of hesitations, Muldoon extended a hand. The old man looked at it, then shook it gingerly.

As the newly arrived doctor attended the last of the wounded and the sweatbox rumbled off towards Rose Hill station, Thomas drew a deep breath. Then he bid farewell to Inspector Muldoon and, his head still smarting from the blow, and his body feeling as though he had just come off a rack, he set off towards home.

Chapter Nineteen

Books lay scattered throughout Sophia's luxurious suite at the Adelphi Hotel. Some were stacked on the small circular smoking table by the fireplace. Others had been thrown haphazardly on the velvet couch. Still others lay in stacks and piles by the large balcony doors. Books had comprised the largest, and certainly the heaviest, share of Sophia's luggage. Nearly a hundred volumes, most accumulated during her time at University in Copenhagen, others acquired in quaint bookshops in Montmartre or Pigalle. A few had been personal gifts from colleagues and carried dedications and inscriptions. Those leatherbound tomes, valued more highly than the others, had been placed with some care on the small writing desk, which stood along one wall.

Sophia rubbed her eyes and dropped a copy of *Medico-Chirurgical Transaction* by the side of her winged armchair. She could feel the tension in the street and even here, in the closeted surroundings of the luxury hotel, the nervousness and irritable energy was palpable. She had heard a group of white-jacketed waiters discussing the murders in low voices as she entered. An evening copy of the *Liverpool Advertiser* brought to her room by one of the maids had illuminated the topic of their gossiping. When she had seen the coroner's name and his outlandish remarks, she had felt an almost insurmountable wave of anger break over her. Pettiness and professional jealousy were one thing. Those were to be expected. But to actively rile up the mob and then unleash them at a community whose only crime was to exist. That was something beyond the usual professional sniping and malice Sophia had experienced for all of her career.

When the maid brought her a cup of tea shortly after ten o'clock, the young girl had told her about the riots which had engulfed the Chinese quarter on Nelson Street. Sophia had imagined Thomas out in the streets, no doubt fighting with a mob of drunken louts who had taken the coroner's comments as gospel truth. The thought of the sergeant swallowed by a horde of marauding rioters had made her as grimly determined as ever to help. She would be of no use on a police barricade, but she could continue unmasking the killer whose actions had given an outlet to the fear, frustration, and hatred that bubbled under the surface of the city.

She got up, stretched, and walked over to her steamer trunk. It was nearly empty now, its contents having already served their purpose. Only a dozen books remained on the bottom, some the most outdated medical textbooks, and some chance purchases that had turned out not to contain as much information or wisdom at Sophia would have wished for.

The corner of a cover bound in dark green dyed Moroccan leather caught her eye. She moved a few journal volumes aside and saw the gold embossed title. *Clinical Notes on Uterine Surgery.* She frowned.

The book had been published three decades previously by an American surgeon, Dr Marion Sims. While the book contained some useful observations about the diseases affecting the uterus and their potential cures, it was not the content of the book which made Sophia uneasy, but its author. Dr Sims was an accomplished surgeon, of that there was no doubt. But his methods of experimentation had made him an unwelcome guest among many European centres of learning. Dr Sims had based most of his medical research on surgical experiments performed on female African slaves in the American South. It had been in the times before the northern States under Abraham Lincoln invaded the South, beating the Confederacy into submission and forcing the emancipation of those tens of thousands of humans who had lived as chattel on plantations throughout states like Georgia, Missouri, and Alabama.

America had come late to the abolishing of the slave trade and slavery, and while some European surgeons and medical experts lauded Dr Sims for his ground-breaking work, others held him to be a butcher, little better than a common killer in the street. A man who had performed gruesome operations and surgeries on pregnant women without anaesthesia believing as he did, that black women did not have the same nervous system as white women and therefore could not truly feel pain. Sophia had inherited the book from her grandfather's collection. She had been meaning to throw it away, but now she picked it up and weighed it in her hand.

The killer had not removed the uterus of either Polly or Victoria. He evidently attached no importance to that organ, unlike Jack the Ripper, who had even preserved some of the uterus of one of his victims and sent it to a newspaper.

Sophia leafed through the book, suppressing a shudder of revulsion at the graphic illustrations. Dr Sims had died nearly a decade before, and Sophia was glad that she would never have to suffer through meeting the odious man at a congress or salon, espousing the beliefs he had held to his dying that the emancipation of the black slaves in America had been nothing less than a crime against humanity.

Finding nothing useful contained in the pages of Dr Sims' work, Sophia made to put the book back in the steamer trunk. Then she hesitated. A voice in the back of her head had awoken as soon as she touched the cover of the book. It was now screaming, but doing so as if through cotton wool, the words unclear, but the volume increasing.

The book fell from Sophia's fingers as she turned, walked quickly to the writing desk, and skimmed through the notes she had taken during Victoria Watson's autopsy.

"What sort of surgeon works to keep people alive but not cure them?" Sophia muttered, thinking back to the words of Detective Inspector Muldoon. She straightened up. All her tiredness seemed to flow off her like a shawl dropped on the ground.

At well past two in the morning, it took a while for Sophia to make the sleepy porter understand what she needed. However, within a few minutes, a growler was summoned and, with Sophia impatiently tapping her feet and glancing out of the rolling fog, it rumbled through the deserted street of Liverpool heading for Rose Hill.

***

Moonlight reflected off the swirls of fog. The streetlights seemed to float freely; their lampposts were not visible. The distant rumble of a growler. The single cry of a baby, quickly silenced by a doting mother. The rhythmic creaks of his hobnailed boots as they hit the glistening cobbles. The volume of his breathing was magnified in the unnatural stillness of the alley. The lantern he held before him only illuminated the path a few feet ahead.

He sensed movement up ahead. He squinted. In the fog, a dark figure was moving quickly across the street. He opened his mouth to call out, but then the fleeting shadow was gone. It had passed too quickly to make out any details. A dark coat, perhaps. The glint of an eye. Nothing else.

The alley narrowed up ahead. Piles of barrels and crates had been put outside an alehouse, now closed, its customers having long since rambled home to sleep. In the distance, the sounds of a gong wagon carrying night soil through the streets of the sleeping city.

After squeezing past the barrels, the alley opened up into a small square where several alleys intersected a broader street. At one side was a small island of paving stones amid the cobbled pathways. Boarded-up windows, crumbling brick warehouses, and temporary shelters built from peeling and rotting wooden boards flanked the square on two sides.

A gasp. Then the sound of running feet. A figure barrelling out of the fog. The beam of a lantern bouncing and flying every which way as the figure collided with Thomas.

"What the…"

Thomas dragged the figure around, feeling the familiar rough wool of a uniform coat.

"Watkins?"

The young man's pale face was made paler still by the glaring light of Thomas' lantern. His helmet had fallen off. The young lad had been trying to grow a moustache, eager to fit in with the other constables. His attempt had gone badly, leaving a mere scattering of scraggly brown hair across his upper lip. His mouth was opening and shutting.

"What's happened," Thomas pressed, shaking the younger man. "Tell me!"

The tin lamp fell from Watkins' hand, its lens shattering on the cobbles and extinguishing the candle inside. The young man pointed towards a corner of the square with his now free hand. He seemed unable to speak.

"Wait here," Thomas instructed, taking on the role of a superior in the face of his colleague's distress and panic.

Squaring his shoulders, Thomas advanced across the square. He held his lantern high above his head, but its beam refused to cut through the roiling fog. Like a ghostly ship appearing from out of the sea mist, Thomas spotted a figure on the ground. Another step. The figure was human. Another step. Then another. The sound of his footfall had changed. He looked down and realised that he was stepping into a spreading pool of blood.

The lantern shook in his hand. She lay with her legs spread apart, her bloody and torn genitals exposed to the summer air. Her dress had been cut and pulled aside like a robe, revealing her torso as well. He stomach was a bloody mess of intestines, ripped and torn as though gnawed upon by a wild beast.

Her head was turned, still in shadow. He did not want to see her face. To see her face would make everything real. He did not want to believe it had happened again. That their failure had cost the life of another innocent. Behind him, he heard Watson's whistle. In the distance, pounding footsteps.

Right now, there was just him and the woman on the ground. Soon there would be constables and detectives and coroners and reporters. But right now, at this time, it was just the two of them. He forced himself to take another step forward. He did not want to, but he needed to see her, to look into her lifeless eyes. He owed her that at least, even if the sight would haunt him for the rest of his life.

He looked up. Her face was wrong. Not haggard. Not the face of Catherine Eddowes, marked by the years and by hardship. Fine porcelain skin. Golden blonde hair, a single ringlet escaping from a tight plait, soaking up the halo of blood, slowly changing colour. Blue eyes, glistening and alive. Slowly, the head turned. Sophia opened her mouth as she looked at Thomas, a gush of blood oozing from between her teeth, dribbling down her chin.

"Thomas..." the voice was choked and faint. "Help me..."

"No!" Thomas's scream shattered the dreamworld, the cobbles and walls of Mitre Square dissolving in an instant, only the grey fog lingering for the briefest of moments.

The sudden scream and violent jerk startled the assassin. Thomas' eyes flew open. The single beam of moonlight which had clawed its way through the grimy window of his room caught the blade of a knife raised above him. He rolled, and the knife fell, its point cutting into his mattress a hand's breadth from his throat.

The assassin let out an involuntary gasp of surprise. Thomas kicked out from his prone position on the bed. He had come home exhausted after the riot and had not even bothered to undress himself, simply falling straight on the bed. His heavy boots connected with the man's kneecap, and Thomas felt something crack and shift. The man screamed and slumped forward, nearly landing on top of the constable.

Thomas rolled out of the way, crashing to the wooden floor. Then he heard rapid steps. There was a second attacker. In the darkness of the room, Thomas rolled under the bed, buying himself a few seconds as the second attacker rushed around the bed, expecting to find Thomas on the floor, but seeing no one there. As the man bent down to look under the bed, Thomas coiled his body and punched as hard as he could towards the broad whiskery face that came into view. He hit the man on the nose, and the attacker recoiled with a scream of pain.

Thomas used the man's momentary inattention to roll out from under the bed and scramble to his feet. The first attacker hobbled towards him, weaving his blade back and forth. Thomas allowed him to come close, then grabbed the arm holding the blade and twisted. He used the man's own weight and the momentum of his swing against him, turning around, ducking under the man's arm while refusing to let go. As Thomas straightened up panting, the man had been turned around, his back to Thomas, and his arm pinioned painfully behind his back.

The second attacker wiped blood from his face and squared off against Thomas. He, too, held a blade, and now he lumbered forward. Thomas used the first attacker as a human shield, ducking behind him as the second attacker lunged for his face. The first assailant was screaming at his partner to help him. The three men twirled across the small room, knocking over Thomas' sparse furniture. Surely the neighbours would hear the racket and send someone down the street to fetch a constable, Thomas thought. But he knew that disturbances were so common across most of the city that people had learned to mind their own business and not become involved.

As the second attacker charged forward again, Thomas and his temporary prisoner were pushed towards the door. Thomas stepped on something soft and suddenly he remembered. He had thrown his coat just inside the door. And in one of the pockets was the Webley. He had been too tired and had forgotten to return it. Fraser and Muldoon had been too busy with the clean-up after the riot to remember to reclaim it.

Thomas dropped to one knee and, with all his remaining strength, he pushed his prisoner forward, letting go of him and allowing him to collide with his charging partner. The two assailants stumbled into each other. One of them tripped over the legs of Thomas' bed. Thomas used the distraction to grab the coat. He felt the weight of the Webley in the pocket.

The first attacker had turned around, the knife he had refused to relinquish still in his hand. Thomas saw his dark eyes glint as he saw his prey kneeling and seemingly unprotected. The large man lumbered forward; he was less than three yards away. As he raised his weapon, Thomas pulled the Webley free, cocked it and raised it in front of him.

The discharge was deafening in the confined space. The bullet caught the assailant squarely in the chest, and he dropped to the ground like a marionette with its strings cut. The second attacker paused. Thomas levelled the Webley, aiming directly between the man's close-set eyes.

"Put down the knife," he said, the steadiness of his voice surprising him.

The man hesitated.

"Put it down! I won't tell you again."

The knife clattered to the floor, and the man raised his hands above his head.

Thomas nearly fell backwards as the door against which he had rested his back was opened with a sudden jerk. He threw back one arm to steady himself, and for a moment, the aim of his pistol flew wide. The surviving assassin reacted with surprising speed. He dropped to the ground and scooped up his knife. The scream of a woman cut the silence of the night. Thomas aimed his pistol and fired a barrage of shots towards the hulking figure of the second attacker. He did not have time to aim, but he heard the heavy body thud to the floor. Then he sprang to his feet and turned, his pistol still raised.

Mary, his neighbour, was screaming, both hands pressed to her mouth. She had come to investigate the noises coming from his room, no doubt remembering how he himself had intervened when she had suffered at the hands of her husband. But Thomas had no time for gratitude. He stuffed the pistol into his waistband and crossed the room, dropping down by the second attacker's side. The man was lying on his back, his eyes wide and wild with pain and fear. Even in the half-light of the room, Thomas could see that at least one of his shots had found its mark. The man was clutching his ample belly.

"Mary," Thomas said sternly, speaking loudly to drown out her continuing screams. "Go and fetch a doctor!"

He heard footsteps on the landing and the sounds of other doors being wrenched open. There was a limit to what people would ignore, even in this neighbourhood. Soon he would have an audience.

"Please…" the attacker moaned. Thomas cradled the man's head and pressed his coat against the man's gut wound, trying to stem the bleeding.

"I don't want to die…"

"A doctor's coming," Thomas said. "You're not going to die."

"Please, don't let me die, I don't want to die," the man burbled, his words were slurred, and from the smell of his breath, Thomas knew that he had been drinking his courage before the attempted assassination.

"He said it wouldn't be dangerous," the man moaned. "He said… He said it'd be a quick job. Charlie… Is Charlie alright?"

Thomas looked across to the first figure. His eyes were open, staring blindly at eternity. He would never close those eyes again.

"He's fine," Thomas lied. "The doctor will take care of you both. Who hired you?"

"I...I don't know..." the attacker's words were becoming fainter, his complexion paler. Thomas knew instinctively that no doctor or surgeon, not even Sophia, would be able to save the man's life. The bullet had torn through his intestines and lodged in his spine. He was already dead, his body was just not ready to accept it yet.

"Charlie," the man said. "Tell Charlie I'm sorry... I told him we should take the job..."

"You can tell him yourself soon enough," Thomas said. The attacker reached out, a scarred fist grabbing Thomas' lapel with surprising force.

"I can't see," the man whispered. "I can't see anything."

He let go of Thomas and stretched out his hand as if trying to focus on it through the gathering darkness.

"I'm scared..." he muttered.

Thomas heard running steps on the stairs. A middle-aged man in a dark frog coat and eyes still blurry from sleep rushed into the room, out of breath. Thomas caught his eye. Then the doctor looked down at the dead man and his dying partner.

The dying man mumbled a few more words, but they were unintelligible. His hand fell to his side. The doctor crossed the room and knelt down beside Thomas. He reached out and touched the man's wrist, holding it gingerly for a few moments, his face screwed up in concentration. Then he sighed and shook his head.

"He's gone," he said, reaching up to close the man's eyes. Then he looked around the room.

"The young woman who came to fetch me told me you're a detective," he said. Thomas nodded.

"Well, this doesn't look like a difficult crime to solve," the doctor said drily. "What happened?"

"They tried to kill me," Thomas said quietly. He stood up and walked over to the door leading to his room. He examined the keyhole and saw the faint scratches and lines in the corroded brass.

"They used lockpicks," he said.

"A big risk to take to kill a single officer," the doctor said. "You must have upset someone."

Thomas nodded slowly.

"Undoubtedly," he said hesitantly. "But who?"

Chapter Twenty

Thomas arrived at Rose Hill station, sitting on the box of an empty drover's cart. It had been the only means of transport that could be found to bring the bodies of the two dead assailants from Thomas' abode to the station dead house. As they drew up to the station house, Thomas looked up in surprise. Sophia was standing beside Inspector Muldoon. The Danish surgeon was pale, her hands clenched convulsively in front of her. As soon as she saw him, she rushed forward.

"The constables said that someone had tried to kill you," she said. "They didn't say if you were hurt or not."

"I'm fine," Thomas said. Sophia grabbed his shoulders and looked him up and down. His white shirt was soaked in blood. Sophia ran her hands across his torso, and Thomas felt an entirely unexpected but not unpleasant shudder at her touch.

"You don't seem to be hurt," Sophia said.

"I told you, I'm fine," he said. "But thank you for your concern."

Sophia glanced up at him, and he saw relief in her eyes.

"The same can't be said for these two," Muldoon said. He had crossed to the cart and was examining the two assailants. "Who were they?"

"One of them was called Charlie, that's all I know," Thomas said. Muldoon nodded.

"Some of the constables will know them, no doubt." Muldoon lifted Charlie's right arm and examined his knuckles. They were cracked and showed signs of repeated cuts and wounds that had healed before being opened again. "A pair of brawlers," Muldoon said, showing Thomas the poorly healed wounds.

"The question is why they wanted to kill me," Thomas said. Muldoon nodded.

"I don't like it one bit," he said. "Killed in the line of duty is one thing. But this was a cold-blooded assassination attempt."

"We should discuss this in your office, inspector," Sophia said pointedly. The sun had arrived on the horizon as Thomas made his way to Rose Hill, and the first pedestrians were stopping curiously, staring at the dead men and at Thomas, caked in blood and looking for all the world like the survivor of a terrible battle.

"You're quite right," Muldoon conceded and led the way into the station house. As they passed the front desk, Thomas gently placed the Webley in front of Sergeant Fraser.

"Four shots fired, sergeant," he said. "Please make a note of that."

Fraser nodded, picking up the pistol, cracking it open, and removing the four spent cartridges and two live rounds.

"I'm glad you're alright, sir," he said.

"So am I, Fraser, so am I," Thomas said as he continued through the watch room following Muldoon.

As soon as Thomas entered Muldoon's office, the old inspector went behind his desk, opened the top drawer, and took out a bottle of whiskey and two glasses. After a quick glance at Sophia, he sighed, reached into the drawer, and took out another crystal tumbler, filling all three glasses.

"A little early perhaps," he said. "But I think we all need it in our own way."

"What happened, Thomas?" Sophia asked, accepting the glass from Muldoon. Thomas swilled the whiskey around in the tumbler, then threw his head back and drained the glass in a single large gulp.

"I got lucky, I suppose," he said. He described how the terror of his dream had awoken him in time to avoid the first assassin's blade. He left out the unsettling transformation of Catherine Eddowes, deciding against upsetting the surgeon.

"I'm just relieved you forgot to hand in your pistol," Muldoon said when Thomas had finished his story. "Without it…" His voice trailed off, but his meaning was plain. If Thomas had not had access to the firearm, he would more than likely be dead.

"But why?" Sophia wondered. "What possible benefit could there be in murdering Thomas in his sleep? Who would stand to gain?"

"Any number of gangs," Muldoon said. "The city's lousy with them, has been for decades. The High Rips, the Lockwoods, the Hibernians, the Dead Rabbits. Every bloody neighbourhood has its very own gang, and all of them consider a dead officer to be merely a good beginning."

"But have they ever acted like this before?" Sophia asked. "Why not simply jump Thomas in the street?"

"She's got a point," Thomas said. "When the gangs have killed a constable before, they've done it in the streets, out in the open where the death can send a message, not sneaking about a bed chamber at night."

"A less risky tactic, perhaps," Muldoon said.

"But why now?" Sophia pressed on. "Has Thomas arrested any gang leaders in the recent past? Have the police moved against any of the gangs and taken their territory?"

Muldoon hesitated.

"It pains me to admit it," he said. "But to be perfectly honest, we lost the war against the gangs many, many years ago. Long before Thomas' time, even. We'll occasionally bring in a low-level gangster or two, but most of the leaders are far too powerful to be touched."

"So why would they want to start a war by killing a detective in his bed?"

The two detectives sat in brooding silence, unable to answer Sophia.

"Maybe we'll learn more once the assailants have been identified," Thomas said, though he knew this to be unlikely.

"It could be our killer," Sophia said quietly.

Muldoon shook his head like an old elephant trying to clear flies from its rheumy eyes.

"Our killer targets young girls. There would be no satisfaction for him in killing Thomas."

"That's why he paid someone else to do it," Sophia said, her tone becoming more excited. "Think about it," she continued. "These attackers were thugs, brawlers. If Liverpool is anything like Copenhagen, or Paris, then men like that can be hired in every ale house for a handful of pennies."

"You think the killer worries that we're getting closer to him?" Thomas said. "I wish I was certain that we were."

Sophia nodded.

"It makes sense," she said. "We know that the killer is not physically strong, so attacking Thomas himself would be far too risky. Much easier, then, to hire a couple of drunks to do his dirty work for him."

"If you're right then we might all be in danger," Muldoon said. "You included, miss."

Sophia brushed the comment aside.

"How many know that I've contributed to this investigation?" she said. "I've not been named in any of the newspapers to my knowledge."

"You're not wrong," Thomas said turning to Muldoon. "Aside from a handful of people, no one in the city even knows her."

A thought occurred to Thomas and looked questioningly at Sophia.

"And speaking of your assistance," he said. "May I ask why you are here at the crack of dawn?"

Sophia opened her mouth to reply but inspector Muldoon cut in.

"Miss Steenberg arrived a few hours ago," he said. "Fortunately, I was still here, but busy with the aftermath of the riot. I asked her to wait in my office, but before we had a chance to converse, the constables arrived with news about the assassination attempt."

Sophia leaned forward in her seat.

"I continued to work on the investigation last night," she said. "After I came back to my hotel, I mean."

"How could you work on the case from your hotel room?" Muldoon asked, a note of amusement in his voice. "I trust you didn't ask any of the maids or porters for help."

Sophia smiled at the inspector and shook her head.

"No," she said. "But something about Victoria Watson's murder puzzled me. You may remember, inspector, that you asked me what sort of surgeon would be trained in what essentially amounts to torture. The flaying of skin from the soles of the feet, the forced amputation of limbs."

"Yes?" Muldoon said, sitting up. "Do you have an answer for me?" There was an ill-disguised note of excitement in his voice.

"I believe so," Sophia said. "There is one class of medical professional who makes their career performing such tasks."

"Who?" Thomas asked eagerly.

"Those who worked on slave plantations in the new world," Sophia said, her nose wrinkled in disgust. "The thought occurred to me when I examined the work of a man whom I'm ashamed to call a fellow surgeon. His name was J. Marion Sims, and throughout his career, he performed numerous medical experiments on African slaves across the American South. And plantation doctors not only performed experiments, they also supervised and even conducted the torture and punishment of slaves."

Thomas' mouth had gaped open. He looked at Muldoon. The old man's eyebrows were knotted in an expression of deep contemplation.

"Slavery has long since been abandoned in the American south," he said hesitantly. "Nigh on thirty years."

"We did suspect that our murderer's physical weakness could be due to advanced age," Thomas said. "That might explain it."

"If our killer worked in America…" Muldoon began.

"Then we need to widen out net," Thomas finished the sentence. "We cannot assume that he has only murdered in this country. He may never have killed here before."

Muldoon nodded.

"We can send a telegraph to the Foreign Office. They can reach out to their general consuls across the Empire. If there have been similar murders elsewhere, we need to know, whether they were committed in New Delhi or New York."

"The Foreign Office must also be able to reach out to our American cousins," Thomas said. "We cannot exclude that the killer is American, if we assume he worked on slave plantations."

"I'll send a runner for the superintendent," Muldoon said. "He won't want to stand in the way of this one."

Thomas felt a sense of excitement, like an electrical current. He looked at Sophia, and there was such warmth and admiration in his expression that the reserved Dane was taken aback.

"I don't suppose you have had any other ideas as useful as that one?" he said with a broad smile to Sophia. She blushed, but then cleared her throat, evidently annoyed with herself, and continued in a brisk tone.

"One additional point occurred to me," she said. "The ways in which the girls were mutilated are clearly significant to our killer, and he is well-practiced in them. If he was indeed a plantation doctor, then perhaps someone with knowledge of such matters would know in which area or region such punishments were routinely carried out?"

"I'm no expert on the plight of slaves in the Americas," Thomas said. He looked across at Muldoon, whose face had suddenly lost all expression, the excited gleam in his eyes fading entirely. "Certainly there must be someone in the city who can help us with such an enquiry?" he asked.

Muldoon did not reply. For a long time, he sat, looking intently at the empty glass in his hand. Then he reached into his drawer, drew out the bottle, and poured himself another dram without offering one to either Thomas or Sophia. The two looked on in bemusement as the inspector emptied the glass, put it down on the table, and then stood up, walking over to the window. He stood for several long moments glaring out at the city, then he slammed his fist into the window frame.

"Damit to hell," he swore. "I knew this would come back to haunt me someday."

"What do you mean, sir?" Thomas asked. Muldoon turned, and there was an expression of great anger and frustration on his face.

"Old sins coming back for me, Thomas," he said. "Old crimes demanding justice."

"I don't understand."

"I know who you need to ask your questions," Muldoon said. "But she doesn't live in this city. Nor will she set foot here even under pain of death."

Thomas and Sophia looked on in confusion as the old inspector walked back to his desk and slumped into his office chair. He avoided their gaze, addressing his words instead to the ceiling.

"This was before your time, Thomas," he said. "Back in '62. I was a young constable, greener behind the ears than you can imagine. One night, we were called to a meeting in Quaker Hall. That's where I first saw her."

"Who, sir?" Thomas prompted as the silence dragged on.

Muldoon rubbed his eyes, his body slumped, his demeanour suddenly exhausted. He looked old. Older than Thomas had ever seen him before.

"Her name's Clarissa Richmond," he said. "She was a black slave who escaped from her owners in Virginia. She made it safely to the North, where she lived as a free woman until 1861. When the American Civil War broke out, she travelled to Europe. She gave lectures and held meetings, trying to persuade merchants and politicians to boycott cotton and rice produced on plantations in the American South. She held speeches about the plight of the slaves and showed the scars she herself had gotten from manacles and whips."

"Some didn't want to believe her. Many wanted to silence her. She found friends in Manchester, the Quakers there have always despised slavery, but our own city was a different story."

"Why?" Sophia asked.

Muldoon sighed.

"What do you think paid for that fancy suite you live in, miss?" he said. "Slavery built this city. Slavery and importing the products of slaves. Rum, molasses, and cotton."

Sophia fell silent, her eyes downcast.

"Clarissa Richmond was not the only one. There were plenty of former slaves who risked everything traveling around Europe trying to raise support for the plight of their brothers and sisters in bondage. But there were many wealthy families in this city who would have become a great deal poorer had their mission succeeded."

"They opposed the abolitionists?" Sophia asked. Muldoon nodded.

"Oh, they did more than that," he said. "That night, some of the other constables and I had been ordered to wait outside the meeting house. We could hear the murmuring of the crowd and Clarissa's loud, clear voice through the closed door. Then he came."

"Who?" Thomas asked.

"He called himself Chester," Muldoon said, an angry scowl on his face. "A big bear of a man with the largest sideburns I'd ever seen. I found out later that his real name was James Bulloch, and he was in the employ of the Confederacy. The most dangerous man in Europe they called him. Filthy spy. He lived here in Liverpool for years, even though Britain was supposed to be neutral in the conflict."

"And no one knew?" Thomas asked. Muldoon laughed.

"Don't be naïve, Thomas," he said. "Everyone knew. He even paid one of the shipyards in Birkenhead to build a secret warship, which a Liverpool crew sailed out of the city, armed to the teeth, and then handed it over to the Confederates down on the Azores. Do you really think that anyone could build and arm an entire bloody battleship without the local politicians and superintendent of police getting wind of it?"

Thomas looked down. He knew the ship Muldoon was referring to. The *Alabama* had been built with money collected from Liverpool's merchant class and had gone on to become the most successful Confederate privateer, raiding Union shipping across the world. The *Alabama* had not met her end until she found herself going up against a more powerful foe, the *Kearsarge*, in the French harbour of Cherbourg. The two ships had pummelled each other for hours until the *Alabama*, under the sheer weight of shot from the *Kearsarge*, finally sank under the waves, allowing the sea to wash away one of the greatest stains on Liverpool's history.

"That night, Bulloch brought orders from the superintendent of police. We were to raid the meeting and disperse the crowd. *Dangerous revolutionary elements*, that was what the superintendent had labelled Clarissa Richmond and her audience."

"And did you?" Sophia asked in a hushed voice. "Did you carry out the orders?"

Muldoon looked away. His fist was still clenched so tightly on the glass that his knuckles were white. He nodded once.

"We stormed the hall," he said. "Clarissa was thrown from the stage and badly beaten. Some of her supporters got her to safety."

"Where is she now?" Thomas asked.

"In Manchester," Muldoon said with a tired tone in his voice. "Most of the other abolitionists went back to America after the war was won and slavery abolished. But Clarissa remained here. I hear that she still advocates for those former slaves who were simply thrown out with only the clothes on their backs by their former masters and who now live in poverty in tenements and slums across the American South."

Sophia's eyes were wide. Her expression was inscrutable, but Thomas sensed a deep sense of anger. When she spoke to the inspector, her tone was clipped and cold.

"Will she be able to answer our questions?" she asked.

"If anyone possesses the knowledge you need," Muldoon said. "Then it's Clarissa Richmond."

"But *will* she help?" Thomas asked. Muldoon shook his head sadly.

"I don't know," he said. "If we go and introduce ourselves as Liverpool constables…"

"That at least is easily remedied," Sophia interrupted. "I will go. She may have no interest in helping you. But perhaps she would be willing to help me."

Chapter Twenty-One

The two cities of Liverpool and Manchester had been connected by a rail line for more than sixty years. In 1830, the Liverpool and Manchester Railway Company dispatched the first steam locomotive, the Northumbrian, from Liverpool Crown Street to Manchester's Liverpool Road Station. The first journey had taken more than eight hours, in no small part due to the death of one of the invited guests—a local MP no less—in a horrific accident. Now, more than six decades later, the route between the two cities was one of the busiest and most heavily travelled in the country.

The train which conveyed Sophia from Liverpool to Manchester's new Oxford Road Station was neither as luxurious nor as well-appointed as the first-class carriage which had brought her and Thomas to London. But as the journey was considerably shorter, taking only a little more than an hour, Sophia was content to sit in one of the public compartments with five other travellers, including a family with two young children.

Sophia spent the journey watching as the suburbs of Liverpool rushed past, rows and rows of terraced brick houses eventually giving way to farmland and the occasional village or small cluster of cottages.

Manchester could be smelt before it could be seen. The factories and spinneries which had made the city rich, and also earned it its nickname of Cottonopolis, discharged vast clouds of pollutants, ensuring that both the city and the land for miles around was permeated with the smell of smoke.

Arriving into Manchester the train crossed a series of viaducts. The soaring brick arches not only served to provide a safe platform for the railway. They also gave shelter to thousands who lived in poverty in tents and huts underneath them, descendants of the occupants of the slum known as 'Little Ireland', which had been forcibly cleared to make way for both the railway and the station.

Sophia joined the bustling crowds pushing out through the station. She carried nothing except a leather satchel containing a folder of the photographs and sketches from the two crime scenes, as well as her own written reports.

A light, dusty rain filled the air as she made her way down Oxford Road towards the Friends Meeting House. The Meeting Houses were akin to Quaker churches, places where the congregation could meet weekly and listen to sermons, but they were also a place for society meetings, even places where revolutionary topics such as women's suffrage could be more freely discussed than elsewhere. The large Meeting House in Manchester had been sponsored by several wealthy industrialists and included several apartments and living quarters, in which supporters of the Society of Friends, such as Clarissa Charlston, had been permitted to live permanently.

The Meeting House was an impressive red-brick manor trimmed with white limestone. It was set a little back from the thronged road, fronted by an ornamental gate, wrought iron fences, and a small garden. As Sophia strolled up the gravel path towards the front door, she looked around the garden. There were granite benches set under ash and elm trees that would no doubt provide welcome shade in the summer. Now, in the grip of autumn, though, only a scattering of reddish leaves clung onto spiky branches, looking like ink lines scribbled against the overcast sky. As Sophia looked, the October breeze tore a few more leaves from their perch, carrying them up and away across the shingle roofs of the city.

The front door opened into a homely reception room. A granite fireplace surmounted by blue Dutch tiles stood against one wall. Clusters of velvet armchairs and small round tables occupied most of the space. The walls were decorated with life-sized portraits of some of those men who had donated a part of their newly won fortunes to the Society of Friends.

"Can I help you, miss?" Sophia turned at the sound of the voice. A young woman had entered the room through a pair of double doors. She was modestly dressed in a simple black skirt and a white lace shirt buttoned up to her chin. Her reddish-blonde hair was pulled back into a ponytail, held in place with a tortoise shell clasp.

Sophia crossed the room and held out a white printed visiting card, which carried her name and titles. The young girl looked at the car with some surprise, noting Sophia's medical title and frowning slightly. Then she seemed to remember herself, looked up and smiled warmly.

"My name is Miss Wilkinson," she said. "I'm the Secretary of the Society of Friends. You have clearly come a long way, so how may I assist you?"

"I have come to seek a meeting with a resident here, Mrs Clarissa Richmond," Sophia said.

The young girl's face fell.

"Do you have an appointment?" she asked.

"I'm afraid that I come on a matter of some urgency," Sophia said. "I had no time to send a telegraph message or letter ahead of time."

"Then I'm not sure..." the girl began.

"May I ask why?"

"Mrs Richmond is not as strong as she once was," the girl said almost apologetically. "She turned eighty years old in the spring, and her eyesight is failing."

"But her mind remains sharp, I've heard," Sophia said, glad the inspector Muldoon had filled her in on any recent news concerning the abolitionist he had picked up from the Manchester constabulary. "I heard that she addressed a large audience of scholars from Victoria University less than a fortnight ago."

"That is true," the secretary said hesitantly. "But she gets tired, and I'm not sure that a private audience without any prior agreements is..."

Sophia lowered her voice and leaned in close to the girl.

"Miss," she said, overlaying a hint of sternness on her voice. "I would not ask were this not of the utmost importance. You have heard about the recent murders in Liverpool, I assume? Those two young girls..."

The secretary's eyes widened, and she looked suddenly frightened.

"It's been all over the newspapers," she said in a whisper.

"I am consulting with the Liverpool Constabulary on the investigation, and I believe that Mrs Richmond may possess key information."

"You are surely not accusing…"

Sophia raised her hand disarmingly.

"Of course not," she said. "I merely believe that the murderer may have worked at some time in his life on a slave plantation. And I wish to ask Mrs Richmond a few questions about her own experiences in such places."

"Well then," the secretary began, hesitating only slightly. "Well, then, I suppose you may see her. But I must insist on accompanying you."

"Of course," Sophia said graciously. Miss Wilkinson nodded, satisfied, and turned around, beckoning Sophia to follow her. They passed through the double doors, entering a spacious hall where the meetings of the Friends were held. Now it had the neglected air of any large communal space not in use. More than a hundred wooden chairs stood stacked against one wall, and the grey light coming in through the large mullion windows that took up the whole of one wall caught particles of dust from the scuffed and scratched floor, thrown into the air by the passage of the two women.

At the far end of the room was another set of doors leading to a small antechamber. Miss Wilkinson led Sophia up a flight of steps to a landing. She knocked gently on one of the heavy, polished wooden doors leading off the landing, waited a moment, and then entered.

The door led directly into a long, rectangular sitting room, tightly packed with furniture. Every surface held gilt-framed photographs; every inch of wall was covered in paintings. Many of the photographs showed a tall and powerful woman with dark, burnished skin and a defiant expression. The woman was often standing next to various dignitaries. Sophia recognised several suited politicians and even members of various European royal families. Some of the frames contained pictures of young children, and several of a handsome, dark-skinned man.

"Emily, is that you?" The voice was powerful but marked nonetheless by encroaching age. It came from an armchair standing close to an ornate fireplace. As Sophia looked, the same woman who had appeared, though much younger, in the photographs, slowly got to her feet, reaching out for a cane. Her white hair was tied back, and she wore an emerald dress, finely made though several decades out of fashion. The woman stretched out the cane in front of her, tapping the ground as she walked forward. Sophia saw that both of her eyes were covered in a grey film of cataract.

"Yes, Mrs Richmond," the young secretary said. "I've brought a visitor."

The older woman hesitated. Sophia could sense that she was close to refusing her unknown guest.

"I am very pleased to meet you, madame," she said. "My name is Sophia Steenberg. I would like to ask you some questions."

Clarissa turned her blind eyes in the direction of Sophia's words, and for a moment, Sophia had the unpleasant sense that, despite her blindness, the former slave could see her nonetheless.

"You are not English," Clarissa said curtly. "Your accent is Nordic. German, perhaps?"

"I am from Denmark."

"Then you've come a long way indeed," Clarissa said and gestured towards the two armchairs by the fireplace. "Will you have a cup of tea with me?"

Sophia glanced at the young secretary, who nodded encouragingly. They waited for Clarissa to settle herself, then Sophia sat down opposite her. Miss Wilkinson poured two cups of tea and then quietly withdrew from the room.

"I visited your country once," Clarissa said. "Not long after the war broke out, back in '63 it must have been. I met your new King," she hesitated her eyes narrowed as she sorted through her memories. "Christian, I think his name was."

"He's the king still," Sophia said.

"He was a worried man," Clarissa said. "That much I remember. He feared that war would soon come to his own shores."

"It did," Sophia said quietly. "A year later."

Clarissa sighed.

"The cruelty of humanity never ceases to amaze me," she said. "If we are not warring, then we are enslaving or torturing. The newspapers say that Victoria's reign brought peace and prosperity, but what good has that prosperity done for those who struggle to feed their families or who die of disease in the slums and tenements?"

"They tell me you are an advocate for female suffrage," Sophia said.

Clarissa nodded.

"Women are of this world too," she said. "Why should we not have a say in how it is governed?"

Sophia smiled.

"I don't disagree," she said. "Even if I suspect it will be a hard fight."

"Anything worthwhile is hard to win," Clarissa said flatly. "Nothing of any value is given freely."

"I can certainly agree with that," Sophia said.

Clarissa turned her face to the younger woman, a puzzled expression playing across her lined face.

"You really can, can't you?" she said. "You sound like a woman with a story to tell."

Without truly wanting to, but led by the occasional grunt and nod from Clarissa, Sophia soon found herself relating her life story to the older woman. She told her of her childhood, sheltered as it had been, as far from Clarissa's own experiences as it was possible to be. She told her of her dreams to study medicine. She told of the fights with her overbearing father, about her empty-headed mother, interested only in attending parties and theatrical performances. She told her how she had, in the end, cut any connection to her family, taken her possessions as an inheritance, and left for America.

At the end of the tale, Clarissa leaned back in her seat, folded her hands atop her walking cane, and smiled.

"I was right," she said. "You really are a woman with a story to tell."

"Not as fascinating as yours, I am sure," Sophia said deferentially.

Clarissa scoffed.

"My story is not about fascination but about pain, Miss Steenberg. Pain and blood and cruelty. I have told my story more often than I can count, but I did not do it for me. I did it because it was necessary. Because I had a debt to those still suffering. I feel that debt still."

Sophia did not speak but watched as the older woman stood up and walked slowly across the room. She ran the tips of her fingers across the gilt picture frames, picking up two of them. Sophia realised that no two frames were identical, and that this allowed their owner to tell apart those photographs which were now only visible in her memory.

"My husband," she said with a fond smile, passing Clarissa the photograph of the smiling handsome man. "Simon, his name was. I met him in Boston, not long after I escaped to the North. He travelled with me to Europe when I first decided to tell my story to the world. But after a while, he grew restless. He felt that he, too, needed to help, but he was never a great orator. When the Union generals finally allowed the formation of coloured regiments to aid in the war effort, he returned to Boston and signed up with the 54th Massachusetts. He wrote me letters all through that dreadful year of 63."

Clarissa's expression darkened.

"I received the final letter in January of '64. A month later, he fell at Olustee. I got a telegram while I was staying in Paris with our daughter. She was not yet two years old and suddenly without a father."

"It must have been hard," Sophia said.

Clarissa nodded.

"Simon died for his beliefs, and I continued to live for mine," she said.

"You still work for the abolishment of slavery."

"With every breath in my body."

"Even after the war between the states was won?"

Clarissa laughed, but there was no humour in the sound.

"You think slavery vanished in a puff of smoke just because that traitor Lee signed a piece of paper at Appomattox?"

Sophia frowned.

"Perhaps not," she said. "But surely the trade with slaves has been outlawed nigh on a hundred years in this country."

"It has," Clarissa said. "But there were still slave plantations in the New World. The slaves in Cuba were only given their freedom five years ago. In Brazil, only three. All that rum and tobacco the English are so fond of, how much of that do you think was produced by black slaves?"

Sophia did not reply.

"You no doubt arrived in this country through the port of Liverpool," Clarissa said, and Sophia tensed. "That is where it used to be unloaded. Two hundred years ago, the Liverpool merchants grew rich from the slave trade, and when they could no longer legally barter in human lives, they found other ways to grow their wealth."

"How?"

Clarissa leaned forward.

"Until very recently, a Liverpool merchant could legally buy rum and molasses from a slave plantation in Cuba. In fact, he would have to buy it because he could not legally own such a plantation outright. But consider now that this greedy merchant wanted rum and molasses, which he could sell cheaper than his competitors. Then that merchant would send a telegram to a Spanish lawyer in Havana. And through that Spanish lawyer, he would set up a corporation headed, not by him, but by the lawyer who, as a citizen of Spain, could still legally own the plantation and the slaves toiling on it. The lawyer becomes the owner *de jure*, and the British merchant the owner *de facto*."

Sophia was horrified.

"Surely, the British state would have investigated such a crime; the judges would have punished it."

"Why would they?" Clarissa asked. "They liked cheap rum too."

Sophia shook her head.

"Astounding hypocrisy," she said. Clarissa smiled.

"Oh, there are no saints in this game, Miss Steenberg," she said. "Do you know why your own country outlawed slavery nearly a century ago?"

Sophia hesitated.

"The call for abolition had been growing…"

"Your king and privy council decided that slavery was no longer profitable," Clarissa interrupted with whiplash speed. "And your king at the time had heard that the British were considering outlawing slavery. He wanted to beat them to it."

Sophia said nothing. She had no retort to make.

"To your country's credit," Clarissa said, a mocking tone in her voice. "You did indeed beat the British to it and gained a great deal of international recognition from it. Imagine that being applauded for simply ceasing the torture and murder of other human beings."

The rhythmic beats of a tall grandfather clock, which stood in a corner of the room, seemed to grow louder as the awkward silence between the two women lengthened.

"Mrs Richmond," Sophia said with hesitation in her voice. "I have not told you the entire truth behind my visit."

"I didn't imagine that you had come all this way just for a cup of tea," the older woman said sardonically. "Why are you really here?"

Sophia drew a deep breath, readying herself for the woman to call for her secretary.

"I did indeed arrive to this country through the port of Liverpool," she said. "As a surgeon, I was asked to aid the Liverpool constabulary with the investigation of two brutal murders."

Clarissa had stiffened in her chair at the mention of the Liverpool constabulary. Sophia hurried on.

"I am sure you have heard of the case. When I conducted autopsies of the two dead girls, something about their injuries struck me. I believe that whoever inflicted those injuries worked, perhaps even for a very long time, as a plantation doctor in the New World. I believe that he honed his surgical abilities through the torture and mutilation of coloured slaves."

A rattling interrupted Sophia's rapid speech. Clarissa's hand was shaking on her cane, causing it to judder against the wooden floorboards.

"You have lied to me," she said in a low voice. "Had you told me from the start who had sent you, I would have refused to see you."

"I am sorry," Sophia said. "There is no excuse I can make. I beg you to know, though, that I only care about catching the monster who has taken the life of two young women and abused them in the most horrid way imaginable."

There was an audible thud as Clarissa set down her cane. Her nostrils were dilated, her face contorted into a dark scowl. Her mouth was working as though she was chewing, and she seemed to be arguing silently with herself.

"Tell me about the injuries," she said, her tone cold and her words clipped.

Sophia expelled a breath she did not realise she had been keeping. She opened her satchel, drew out the folder containing her report of the autopsies of Polly and Victoria. She read the description of their injuries, every word, every twisted and gruesome detail. Occasionally, she glanced at Clarissa, but the old woman did not flinch or move a single muscle as the laundry list of mutilations was read out.

When Sophia had finished, she sat in silence for so long that she began to wonder whether she was being dismissed. Then Clarissa seemed to sag in her chair. She laid a hand over her unseeing eyes and began to speak in a low voice.

"I can assure you, miss, that every injury you describe has been inflicted on a slave at some point in the past. I worked on cotton plantations in the American South, and the preferred punishments there were whippings and canings. But I know that in the Caribbean, and in particular in Cuba, the punishments meted out on the sugar plantations often involved forced amputations. Sometimes, a slave would have their arms or legs run through one of the big presses used to crush the sugar cane. Other times, their skin would be scalded with boiling molasses that sticks like tar. But the flaying of the feet, that was the favourite punishment of the Cuban slave drivers. A punishment enacted on slaves who had conspired to run away from their plantation. A twisted joke of sorts. After all, who can run on flayed feet?"

"You believe that this killer may have worked at one such plantation?" Sophia asked.

"It is possible," Clarissa said. "Forced amputations were often performed by plantation doctors. They could remove the limb and cauterise the wound so that the slave could still work."

"It's madness," Sophia said quietly. "Utter madness."

"It is how this world of yours was built," Clarissa said. "Your people built it upon the backs of mine. Perhaps you are better than your ancestors, miss, I do not know. But you too used me for my knowledge."

Sophia looked down, a flush of blood reddening her cheeks.

"It is time for you to return to Liverpool," Clarissa said. "Remember, the animal that ripped children from their mothers, tortured, mutilated, and murdered, is only asleep. It is not dead or truly banished. And it may one day reawaken."

Chapter Twenty-Two

Sophia arrived back at Rose Hill station shortly after four o'clock in the afternoon. She felt exhausted. The conversation with Clarissa Richmond had been far more draining than anything she had experienced since arriving in Liverpool. The guilt still hung like a cloud around her; she felt tainted as though bearing the Mark of Cain. Everywhere she walked, she fooled herself into thinking that passers-by could see the guilt written, as though in ink, upon her finely chiselled features.

As she entered the station house, she was nearly knocked over by a pair of constables rushing out the door. They apologised profusely, helping her steady herself, but then ran off, sprinting up the street in the direction of St George's Hall. As she opened the door, she could hear Muldoon's raised voice.

"Parker and Renfield, you two run along to the Central Library. We need every issue of the Calcutta Gazette from 1887 through 1888. If the librarian objects, tell him to come and talk to me directly."

"Shaw, you go with them," she heard Thomas' voice, excitement and eagerness on every word. "Get every copy of the Savannah Morning News from 1890 that you can lay your hands on."

Sophia shook her head, confused, and pushed through the throng of constables filling the watch room. As she cleared the front row of constables, she saw that all the tables and chairs had been cleared and pushed with some haste against the walls. Thomas and Muldoon were squatting in the large open space, dozens of slips of paper laid out in front of them. The yellow paper slips were easily identifiable as telegraph messages, and each one had been secured with a pin to a vast map of the world, measuring more than eight feet on a side. Thomas looked up.

"Miss Steenberg," he said with a broad smile. "I believe your theory may have been correct."

Sophia was flabbergasted. She opened and closed her mouth several times, trying to decide what to say. Finally, she settled on a single word.

"What?"

"Alright, you horrible lot," Muldoon shouted at the constables. "Don't you have beats to go to? Those not assigned a route, can stay and help out, everyone else can clear out."

There was a clamour as the constables rousted themselves, put on their helmets, picked up truncheons and lanterns, and gradually made their way out of the cramped room.

"Good grief, it's like the Zoological Garden in here," Muldoon said, as he sorted through a slim stack of telegraphs not yet attached to the map. "Here's one more. Last year, near Valetta on Malta." He leaned down and fastened the slip of paper to the map.

"What is all of this?" Sophia asked. Thomas looked up, saw her standing awkwardly, and rushed over to grab one of the scuffed and scratched chairs used by the constables. He placed it in front of the map, and she sat down gratefully.

"We started receiving replies from both colonial and foreign police forces just after you left," he said.

"They've been pouring in like rain," Muldoon said gleefully. Sophia suddenly understood their meaning and leaned forward eagerly, feeling her exhaustion melt away.

"Our killer?" she asked. "He's killed before?"

"Oh yes," Thomas said grimly. "If these poor girls were all his victims, then he has killed no less than seventeen before even arriving in our fair city."

"Seventeen?" Sophia said, stunned. "He's an even bigger madman than we thought!"

"But a consistent one, thank God," Muldoon said with a twisted grin. "The feet gave him away. There are some minor changes between each murder, but the flaying of the feet is consistent throughout."

He pointed to the map.

"The most recent murder was only a few months ago, in Cauville-sur-Mer. It's a small village on the Normandy coast. Before then, there were two girls near Alexandria. Before then, a girl found in the slums of New York. Before that, three girls were all found in the suburbs of Calcutta. Cape Town, Valetta, and even a girl on Burma back in 1889."

"No wonder he wasn't discovered," Sophia mused. "So many different places."

Thomas nodded.

"None of the murders were solved, and none of the investigators suspected that the killer was moving so freely between countries and jurisdictions."

"How far back can you trace him?"

Muldoon planted a thick finger on a slip attached to a large island in the middle of the Caribbean Sea.

"December of 1886," he said. "A young girl, a prostitute, was murdered and her body dumped on the outskirts of Havana. The mutilations are near-identical to those inflicted on Victoria Watson."

Sophia clapped her hands in triumph. The two police officers looked at her in surprise.

"I can explain why these murders began," she said, her cheeks flushed not with shame, but with the thrill of discovery.

"Oh?" Muldoon said, his brow furrowed.

"The murders began because he ran out of legal victims," she said. Thomas glanced quickly at Muldoon.

"What do you mean?"

"In October of 1886, the Spanish Crown passed a decree that outlawed slavery on the island of Cuba."

Thomas' mouth fell open in surprise. Sophia could see the conclusions beginning to form behind his eyes.

"Clarissa Richmond agreed to meet with you?" Muldoon asked sharply. Sophia nodded.

"The flaying of the feet was a punishment favoured by those who ran sugar plantations on Cuba until the abolishment of slavery in 1886."

"When our killer lost his pool of ready victims," Thomas said.

"But his compulsion was not satisfied," Muldoon said slowly. "He had spent so long killing and maiming without consequence that it had become a habit."

"A perversion," Sophia clarified. "Are you familiar with a German scholar by the name of Julius Koch?"

Thomas smiled.

"I think you can assume that we are not," he said. Sophia rolled her eyes.

"Dr Koch is an alienist, an expert in the diseases of the mind rather than the body. I was fortunate enough to listen to one of his lectures in Paris. He has proposed the identification of a novel form of psychopathology, which he terms psychopathic inferiority. People who are inflicted in this manner are not insane in the traditional sense."

"You mean they're not balmy?" Muldoon said with a twisted smile.

"Not in the sense that they are subject to hallucinations or manias," Sophia continued, ignoring Thomas's snort of laughter. "Instead, they have abnormalities in their behaviour. They can be primal, violent, sadistic, and eccentric, but they, unlike those poor souls in Bedlam, for instance, are in full control of their faculties. They commit acts which, to us, may be inexcusable, cruel, and horrific, but to them the acts are logical and sensible."

"Still sounds like insanity to me," Muldoon grumbled.

"No," Thomas said, raising a hand. "I think I understand the difference. A few years ago, I arrested a man who had murdered both his wife and young child. He was raving, shouting, and screaming about how demons had possessed his victims. How he had seen them come alive with red eyes and fiery wings. In the end, he was confined to the asylum rather than hanged."

"Yes!" Sophia said, pointing excitedly at Thomas. "You are precisely right. That unfortunate soul was truly insane, suffering from delusions and hallucinations, and so not responsible for his actions. But I believe that our killer suffers from no such hallucinations. He does not do what he does because of some external imagined force, but because of a deep defect in his personality."

"A born killer, in other words," Thomas said. Sophia nodded sadly.

"Yes," she said. "But one who was allowed to quite legally satiate his obsession with no recourse from the law."

Muldoon looked down as she glanced at him. She saw his knuckles whiten.

"Did…" he began, then he hesitated before rushing on. "Did Mrs Richmond mention me?" he said.

Sophia frowned.

"No," she said. "I don't believe so."

"I always wondered," Muldoon said quietly. "I wondered if she knew who I was. Who I had become. That one of the constables who took orders from a scoundrel like James Bulloch had risen to become a detective inspector."

Sophia looked at Muldoon and felt a stab of pity.

"I do not believe that Clarissa Richmond sees any benefits in forgiving those who wronged her and her people," she said. "I can't say I blame her."

Muldoon sighed heavily.

"No," he said. "No, neither can I. Perhaps that is my punishment. To know that I cannot be forgiven for that particular sin."

Sophia glanced at Thomas, but he was not looking at her. He was watching the older inspector with a tenderness that Sophia had rarely seen on his face. She remembered that Thomas's own father was long dead.

"This explains our killer's motivation," Thomas said, his voice slightly raised to penetrate the gloom that had settled upon the inspector. "But it does not help us catch him."

"Maybe not," Muldoon said, shaking himself out of his reverie. "But perhaps we'll strike lucky with the newspapers."

"Newspapers?" Sophia asked.

"Thomas' idea," Muldoon said, smiling broadly. "Most of the cities where our killer struck were port cities, like Liverpool. Every newspaper printed in a port town prints the names of arriving ships and their passengers."

"So, if we compare newspapers printed at the time of the murders across these different cities," Thomas said, pointing to the map, "then we may perhaps find a name that appears several times."

Sophia frowned. She understood the logic, but also the sheer scale of the proposition.

"That must be hundreds of papers," she said. "Thousands even."

"I didn't say it would be easy," Thomas said a little defensively. "But what else can we do?"

Sophia bit her lip.

"Could you perhaps reach out to the authorities in Cuba?" she asked.

"I doubt that former slave owners would have kept many records after the abolition," Muldoon said. "And even if they did, you are talking about even more documents going back decades. Our killer could have worked across several different plantations all over Cuba and even elsewhere in the Caribbean."

"A needle in a haystack, in other words," Thomas concurred.

"Our killer surely has another identifying trait," Sophia said. Thomas looked at her encouragingly. "He must be wealthy," she said. "Not only is he a well-educated doctor, but judging from the sheer scale of his murderous spree, he must have spent a fortune travelling throughout the world."

"Yes," Muldoon said. "And that is odd enough in itself. What possible purpose could there be to these rambling journeys?"

"Could he have travelled so frequently simply to avoid detection?" Thomas asked. Muldoon frowned.

"I have known killers who very carefully sought to cover their tracks," he said. "But this feels different."

"I cannot see a pattern in these journeys," Sophia said, staring at the map. "There is no logical progression from one country to the next."

"The travels may make sense to the killer," Thomas said with a shrug. "As you said, what appears illogical and senseless to us may be perfectly sensible in his twisted mind."

Sophia sat back and for a long moment she remained silent, fearing the sentence that she knew she would have to utter. She did not want to speak, because to speak would be to add further pressure on the already exhausted detectives squatting on the floor in front of her. After several long moments, she finally cleared her throat and opened her mouth.

"The travels raise another possibility," she said quietly. "A grim one."

Thomas nodded without looking up.

"I know what you mean," he said. "There is no evidence that the killer intends to remain here in Liverpool. If we do not catch him, he will no doubt vanish to some other country, maybe in the Far East or Africa or the Americas…"

"…And we'll never catch him," Muldoon said darkly.

"And he'll be free to continue his twisted spree," Thomas concluded.

All three sat for a moment, feeling the weight of their responsibility settling upon them. This was no longer merely about avenging and seeking justice for the senseless killing of Polly and Victoria. To allow this killer to slip away as the Ripper had slipped away from Abberline would condemn who knew how many innocent girls and women from across the world to a similar fate as the two girls in Liverpool, and the seventeen others across a dozen countries.

Sophia sighed and rubbed her eyes. She suddenly felt the tiredness and the exhaustion again. The excitement that had filled her seemed to be leaking out like air from a punctured balloon. She tried to focus.

"Clarissa Richmond did mention one other point of interest," she said. Muldoon and Thomas sat up. "I don't know how useful it will be, but she said that some of the merchants in this city illegally invested in the sugar plantations in Cuba for years before the abolishment of slavery."

Muldoon nodded, dropping his eyes.

"An open secret again, I'm afraid," he said. "We were never empowered to prosecute them. The superintendent of police at the time was very clear on that."

Thomas turned his head to Muldoon, his forehead wrinkled.

"If there is this connection between the sugar plantations where we believe our killer worked and our city," he said slowly. "Is it then impossible that the killer may have originally come from here? That these murders are not simply two more in a long line, but different somehow."

"A home-coming celebration," Sophia said.

Muldoon looked at the two young people sceptically.

CHAPTER TWENTY-TWO

"Perhaps," he said. "But you'd have a devil of a time proving it," he said.

Thomas raised his eyebrows.

"You're not telling me you didn't know which families participated in this trade," he said.

Muldoon did not reply for a long moment. Then he seemed to deflate.

"Of course, we knew," he said. "But there were dozens and dozens of them. Not exactly a narrow list of potential suspects. And just because one of these families may have employed our killer to work on some distant island, does not mean they knew him."

"But it doesn't exclude it either," Thomas pressed. "And it would explain our killer's education and wealth."

"Many of these families remain both wealthy and powerful, Thomas," Muldoon said warningly. "We can't just seek them out and demand that they provide us with a list of everyone they've ever employed. Especially as these employments were not strictly speaking legal at the time. I doubt they kept records."

"But what if the killer was not employed by the family, but rather was part of one of the families," Thomas pressed. "Surely they would know if they had shipped a family member off to the Caribbean."

Muldoon shook his head.

"We can't just go at this blind, Thomas," he said. "My career may be nearly over, but yours is just beginning. I don't like it any more than you do, but if you tangle with the rich and powerful, then most likely you'll never make it beyond detective sergeant. In fact, you might be lucky to keep your job at all."

Thomas had reddened. When he answered the inspector, Sophia could hear the barely controlled anger in his voice.

"Damnit, inspector," he said. "What's the point of us if all we do is to catch drunkards and pickpockets. Don't you want to see justice done for Polly and Victoria?"

"Of course, I do..." Muldoon interrupted, but Thomas cut him off.

"Then shouldn't we explore every possible lead, every avenue of inquiry?"

"Not without a clearer idea of what we're looking for, Thomas," Muldoon said, raising his voice to match his subordinates. "You're young still, and untried. Don't bite off more than you can chew."

Thomas opened his mouth to answer back, but to his surprise, Sophia cut him off.

"There may be a way to further narrow down your pool of suspects," she said. The two men looked at her, ruffled feathers settling. The echoes of what had almost been said still hung in the air.

"Yes?" Muldoon said curtly.

"Dr Koch, the German alienist who proposed the theory of the psychopathic inferiority, has some interesting ideas about how a man with that kind of perverted mind develops. Mind you," Sophia said. "These are theories. Barely published and entirely untested."

"At this stage, I'm willing to try anything," Muldoon said in a tired tone. "Even the ramblings of some German quack."

Sophia suppressed a smile and continued.

"Dr Koch believes that such people do not simply develop their affliction because of some incident or event. He believes that they are born with it."

"And how does that help us?" Thomas asked.

Sophia frowned, trying to order her own thoughts to properly explain them to the two detectives.

"Anyone who has such a defect of the mind would tend to display cruelty, even in childhood. Pointless cruelty, not merely bullying or misbehaving. In Paris, Dr Koch discussed a patient of his who, at the age of six, had killed and skinned the family dog. For no reason. He came from a stable and loving home, there was no explainable reason for this action. No reason, other than the enjoyment the child derived from the act."

"Mother of Mary," Muldoon said quietly.

"If the killer was born and grew up in this city, then his behaviour may have been noticed. It may even have reached the ears of the police."

Thomas looked at Muldoon.

"The old arrest ledgers," he said. Muldoon nodded.

"It's a place to start," he said. "You are welcome to remain, miss," he continued, turning to Sophia. "But I fear it will be a long evening and night of looking through old and dusty books."

Sophia smiled; her eyes glazed.

"Thank you for the offer, inspector," she said. "But after my travels today, I must admit that I am rather looking forward to a quiet dinner and an even quieter evening at the Adelphi."

Chapter Twenty-Three

It was wise of me to wait outside the detective sergeant's squalid quarters last night. If I had not, I might have assumed that those two drunken fools I hired in The Greyhound had been successful. Imagine my fury when I saw the sergeant appear, bruised and battered for sure, but depressingly alive. With him alive, I will have to adjust my plans. I decide to do what I do best. I spend the day stalking the sergeant and my intended. I see her leave the station house and rush to Lime Street, but the street is far too busy with early morning traffic to make an attempt. I wait patiently by the rail station until, in the afternoon, she finally returns, her face drawn.

But again, the street is far too busy, even under a dark and grey October sky. I see her return to the station, and I take up my vigil, concealed in an alley across from the station house. The sense of urgency is beginning to take hold again. I cannot remember a time when it did not. As certain as the passing of the seasons, it returns again and again. My exile was in some ways a blessing in disguise. As angry as I was and still am to have been robbed of my future and sent to live in that fetid swamp, it nevertheless allowed me to indulge myself whenever I pleased. It was easy. Whenever the urge grew too strong, there was always someone who had been careless. Maybe dropped one of the heavy baskets with sugar cane. Maybe fallen asleep from exhaustion in the field. Maybe even tried to run. The overseers didn't mind that the punishments sometimes went too far. That sometimes those being punished could not be brought back from the brink.

Damn this town and damn that sergeant. My trinity needs to be completed. And it needs to be completed quickly. I have no desire to stay here any longer than I must. Once it's done, I can leave. Maybe I'll go back to the Americas. I had liked Savannah. There they still remembered the old ways and as long as I never hunted white girls, no one asked any questions or started any investigations.

In the early evening, I track her back to the Adelphi. I had planned to engage her in polite conversation, maybe share a meal with her. I would gradually build trust with her and then, when she least expected it, I would strike. But I don't have time for that. As I sit in a public house across the street from the hotel, a plan slowly takes shape. I squint out through the narrow dusty windows. I find what I'm looking for standing right outside the pub, sheltering from the rain under an awning. Perfect.

* * *

Sophia felt a great need for solace and sleep, but hunger drove her to the restaurant on the ground floor of the Adelphi. One of the uniformed waiters showed her to a table. Within two minutes of arriving, she was being served a steaming bowl of spiced Mulligatawny soup followed by an entrée of dover sole, steamed and served on a bed of roasted vegetables with a tarragon sauce. The portions were small, but with no less than eight courses served as part of the standard evening menu at the hotel, a dinner service could take hours. Sophia looked around while she ate. The waiter had positioned her in one of the corners of the room, and her seat gave her a commanding view across the entire dining hall. A central table housed more than a dozen couples, the women in colourful evening wear, the men in top hats and tails. She tilted her head and recognised them as Americans by their drawling accents. They had just ordered oysters and champagne, and the high-pitched laughter of the women showed that the occupants had already been well lubricated even before the champagne arrived.

The main courses included a veal medallion in a port reduction and roast capon with a herb and chestnut stuffing. Between each dish were sorbets and water ice to cleanse the palate and the meal was finished with sumptuous desserts including a vanilla blancmange with raspberry cream and a selection of fruits, nuts, and cheeses.

Nearly three hours had passed since Sophia sat down when she finished the last mouthful of ripe blue Stilton cheese and emptied her small glass of Portuguese fortified wine. Smiling contentedly at the waiter as he bid her goodnight, she left the dining room feeling comfortably full. She made her way up the red-carpeted stairs, pausing on every landing to catch her breath. The exhaustion she had felt ever since returning from Manchester had, along with the food and wines, made her light-headed. Colours seemed blurry, the whole world at once both sharper and more diluted than normal.

She sank into one of the comfortable armchairs as soon as she had locked the door to her suite behind her. A maid had lit the fire in the grate, and its merry crackling almost immediately put Sophia into a fretful sleep. Strange images chased through her mind as she teetered in the shadowland between sleeping and waking. The faces of Polly and Victoria swam before her, the mouths opening and closing silently, their eyes wide with fear. They were replaced by Thomas' chiselled features. He was a handsome man, despite his injured ear. It gave him a rakish appearance, and certainly frightened some people, but his deep brown eyes contained great kindness. In her dream, she reached out a hand and delicately stroked his unshaven cheek, feeling the stubble scratch against her fingertips.

"What are you doing with your life?" Thomas' face changed, the features becoming sharper, a thin face, all angles. The kind brown eyes turned blue and cold.

"Why are you always such a disappointment?" her father's voice was low. He never shouted. Never. Even when provoked by his family or by business partners, he merely grew quieter the angrier he was.

"It is my life to do with as I please," she pleaded, her voice no longer the confident tones of a grown woman, but the lighter voice of an adolescent.

"As long as you live under my roof and wear the dresses that I have bought you, you will do as I tell you."

"Please, father…"

"Not another word. Stop pestering me with these nonsense fantasies of yours."

"They're not fantasies!"

"They're fantasies if I deem them to be so, Sophia. Whatever wretch would ever be desperate enough to seek out medical advice from a woman. It is a business best left to men."

"But…"

"Be quiet, you silly girl."

She struck out at the sneering face, but it refused to dissipate.

"I'll show you!" the petulant words of a much younger girl.

Sophia jolted awake. She stared around wildly, seeking out the disturbance that had dispelled her nightmare. Someone was knocking insistently at her door. Sophia glanced at the grandfather clock. Ten minutes to midnight. The balcony windows showed only darkness with the faint glow of the streetlamps burning below.

She shook her head and staggered to her feet, grabbing the back of the chair for support. She stood for a moment, forcing her body to follow instructions, and then she walked, with slow but measured steps, across the room and opened the door. She was greeted by an absurd scene. One of the night porters was holding an adolescent boy by the ear. He had evidently just apprehended the boy and was shaking him violently. The boy's face was screwed up in pain.

"Stop that," Sophia snapped, reaching out and firmly pulling the porter's hand away from the boy.

"Begging your pardon, miss," the porter said, his expression furious. "He must have snuck past me. Some of these street urchins like to sneak in here at night and wake up whole floors for sport. Or perhaps you wanted to see if the room was empty so you could break in and rob it, you little sneak thief," he snarled at the urchin.

Sophia looked at the boy. He looked indistinguishable from the many young children she had seen hanging about the city's streets, alleys, and squares. He was wearing a stained white shirt and trousers held up with rope. His overcoat was overlarge and so greasy and worn that it shone and glittered like a black mirror. He wore a knitted cap pulled down low, with a thatch of auburn hair sticking out from underneath it in every direction.

"What do you want?" she asked him, trying to inject a note of kindness in her voice.

"Please miss," the boy said. "I've got a message for you…"

"Don't lie, you little perisher," the porter interrupted cuffing the boy around the ears. "If you had a message for a guest, why didn't you give it to me?"

The boy clutched the livid red mark on his cheek where the man's palm had landed, tears welling up in his eyes.

"He told me to go directly to Miss Steenberg in Room 506," he said, his voice shaking as he tried to suppress his tears. His breaths were short and sharp. Sophia looked hard at the night porter.

"As this boy knows who I am," she said. "I think we can safely assume that he's telling the truth. You may return to the front desk. If I have any further need of your services, I shall call for you."

She turned to the boy, pointedly ignoring the porter. The man opened his mouth to argue, but before he could speak, and still without looking at him, Sophia said. "Good night," in a tone that brooked no argument.

When the porter had left, Sophia looked the urchin up and down. Then, leaving him standing nervously by the door, she crossed to one of the small tables by the balcony doors and picked out three plump oranges from a silver fruit ball. She brought them to the boy.

"Have these," she said. "You look hungry."

The boy's face lit up at the sight of the sweet fruits. He quickly stuffed two of them in his pocket and began to tear the peel of the third with his chipped and frayed fingernails.

"What message were you told to bring to me?" she asked. The boy, his mouth already stuffed with segments of the orange tried to speak but had to chew thoroughly and swallow before he could get the words out.

"Thomas said that he needs you by St James Park," he said. Sophia stiffened.

"Thomas?" she said. "Thomas O'Callaghan, the detective sergeant?"

The boy shrugged.

"What's happened?"

"Dunno, miss?"

"Has there been another murder?"

At the sound of the last word, the boy's face grew blank, and he replied with the standard words that seemed to be imparted in every member of the city's underclass at birth whenever a crime was mentioned or even alluded to.

"I don't know nothin'."

Sophia sighed, realising that the boy would not be able or willing to provide any further information. She glanced again at the clock. The hour hand quivered only two or three minutes from midnight. If Thomas had summoned her at this time of night, there could only be one reason. Another girl had been murdered; another body found.

The boy had finished the orange, but was hanging around expectantly in case any further gifts of food were forthcoming. Sophia grabbed her purse, picked out a few coins without really looking at them and pressed them into the urchin's hand.

"Thank you," she said distractedly, her mind already racing ahead. "You've done a good job." She patted him a little clumsily on the top of his knitted cap and half-guided, half-pushed him out of the room. Then she began running, every thought of sleep and exhaustion forgotten. Before the clock struck the midnight hour, Sophia was in a growler, its driver having been paid enough money to ensure that he ran the horses at a full gallop through the city's emptying streets.

Chapter Twenty-Four

The small, cramped space with the leaking roof and the clapboard walls could hardly even be called a room, let alone a home. But a home it was nevertheless for half a dozen children and adolescents, the youngest only just seven, the oldest well into his fourteenth year. All of them were orphans either by circumstance or by choice. Disease, starvation, and the privations of life often claimed the lives of mothers, and when so many of the fathers of Liverpool spent their time in faraway places with strange names, hundreds of children were abandoned in a limbo between childhood and adulthood. Some went to one of the orphanages around the city, but the strict regulations and spartan conditions of such places did not suit all temperaments.

Many of those who went or were sent to orphanages for their own good, ended up fleeing from them in the dead of night. Others had grown up in homes where drink and violence were the order of the day. And one day they had had enough and decided that such parents—who only hurt them and each other—might as well be considered dead and gone. Such children, forgotten and neglected by society, banded together. Some formed small gangs, a complex network of feuds and alliances governing which area of the city you could move freely through. Walk down the wrong street in the territory of a rival gang, and you might end up on the business end of a blade.

Some of the gangs of children and adolescents banded together with older thieves and housebreakers. The younger children could always find work as lookouts. Some specialised in distracting marks and targets as they walked down the street. A fancy gentleman was always easy to trick with a hard-luck story from a wide-eyed child, especially if the gentleman was in the company of his wife. And before he knew it, he would find both his purse, pocket watch, and handkerchief gone, and the child and its invisible partner would be away down the back alleys before the cry for the police even went up.

The little group who called the abandoned shed located in the backyard of a tannery home comprised four boys and two girls. They sat around a small fire, merely a few sticks of kindling burning in an old and rusted tin can. The two girls, Eve and Rosie, were sisters, aged ten and twelve. Their mother had died giving birth to their younger brother, and the loss of both wife and son had driven their father to despair. He had found salvation at the bottom of a bottle, but gin cost coins, and soon he had sold everything the family owned. When a gentleman had sought him out and paid the right price, he had sold his daughters too, at least for a night, and after that, the girls had run away. They were quiet and always sat close together, spending their days selling small bunches of flowers and sometimes helping the baked potato sellers drum up business in exchange for a few coins.

The oldest boy was already an experienced fence. He had earned the nickname Claret as he, by way of nature rather than inclination, appeared, with his ruddy complexion and rather bulbous nose, like a man who was overly fond of drink. But his looks were a benefit in his line of trade. Thieves underestimated him because of his good-natured appearance, and were often too trusting when counting the coins he paid them for their stolen loot. Sometimes it was hours and even days before they realised that he had quickly switched out good coins for bad ones, and shillings for pennies.

The two youngest boys, known by general acclaim simply as the Muckies, were mudlarks and spent their days on the tideline of the Mersey, going through sewage and household waste looking for lost coins, jewellery, but also pieces of coal, scraps of cloth and bones, anything that could be sold to raise a little specie.

The final urchin sitting around the fire was holding a scratched and scuffed brass pocket watch close to the flame, looking at it, his slightly upturned nose wrinkled in disgust.

"Hardly worth the bother pinchin' it," he said throwing it down. "And he looked like such a well-dressed toff too. What'd he want to go around with a natty thimble like that. I won't get more than a few pence for it."

"Don't feel too bad, Skittles," Claret said. "That's still better than what the Muckies brought in." He looked sternly at the two youngest members of the group. They simultaneously hung their heads in shame. A full day on the riverbank had resulted in nothing more than a single farthing and a few pieces of coal, which had already burnt out in the rusty tin can.

"Go easy on them, Claret," Rosie said quietly. At twelve years old, she had adopted the role of overbearing older sister to the two young boys. At mealtimes, she made sure that they got their share, even if it meant arguing with Skittles and Claret, who, as the two oldest boys, naturally assumed that they were the leaders of the little cadre.

"And where the hell is Moe?" Skittles asked, his tone showing that he was still annoyed at the nerve of a wealthy mark carrying such a very worthless pocket watch.

"I saw him hanging around by the Adelphi," Claret said. "A couple of hours ago, but he waved me away."

"Maybe he spotted a mark," Eve said, her eyes widening in anticipation. Like Skittles, the absent Moe was a pickpocket, although unlike Skittles, he specialised in ladies' purses rather than pocket watches. The purses were often carried on light brass or silver chains, and for this purpose, Moe always carried a small pair of pliers. In a milling crowd, he could quickly snip the chains, stuff the small purse down his trousers, and walk away, hands behind his back, whistling merrily as his mark looked around aimlessly for the culprit.

The group listened as the thudding of raindrops on the tin roof intensified. The light, misty drizzles of the evening had been replaced by a proper autumn rainstorm. Claret stood up and, using rags taken from a pile in the corner, he tried to locate and plug any gaps along the walls, fighting a losing battle against the rising wind.

"If he doesn't come back soon, he'll get drenched," Rosie said, a worried tone in her voice.

"He'll be fine," Skittles said breezily.

A clatter made the group look around. Occasionally, constables would raid such places where the street children congregated, especially if something valuable had been stolen anywhere in the city. But since Skittles had struck up his unlikely friendship with Thomas, these raids had become far less frequent.

The room had no door as such, but instead a thin piece of clapboard had been set in front of a gap in the wall and secured with twine. As the children looked on, the board was pushed aside and Moe staggered in. He was, as Rosie had predicted, drenched to the skin, but there was a triumphant gleam in his eye. He shook the rain off his over-large coat, pulled off his knitted cap and squeezed the water out of it.

"Evenin'," he said casually, then dug into his pockets and drew out two oranges, rolling them across the floor where they came to rest at Rosie's feet. The two girls let out squeals of joy, and both Skittles and Claret patted Moe on the back. The fruits were a rare treat, and they were soon divided between the members of the little gang, Rosie predictably intervening to wrench a few extra segments out of Skittles' hands to pass them to the Muckies.

"Did you rob a coster?" Skittles asked Moe, grinning broadly and using the common slang term for the fruit and vegetable sellers that placed their barrows on street corners or squares throughout the city.

Moe shook his head, the lower part of his face covered in a mixture of grime and sticky orange juice.

"Met a madman," he said, smirking. Skittles frowned.

"What do you mean?"

"Strangest thing," Moe said, settling back on the hard ground and picking strands of orange from his crooked teeth. "I met this geezer outside the Bells, that pub across from the Adelphi. He gave me a whole six-pence just to wait around until midnight and then bring a message up to one of the guests."

He triumphantly drew out the sixpence from his pocket and flicked it to

Claret, who caught it and held it close to the fire, making sure that it was not a dud coin.

"Come on," Skittles said, disbelief etched in every line on his face. "A whole six-pence just for bringing a message? Pull the other one."

"God's honest truth!" Moe said, his eyes wide. "Couldn't believe it either."

"And he gave you a couple of oranges too?" Skittles said, his tone still disbelieving.

"Na," Moe said casually. "The lady gave me those."

"What lady?"

"The lady I had to bring the message to, ratbag," he said, sticking out his tongue at Skittles. Skittles lashed out quick as lightning, and soon the two boys were rolling on the ground, trying to land blows on one another.

"That's enough, you two," Claret said without raising his voice. Skittles, grinning, pushed Moe aside and retook his place at the fire.

"I'm not lying," Moe panted. "She really did give me the oranges." He kept quiet, at least for now, about the three pennies she had also pushed into his hand. Those would buy a few glasses of gin and maybe a pipe or two of tobacco later on.

"So did the geezer want you to deliver a love note to his intended?" Skittles said, his grin widening.

He turned to Rosie, fell on one knee and grabbed her hand.

"Oh my darling," he said in the rather neighing tones the children associated with the well-to-do members of society. "I simply must gaze upon your pretty face." He bent and kissed Rosie's hand with an exaggerated gesture as the Muckies and Rosie's younger sister burst out laughing.

"Shut up, Skittles," Moe growled as he reached out and pulled Skittles back to his seat. "The message didn't make much sense to me, but it must have meant something to her. It got her all in a flap."

"What was the message?" Claret asked curiously.

Moe scrunched up his face as he tried to remember.

"Something about Thomas wanting to meet her down by St James," he said unconcernedly. Claret shook his head.

"Madman," he said. "City's full of 'em."

Skittles frowned as the group began to discuss what to purchase with their newly won sixpence. This was normally a discussion that Skittles would have enthusiastically taken part in, but now he felt a chill run down his spine. Something did not feel right.

"Who was the lady you had to bring the message to?" he asked Moe.

Moe looked up distractedly from the conversation.

"What?"

"The lady," Skittles repeated. "The one you gave the message to. Who was she?"

Moe hesitated.

"Strange name," he said. "Foreign. She weren't Scouse, that's for sure," he mouthed silently as he tried to remember.

"Steen," he said. "Steen…something."

"Steenberg," Skittles completed the name.

"That's the one."

Skittles had gone white.

"She's that Danish woman who's been going around with Sergeant O'Callaghan," he said.

"Thomas O'Callaghan?" Moe said. "That must be the Thomas in the message, then."

"But was it Thomas that gave you the message?" Skittles pressed. Moe looked annoyed.

"No, of course not," he said. "This toff had both his ears for a start."

"How did he look?"

The conversation around the fire had died down as the group's attention were drawn to Skittles. The easy-going boy was tensed, his expression drawn.

"What's wrong, Skittles?" Rosie asked, but Skittles held up a hand to silence her.

"Come on, Moe," he said. "What did he look like?"

"I dunno," Moe said, confused by Skittles' unwarranted interest. "I didn't see him properly. He was an older gent, well-dressed. Red face, looked like he likes a drink or two."

"So, you're sure it wasn't Thomas?" Skittles said, his eyes not leaving Moe's face.

"Yes, damnit!" Moe said exasperatedly.

Skittles stood up with a suddenness that shocked the group.

"I've got to go," he said, turning to the doorway.

"Don't be stupid," Claret said. "You'll get soaked out there."

Skittles did not reply. Instead, he crossed the room, pulled aside the clapboard, and ducked through the opening into the driving rain.

Chapter Twenty-Five

The archives of the Rose Hill station were situated in a long, low room off the central watch area. The room was crammed with narrow wooden shelves running from the floor to the ceiling. It was lit with gas lamps set along the walls and, during the day, by what natural light could fight its way through decades worth of grime covering the narrow windows. The archives contained dozens of heavy leather-bound tomes, the arrest books containing details of every apprehension and arrest made by the Rose Hill force for more than fifty years, since the requirement to keep records of such matters had been instituted by Parliament. Along with the copies of records from trials, hearings, and even copies of confessions given before executions by the condemned, the arrest books represented a treasure trove of information about the nature and composition of Liverpool's underworld.

While half a dozen constables were occupied outside reading through newspaper after newspaper, trying to identify a connection between the many different places and ports where the killer of Polly and Victoria had struck before, Muldoon, Thomas, and Sergeant Fraser had withdrawn to the archive room. There, they pulled tome after tome from the shelves, reading through the cramped ink-splattered pages, looking for names associated with those families who Muldoon believed had at one time been associated with the Cuban sugar trade.

As darkness fell, Muldoon despatched a constable to fetch supper from one of the stalls, and the officers working in the watch room were treated to a rare meal of pies and baked potatoes on the detective inspector's dime.

"I've got one," Thomas said, consulting Muldoon's handwritten list of surnames numbering more than two dozen. "Tomlinson, Peter William. He was brought in back in '71."

"Crime?" Muldoon asked looking up excitedly. So far, despite hours of searching, the arrest records had provided few clues.

"Embezzlement," Thomas said hesitantly. "Looks like the magistrates dismissed the charges, though."

"Money changed hands, no doubt," Muldoon said. "And in any case, it's a tall step from embezzlement to dismemberment."

Thomas nodded, and the three men returned to their reading. Every once in a while, one of them would call out after spotting a name from the list Muldoon had drawn up. More often than not, however, the page simply recorded a petty criminal who happened to share a surname with one of the merchant families, and the case could be discounted.

"I think I might have something," Fraser said, his tone distant as he narrowed his eyes and scrutinised the page in front of him.

Thomas and Muldoon looked up, grateful for the interruption. When Fraser did not elaborate, Thomas got to his feet, stretched painfully after many hours of sitting on an uncomfortable and rickety wooden chair. He looked over the duty sergeant's shoulder. Then he frowned.

"I've never seen this before," he said. Muldoon got ponderously to his feet and joined the two men. They were staring at an arrest report which carried the date of July 7th, 1859. However, rather than contain information, large sections of the report had been entirely obliterated with thick bands of ink. Muldoon ran his fingers across the page.

"It's been redacted," he said.

"Not the name of the perpetrator," Thomas said, pointing to the top corner of the page. "Arthur Burges Jr."

"I recognised the name from the list," Fraser said.

Muldoon nodded slowly.

"The Burges family certainly did plenty of trade with the Cuban plantations back in the day," he said. "It'll be before your time, Thomas, but they owned a big warehouse down on Stanley Dock. Lived in a big mansion."

"I've never heard of them," Thomas said.

"The family fell on hard times about five years back," Muldoon said. "After Burges Sr died without heirs, the debtors closed in. Turns out he had borrowed far more than he owned, so they took everything. The stock, the warehouse, even their home."

Thomas frowned and pointed to the name.

"But he had an heir," he said. "Says right here. Arthur Burges Jr must have been his son."

Muldoon squinted at the name and then closed his eyes, trying to remember.

"I can't remember any son," he said. "Maybe Burges Jr died."

Thomas shrugged.

"But what's he doing in this arrest report?"

"Someone didn't want anyone to know, that's for certain," Fraser said. Muldoon narrowed his eyes.

"I've seen this before," he said. "Sometimes we've changed arrest reports if the case was settled without recourse to the magistrates."

"You mean, if someone got paid off," Thomas said. Muldoon nodded.

"Don't play too high and mighty, Thomas," he said. "We've all taken backhanders now and again."

Thomas smiled ruefully. Corruption, though less widespread than it had been in earlier times, was still commonplace in the constabulary.

"Well, this doesn't help us much," Fraser said, pointing to the obliterated information on the page. Muldoon looked at it speculatively. Then, with a sudden movement, he left the room, returning a few moments later. He pulled a switchblade from his pocket and, leaving Thomas and Fraser to look on in surprise, he cut the heavy page from the ledger.

"Back in '59 there wasn't more than a dozen electric lightbulbs in the whole of Liverpool," Muldoon said walking quickly from the archive room with Thomas and Fraser following him. "The only way to see what was written under all this ink splatter would be to shine a light through the page, but if you tried that with an oil lamp or a lantern, you'd char the paper or light it on fire. Whoever covered up this information probably thought that the ink would do the trick."

Thomas grinned, realising what his inspector intended to do. The three men barged into Muldoon's office, the only one in the building to be lit partly by a gas-powered lamp hanging from the ceiling, but also by an electric desk lamp, an innovation, less than five years old. Muldoon removed the screen from the lamp, revealing the incandescent light bulb. He flipped it on, and all three men had to blink and look away from the bright light source after hours spent in the musty darkness of the archive room.

Muldoon held the cut-out page from the ledger in front of the light bulb. The sharp, bright light shone through both paper and ink, revealing faint letters underlying the thick bands of ink that had been brushed on top of every part of the page, which had been considered sensitive.

Thomas and Fraser grinned, patting Muldoon on the back as the older inspector began to read out words aloud. Not every word was legible, but there was enough information preserved for the three men to be able to reconstruct the narrative, written down by an unknown constable more than four decades previously.

"Master Arthur Burges Jr apprehended in…after…complaint levelled at the instigation…Miss Eliza Smallwood, daughter of…of Chester…accuses… Burges Jr of obtaining carnal knowledge forcibly and…with an edged weapon."

"Edged weapon…" Thomas breathed quietly.

"Smallwood," Fraser mused. "Smallwood." Then his face paled, and his eyes widened. "You don't think that means…"

"Yes," Muldoon said. "Lord Smallwood, Earl of Chester," he pointed to the fragmented title.

"Bloody hell," Fraser said.

Thomas ran his hand across his unshaven jaw, his mind reeling.

"He tried to force himself on her," he said. "And when she refused him…"

"He threatened her with a knife," Muldoon completed the sentence.

"But why cover this up?" Thomas asked. "Lord Smallwood could have brought him to trial. He would have hanged for that."

Muldoon bit his lip.

"The old earl was a powerful man," he said. "A big landowner, but he still did extensive business with the merchant families of Liverpool. A good deal of his fortune was invested in trade with the colonies."

"Could Burges Sr have bribed him to keep everything quiet?" Thomas asked.

"Perhaps in exchange for exiling his son," Muldoon said, nodding emphatically.

"Then we have him!" Thomas said excitedly springing to his feet. "Burges Sr used his connections in Cuba to get his son employed on one of the sugar plantations where he remained until…"

He looked at Muldoon.

"You say the family's fortunes began to crumble around five years ago?"

"Yes."

"Around the same time our murders began," Thomas said pointing towards the watch room. "Without his father's money and with slavery now abolished in Cuba and the plantations under new management, Burges Junior had nowhere to go."

"Hold on," Muldoon said, raising a hand in warning. "If Burges Junior is the killer, then how did he move so freely between dozens of ports. With his family bankrupt, he would be without funds too."

Thomas shook his head, unable to explain this final mystery but unwilling to surrender the exhilaration of discovery. He crossed to the door, flung it open and half-walked, half-ran into the watch room. Piles of newspapers, collected from the Central Library much to the chagrin of the librarian, littered every flat surface. More than a dozen constables sat around, pouring through the papers, transcribing lists of arriving passengers in the ports where the murders had occurred in notebooks.

"Listen up," Thomas said clapping his hands together. "Have any of your come across the name Burges? I'm looking for an Arthur Burges or Arthur Burges Junior, or any name to that effect."

The room filled with rustling as the men consulted their notebooks, flicking through pages of names and dates.

"Got him," a constable called. "An Arthur Burges arrived in Valetta four days before the killing of a girl last year."

Thomas punched the air. He turned to Muldoon, his eyes shining.

"You see?" he said triumphantly. "What ship was he a passenger on?" he asked without turning back. The constable hesitated.

"He wasn't a passenger, sir," he said. Thomas wheeled around.

"What do you mean?"

"He's listed as a crew member of the post ship *Victoria*," the constable said. "Ship's surgeon."

"That's how he did it!" Muldoon exclaimed. "The devil didn't pay for his own passage! He worked for it!"

"I've got him here too," another constable called out. "Arriving to Calcutta aboard the post ship *Prince George* back in '88. Also listed as the ship's surgeon."

"Another post ship," Muldoon nodded. "He found work with the postal steamer service."

Thomas nodded.

"But we still don't know what he looks like," Fraser interjected. "How can we put out a description of him?"

"We can't," Muldoon said. "But if he still uses his real name..."

"In his hometown?" Fraser said. "He can't be that arrogant."

Thomas waved his hand as though dislodging an irksome fly.

"We don't need his description," he said. "We know who he is, but we still don't know what he wants. Why did he return to the one place on earth where he was most likely to be...recognised..." he fell silent and for several long moments he stood, hand raised and mouth hanging open. Then he slowly turned to Muldoon.

"Did you say that his family owned a warehouse on Stanley Dock?"

"Yes, I..." Muldoon blanched. "You don't think..."

"Why not!" Thomas exclaimed. "Where did the family live?"

Muldoon shook his head then gazed wildly around the room at the faces of the constables.

"Any of you," he shouted. "Who remembers where the Burges family lived until Burges Senior died?"

The constables looked at each other in confusion. After a deal of hubbub, a conclusion was reached and presented to the irate inspector.

"Somewhere around Sefton Park, sir," one of the older constables offered hesitantly. "Big place. It got sold to pay off the debts, but it's derelict now."

Muldoon turned to Thomas, his moustache quivering.

"He's been leaving dead bodies right on his family's doorstep," he said, his voice shaking. "This is about revenge."

Thomas nodded slowly.

"His family sent him into exile, and he couldn't avenge himself upon them in life…"

"…so he's been leaving evidence of his bloody skills at the places they once frequented."

Thomas' mind was racing ahead to the inevitable conclusion.

"We need constables at every business, every property, every single place in the city ever owned by the Burges family."

Muldoon nodded.

"We need to know how long he's been here as well," he said. "There may have been other cases we have missed, any attempts or assaults."

"Easy enough," Fraser said, crossing to his desk and drawing out copies of the *Liverpool Advertiser*. He flicked through the papers for a few moments, then folded down a page of one of the most recent editions. "Here he is," he said. "Listed as arriving on the mail steamer *King Orry* from Le Havre…" he cut off abruptly and looked up at Thomas in shock. He pointed to the page.

"Sir," he said. "You better take a look."

Curious, Thomas walked over the duty sergeant and looked at the list of arriving passengers and crew. He felt a sense of pure cold dread run down his spin.

"Miss Sophia Steenberg," he read.

"What?" Muldoon said, nearly knocking over a stack of newspapers in his haste to join his subordinate.

"Miss Steenberg arrived on the same ship," Thomas said, his expression drawn.

"But that's a miracle," Muldoon said. "Miss Steenberg can provide us with a physical description of him, surely."

Thomas nodded slowly. The idea of Sophia spending days on a ship with a man as twisted and cruel as Arthur Burges Junior gave him a sense of deep apprehension. But he told himself, she was safe now, away from Burges and his perversions.

The creak of the heavy front door to the station house made him look up. In the doorway, framed in sheets of driving rain, was Skittles, the young boy out of breath, bent double and wheezing.

"Bloody hell," Thomas said, walking over and grabbing the boy by the shoulders, dragging him in out of the rain. Heavy droplets splashed on the doorstep and soaked his shoes and the bottom of his trousers before he slammed the door. "What do you think you're doing?"

Skittles was still wheezing, having run through the city at a dead sprint. He raised a hand, washed cleaner than Thomas had ever seen it by the rain.

"Get the lad a chair," he shouted, and one of the constables brought a wooden chair with ill grace. The young thief collapsed upon it, clutching his side.

"Something…" he wheezed. "Something's not right with Miss Steenberg."

At the sound of the name, Thomas felt as though he had been stabbed in the stomach with a shard of ice.

"What's happened to her?" he asked, shaking Skittles so hard that droplets of water rained off his greasy overcoat, pooling underneath the chair. Skittles looked up and Thomas could see from the boy's hardened features that the situation was grim.

"Someone sent for her pretending to be you," he said. "They paid one of my mates to bring her a message from Thomas to meet at St James cemetery."

"When?"

Skittles shook his head.

"Not long ago," he said. "Maybe half an hour."

"Did she go?" Thomas said insistently. "Did Sophia go to meet this person?"

"I don't know, I think so."

"What did he look like? The man who paid your mate to deliver the message?"

"Older man," Skittles said. "That's all my mate could remember. An older man with a red face."

Thomas felt Muldoon's hand land on his shoulder.

"Easy, Thomas," the inspector said. "I know what you're thinking, but just because her and Burges were on the same ship…"

"It was him," Thomas said. "I know it. Sophia's his next victim."

"We can't know that…"

"Who else would send for her in this city?" Thomas shouted. He stared wildly around. "Get everyone together and go to St James," he said. Then he stood up, letting go of Skittles who slumped in the seat, still winded from his mad race through the city. "I'm going to go ahead."

Muldoon opened his mouth to argue, but seeing Thomas' expression, he closed it again. Without a backwards glance at the room full of constables, Thomas brushed past the inspector, tore open the front door of the station house, and ducked into the rain. Muldoon stood for a moment, indecisive. Then he sighed deeply and turned to Fraser.

"Get a squad together," he said. "And get them armed."

Chapter Twenty-Six

Steam rose from the panting horses as they halted by the wrought iron gates leading to St James Cemetery. The cemetery was located in a large pit, a former openwork sandstone quarry in the eastern part of the city. The quarry had been opened during the reign of Henry VIII, and its stones used to construct the civic buildings and merchant manors, which turned the city of Liverpool from a small fishing village to Britain's gateway to the world. The quarry had long since ended its operations, after which the large overgrown scar in the landscape had been co-opted into a burial ground. More than thirty thousand bodies lay, layer upon layer, under its sod. In the summer, the citizens of Liverpool took strolls and held picnics atop the bones of their ancestors, casually reading the inscriptions of men, women, and children long past.

Memento Mori, Sophia thought as she pushed open the gates, the creak of their hinges, audible even over the rain. The cemetery was a place of death, but also of life. In summer, a fertile undergrowth of wild garlic and knotgrass blanketed the old graves. In autumn, people came to pick mushrooms from beneath the sturdy oak and ash trees planted at intervals throughout the park.

Passing through the gate, Sophia nearly slipped down a series of steps cut directly into the sandstone rock. She paused. The path down to the cemetery led at a steep angle through tunnels originally cut by the quarrymen. The tunnel mouth looked dark and foreboding. She looked back over her shoulder, intending to ask the driver for a lantern or light, but he had evidently not wanted to hang around in the foul weather. She could hear the sound of hooves growing fainter. She squinted through the darkness and rain. From her vantage point, she could see directly down to the cemetery, its thousands of gravestones emerging from out of the darkness like so many grinning teeth. There was no bobbing lantern, no movement of constables. She hesitated.

She could not hear the point of the Liston knife cut through the fabric of her dress. But she felt the point of the blade. It had not broken the skin, but was resting, almost lovingly, directly against her side. If the knife was pushed, it would pierce her liver and exit through her abdomen.

Sophia did not move. Her eyes remained fixed on the tunnel mouth as she thought. She had passed a tall memorial stone commemorating a sea captain and his wife, set close to the gate. Whoever was now holding a knife to her must have stood behind them and awaited her arrival.

For several long moments, she remained still, hardly even daring to blink. If she listened carefully, she could hear breathing overlaid on the lashing rain. But much more, she could feel that indescribable sense of another human being standing too close. But she was not dead yet. And in that, perhaps, was a faint hope of escape.

"Good evening," she said, and she was surprised at how steady her voice sounded. Shaking a little, perhaps, but not more so than one might expect in the freezing autumn rain.

She felt the point of the knife withdrawn slightly.

"I'm pleased you came," a voice behind her replied. Sophia blinked. She recognised it. It took all her willpower not to wheel about and confront the man who had now not only threatened her, but also had the lives of Polly and Victoria and God only knew how many other innocents on his conscience.

"You wanted to see me, Doctor Burges," Sophia said.

"I'm glad you remember me, Miss Steenberg," the voice said, a hint of amusement in the tones. Sophia gritted her teeth. She was not going to play his games.

"I think the police may want to talk to you," she said. "I'm sure they'll be here soon."

"I'm certain that they won't," Arthur Burges Junior replied casually. "Sergeant O'Callaghan and that fat inspector are no doubt still warm and comfortable at Rose Hill."

"I told them I was coming here," Sophia tried, desperate for any leverage over the man holding her life in his hands. Burges laughed softly.

"No, you didn't," he said. "You received a message from Thomas, and off you ran. But I cannot exclude chance witnesses, so if you do not mind, miss, please accompany me down to the cemetery. Down there, there aren't any witnesses but the dead."

Sophia refused to move.

"I won't ask you again," Burges said. "Walk."

She felt again the point of the Liston knife. Burges slowly increased the pressure on the blade, and with a small gasp, Sophia felt it cut her skin and draw blood. She stumbled forward.

The two walked awkwardly through the narrow tunnel leading to the cemetery. Burges did not lower his knife but maintained pressure on its needle-sharp point. Sophie felt a small trickled of blood run from the wound and absorb into the fabric of her dress.

"What do you want?" she asked as they walked.

Burges did not reply.

After what felt like weeks, but which in reality were only moments, they emerged onto the wide flat plain at the bottom of the old quarry. Cobbled pathways ran crisscross throughout the cemetery, binding together these ancestral memorials. There were stones of every size, quality, and material, from extravagant sculptures carved from Italian marble to humble markers of sandstone bearing only a name and a date.

Burges led Sophia down one of the central avenues before branching off on a narrower path. Sophia tried to focus on the gravestones as they passed them, anything to remove her mind from its current predicament. The rows of graves, markers, memorials, and cenotaphs reminded Sophia of the Père Lachaise Cemetery in Paris. The great leveller, they called it. The place where all journeyed to in the end, whether rich or poor, man or woman.

"Stop." Burges's command was followed by a forceful push. Sophia slipped on the rain-washed cobbles and fell to her knees. She looked up, water streaming down her face now mingling with tears of fear, pain, and sheer fury at the man who dared to take her life into his hands. She looked at a large mausoleum built in the style of a Greek temple, but to a far smaller scale. Decades of rain and wear had greyed the white marble, lending it a patina of antiquity. Above its doorway, she saw the single name. Burges.

"The hallowed resting place of my line," Burges said behind her. Sophia closed her eyes for a moment, then took a deep breath and slowly turned around, her hands and knees remaining on the ground.

She recognised Arthur Burges easily enough. An older man in his middle age, his face ruddy and red from years of drink, his white sideburns tinted yellow by nicotine. But his eyes were not as dull or watery as they had been when she last saw him, half-drunk on cheap whiskey, aimlessly trying to stitch up a sailor's gaping wounds.

"What do you want?" Sophia asked, holding his gaze, refusing to allow her eyes to flitter to the Liston knife Burges held loosely in his hand. Burges looked away from her and up at the towering façade of the mausoleum.

"My saintly parents were the last to be interred there," he said conversationally. "After father died, the creditors came calling. Turns out he had spent most of the family fortune on good liquor, women, and the cards. Everything was mortgaged, so everything was taken. It killed Mother. She was quite mad by the end, I heard."

"Why did you come back?"

Burges smiled at her. It was not the mad leer she had expected. It was a pleasant smile, slightly patronising perhaps, but friendly and open.

"I never wanted to leave," he said. "My exile was my father's will."

"He sent you overseas."

A shadow seemed to pass across Burges's face. The smile faded.

"A single youthful indiscretion and my life was over," he said. "A single misstep!"

Sophia fell backwards as Burges screamed the last sentence at her. For the first time, she saw the madness in his eyes. She raised her hands to ward off the knife, but the strike never came. Burges seemed to wrestle with himself, forcing his temper back under control.

"I was a gifted surgeon, you know," he said. "Trained at the Royal Liverpool College. I even attended anatomy classes in London."

Burges walked past Sophia, his hand still holding the knife by his side. He ran his free hand over one of the pillars which supported his family's cenotaph.

"I could have been great," he said. "And a great scholar. Barely twenty-five and already I was establishing my reputation."

His tone was muted and so low that Sophia had to strain to hear.

"But there was no career where they sent me," he said. "Only pain and shit and piss, and blood. A never-ending supply of blood."

"It must have been hard leaving everything you knew behind," Sophia said, desperate to keep Burges talking, her teeth chattering from the rain and the cold radiating off the ground. The killer did not turn around. For a long moment, he remained still, staring unseeingly at the monument raised to the extinct glory of his family.

Sophia used the opportunity to glance around. Her dress was soaked through and heavy, her boots ill-suited to a run on the slippery cobbles. She could not outrun him; of that she was certain. But perhaps she could hide among the cenotaphs and memorials, playing a game of cat and mouse for long enough until… Until what? If Burges was right, then neither Thomas nor anyone else knew of her predicament. Dawn was hours away. She could not hope to evade Burges for that long, and all he needed to do was to wait for her by the only path out of the cemetery. She could no more climb the steep sandstone cliffs that encircled the quarry than she could walk on water.

"It was hard at first," Burges said. Sophia jumped. She had not heard him move; she had been too focused on potential avenues of escape. He was no longer standing by the cenotaph but kneeling right next to her, his mouth close to her right ear.

"But over time I grew to see the attractions of that purgatory," he said. "It changed who I was, who I wanted to be. It robbed me of my status, but it gifted me something else. It gifted me skills no other surgeon ever had the chance to develop."

Burges ran the Liston knife almost lovingly along Sophia's cheek. She remained motionless, trying to control her breathing. Fear rose up in her like boiling water. Her eyes stung, threatening to overflow. But she did not want him to see fear upon her face.

"To practice one's skills not on some stiff in the dead house, but on a living, breathing human is a gift which cannot be measured," Burges said, his eyes not leaving Sophia's face.

"You're a murderer," Sophia said quietly. "Just a common murderer."

"Common?" Burges laughed softly. "Anyone can kill. Even your sergeant has taken lives. Killing is merely a by-product, satisfying in itself, but not nearly as satisfying as producing a great piece of art."

Sophia was shaking now with anger as well as cold.

"Is that what you call it?" she spat. "What you've done? Art? Killing and mutilating innocent girls! It isn't art, it's an abomination!"

"You must say that, I'm sure," Burges said. "To preserve your sense of humanity. Most people cling to it, spending their lives fighting to suppress those animal instincts that lie right beneath the surface. Those instincts they know deep down are far more natural. I have merely embraced them and become something else."

Sophia turned her face now to look directly at Burges, defiantly, expecting at any moment the Liston knife's caress.

"And what have you become, then?" she said.

"A hunter," Burges said. "That which we all have a capacity to be, had we only not forgotten."

"You're no hunter," Sophia said. "A good hunter feels sympathy for his prey! Did you?"

Suddenly she was flat on her back. Burges had pushed her back and was holding her down with his forearm across her chest. She felt the point of the knife under her ribs and gasped.

"Sympathy?" Burges hissed in her ear. "Who showed sympathy for me when they sent me away from this town? I knew that I had to return. I knew that I wanted to humiliate my family, even in death. I wanted to leave corpses of dismembered whores all across the places they loved, owned and built. The places that should have been my inheritance."

Sophia wriggled madly on the ground, but she could not find enough leverage to push off the older man. But Burges, too, was breathing heavily, winded even from this short struggle. *He's weaker than he appears*, Sophia thought. *The knife is his only advantage.*

"But then," Burges continued, and his voice took on an almost dreamy tone. "Then I met you. From the moment I saw you tending to that sailor onboard the *King Orr*, I knew you had to be the final one. My final masterpiece in this city that spurned me."

Sophia was only half-listening, focusing her energies on trying to throw off the madman before he could sink the knife into her chest. But she still managed to gasp out a single word.

"Why?"

"Because you are what I wanted to be but never could," Burges panted. "You told me yourself in that stinking sick bay. A surgeon, like me. An exile from your home, like me. But you had not been banished to some backwater, no! You had taken control of your own fate."

Sophia let out an inarticulate scream of fear and rage, struggling to free her arms, but Burges' weight continued to press down on her.

"Do you think your sergeant will grieve for you?" Burges panted. "When they call him to view your corpse in the morning?"

Sophia screamed again. There were no words. Her fear and anger, fusing into an alloy far stronger than any steel, went far beyond words. The scream was a primal thing. She arched her back and forced her arms down her side, grabbing Burges' wrist, preventing him from penetrating her side. She could hear him cursing, but the words were growing muted. The pounding rain seemed to drown out every other sound, but overlaid on its staccato rhythms, she could hear another refrain. Pounding footsteps.

She looked around and, in the gloom, she saw a figure tearing around the corner, barrelling past tomb stones and cenotaphs.

"Thomas!" the shout was both plea and warning. Burges, unable to force in the knife and confronted now with a spectator, changed his tactic.

Thomas saw Burges roll off Sophia, shielding his own body with hers as he dragged her up by her hair, his blade pressed to the pale white flesh of her throat. Her dress was torn, her hands scratched. Her hair was dripping, water running in rivulets down her face. But there was defiance in her eyes, despite the deadly weapon at her throat.

"Stop right there, sergeant," Burges panted. He was a short man, as short as Sophia, and he used it to his advantage. She stood before him like a shield, and in the dark cemetery, Thomas could only see the murderer as a shadowy outline. Panting, Thomas came to a halt less than fifteen feet from the killer and his hostage.

"Just give up, Burges," he said. "There's no getting away from this."

Burges's breathing was ragged. Sophia felt his head turn right and left, seeking an escape. *A cornered animal,* she thought. *A cornered animal is the most dangerous animal of all.*

"Let him go, Thomas," she said. Thomas blinked.

"Let him go," Sophia repeated. "He's done what he came to this city to do. He's done."

Her words penetrated Burges's preoccupation with his own escape. For a moment, he hesitated, shocked by her attitude.

"I have not," he said. "One whore in that warehouse my father spent his every living moment filling with rum and sugar, the foundations of the family fortune. A second whore on the front step of that house they sent me from. And a third and final prey, the finest I've ever hunted, laid before the resting bones of my family." Burges spoke as if in a trance, and Sophia realised that if he could find no way to escape, or to complete what he saw as a mission of near cosmic importance, he would kill both her, and himself to ensure its conclusion.

"Don't do anything stupid, Burges," Thomas said, a threatening note in his voice. "There are worse things in this world than the rope."

Sophia saw the sergeant slip a hand into his pocket. The hand came out ringed with a set of brass knuckles. His other hand clutched his rosewood truncheon. He had left the station house without a pistol, and in any case, he would not have dared attempt to shoot Burges while he was shielding himself behind Sophia.

"Shut up," Burges mumbled. "Shut up, I need to think."

"There's no way out," Thomas continued. "If you drop the knife, I'll speak to the magistrates. A posh fellow like you, they'll want to go easy on you. If they find you mad, you might even escape the noose…"

"And end my days screaming and drooling and shitting myself in the asylum?" Burges shouted over the ever-increasing thunder of the rain. "I'm warning you, Sergeant. One more step and Miss Steenberg dies."

"I'm warning you, Burges," Thomas threw back. "If you hurt her, I won't bother with an arrest, I'll kill you where you stand."

"Empty threats," Burges jeered.

For a moment, the three stood silently, each person seeking a resolution. Sophia slowly lifted her right leg, allowing more of her weight to fall against Burges. Thomas grasped his truncheon so hard he thought he might end up leaving fingerprints embedded in the wood.

Sophia looked at Thomas, and for a moment, he caught her eye. Her crystalline blue eyes locked into his warm brown pair. An understanding passed between them like an electric charge through a wire. He knew in that instant what she intended to do and braced himself to respond.

As Burges drew breath to hurl another insult at Thomas, Sophia stamped down hard, scraping the inside of her booted foot against Burges's shin. The blow scraped a clear five inches of skin from his leg, sending a spasm of pain through his body. In the same movement, she flung up her hands, grasping Burges's wrist and forcing the knife away from her throat.

Burges struggled for only a second, but Thomas was already moving, quickly crossing the ground between them, his head down. Burges sensed him approaching and, rather than fight with Sophia, he grabbed her by the shoulders and shoved her hard, sending her into the oncoming detective sergeant. The force of the shove and the slippery footing sent both of them to the ground in a pile of limbs. Sophia landed on top of Thomas, his body cushioning her fall. She rolled off him in time to see Burges's figure vanish between two man-high tombstones.

"He's running," she panted. Thomas was swearing loudly, struggling to get back on his feet, his brass knuckles scraping against the cobbles.

"Damn him," he panted as he finally drew himself up, picking up his truncheon which he had dropped. It had rolled away to come to rest against one of the pillars of the Burges's mausoleum.

"Stay here!" he shouted at Sophia as he took off at a run after Burges whose shambling form had been swallowed entirely by the night.

The rain stung him as he ran, his Hornburg long lost, his auburn locks glued to his scalp by the water. The cemetery was a confusing spider's web of pathways and avenues with no lights or lamps. Any candles left by mourners had long ago been extinguished by the wind. With the moon hiding its face behind a vaporous shawl, the cemetery was left in near total darkness, the only light being what dim echoes of Liverpool's own radiance, from streetlamps and windows, could be reflected back off the low-hanging clouds.

Thomas stumbled several times and was eventually forced to slow down. He listened, his head moving from side to side. Occasionally, he turned around, twirling like a ballerina, aware that Burges might attempt to sneak up behind him. There were no footsteps, no breathing, no human sound at all.

Thomas stopped, standing as still as one of the cenotaphs, thinking carefully. Burges did not want to kill him. Not really. He would kill him, if he got the chance. But his quarry, his prey, was Sophia. Thomas spun around. Burges would try to circle around to attack her again.

Thomas sprinted to the right, emerging from a narrow pathway between headstones into an unused corner of the cemetery. Wild garlic, rotting leaves and falling twigs covered the ground. Only a few headstones stood here, some of the oldest, dating back to the very first years that the cemetery had been in use, nearly two-hundred years ago.

Thomas squinted through the rain and the darkness, trying to locate the entrance to the cemetery. From there, he would be able to find his way back to Sophia.

As Thomas passed a gnarled old oak standing by the edge of the abandoned patch of land, he caught a movement out of the corner of his eye. He turned instinctively, throwing up his arm. In doing so, he deflected the point of the knife, which had been aimed at his liver, spoiling Burges's aim. But the edge of the knife cut cleanly through both the sleeves of his jacket and shirt and left a long gash on his arm. Thomas shouted in alarm and pain. His movement had unbalanced him, and Burges took his opportunity, kicking out at the sergeant's legs.

Thomas fell into the mulch of leaves and twigs, feeling them scratch his neck and face. He was disoriented, but Burges's laboured breathing helped him locate the man. The killer must have been holding his breath as he had passed, trying to remain unseen and unheard until the moment was right.

Thomas kicked out blindly, scissoring Burges's legs out from under him. Thomas used his enemy's momentary distraction to scramble to his feet. He had dropped his truncheon; it was long gone among the bracken and mulch. He would have to wait for daylight to retrieve it.

Across from him, with less than six feet of space between them, Burges had also gotten back on his feet. Unlike Thomas, he had maintained hold of his weapon. The point of the knife weaved in lazy figures of eight. Burges held it at stomach level, the blade levelled slightly upwards.

Thomas tried to assess his enemy. Burges was nearly a full head shorter than him and at least three decades older. But the madness that shone clearly from his dark eyes and the heavy knife levelled the playing field. Thomas cursed quietly at his lost truncheon. He felt the reassuring weight of the brass knuckles, but they were close-quarter weapons and he did not want to get within arm's reach of the blade in Burges's hand. Burges might be a surgeon rather than a brawler, but a knife was a knife.

Thomas realised that the best option open to him was to play for time. The squad was on the way. Muldoon was coming, along with Sergeant Fraser no doubt dragging behind them half of the Rose Hill watch armed to the teeth, and eager to settle a score with the killer. Thomas did not need to defeat Burges. He just needed to wait him out.

"There's something I don't get, Arthur," Thomas said, still breathing heavily. The two men had begun circling each other like two feral cats eying each other up, each one trying to decide how best to hurt the other while avoiding as much injury as possible.

Burges did not reply, but Thomas continued.

"You could have gone anywhere," he said. "You could have left that sugar plantation and gone to America and made your own way. Made your own fortune. Why didn't you?"

Burges still did not reply, but Thomas could sense the killer's agitation building. Burges suddenly feinted towards Thomas' midriff with the blade, but Thomas jumped back out of range.

"You know what I think, Arthur?" Thomas asked.

"What?" Burges spat. He lunged again, but Thomas sidestepped the charge.

"I think you were afraid."

Burges blinked, for a moment shocked. Then he grinned.

"Afraid?" he said. "I have brought more fear than you can imagine. I have seen primal fear, that dark clawing knowledge that everything is lost. That your fate is no longer yours. I have seen it, and I have caused it more times than you can imagine."

"I'm sure you have," Thomas said. His shoulders were tensed. Burges lunged again, but Thomas again easily sidestepped the charge. He was beginning to get a feel for how the killer moved. He favoured his left leg over his right. He lowered his shoulder a few inches just before he charged, tensing the muscles in his neck. Burges was no fighter. He had killed, but had never needed to fight. He was predictable.

"But I think you feared what would happen if you failed," Thomas said. "I think part of you knew that you would. Were you really ever more than that pampered little prince they exiled from the city so many years ago?"

"Shut up!" Burges snarled. His temper was rising. He needed to kill the sergeant to return to the hunt. He was a hunter. He knew that, had always known that. But Thomas was like an irksome fly he could not swat, and he dared not launch an all-out assault on the taller and stronger policeman.

"Do you still feel like a hunter, Arthur?" Thomas said and for the first time, his stoney expression broke into a mocking smile. "How does it feel to face someone head on, not someone who trusted you or who had their back turned?"

"Shut up!" Burges screamed in the wind. He pulled his scalpel from the inner pocket of his jacket and flung it at Thomas' grinning face with his left hand. It was a weak throw, the handle of the knife glancing against Thomas' shoulder before it fell to the ground.

The sergeant's grin widened, and he began to laugh.

"Shut your mouth!" Burges screamed, his eyes moving wildly as he fought an internal battle. attack or flee.

"Tell you what, Arthur," Thomas said. He straightened up, his hands hanging loosely by his sides. He spread them wide. "Why don't you prove what a great hunter you are. Kill me."

Burges hesitated. Thomas's laugh echoed in his head.

"It's a trick," he mumbled.

"There's no trick," Thomas said loudly. "You'll never have a finer chance than this, Arthur Burges."

The laughter continued. Thomas had closed his mouth, and yet the laughter rang like church bells inside Burges's mind.

He let out a scream of rage, merging with curses and insults, and launched himself forward. He drew his arm back, aiming to plant the Liston knife in Thomas' abdomen. He would gut the sergeant. Perhaps that would end the laughter and soothe his humiliation.

As Burges charged forward, Thomas' left hand shot out, grabbing the killer by the wrist, stopping both blade and charge dead. Burges had time only to blink a single time. Then Thomas's right hand, fingers clad in brass, and moving like the unstoppable progress of time itself, connected with the side of Burges's head. The older man was flung sideways, his vision flashing and sparking like a dying lightbulb.

He fell hard against one of the headstones. The Liston knife fell from his hand, landing with a soft thud in the grass. Rain merged with a rivulet of watery blood seeping from a gash in the side of his head. His breathing was shallow. But he was alive.

Thomas sank onto his haunches. With a shaking hand, he removed the brass knuckles, slipping them into his vest pocket. In the distance, he could hear shouts. Beams of light from dozens of lanterns cut through the night as

CHAPTER TWENTY-SIX

Muldoon and his men made their way down the steep path to the cemetery.

Soon, there would be noise. Noise and bustle. But for now, there was only him. He glanced at Burges and at the knife. Slowly, he reached out, running his fingertips along its bone handle. He did not know how, but suddenly he had the knife in his hand. Its weight both reassuring and alluring. The blade had been honed to perfection. Thomas knew even without trying that he could balance the blade on a single outstretched finger, so perfectly matched was the weight of the stubbier handle to the longer blade.

Droplets landed along the sharp edge, causing a gentle ringing like little silver bells. They seemed to call out. Thomas glanced at Arthur Burges, still lying unconscious in the dirt. How easy it would be to finish him. His death would be simple to explain. *I got the knife from him, sir, but he kept coming at me. I must have caught him in the chest in the melee.* Who would care? There would be justice and retribution. What else was really needed?

Sophia and Muldoon found Thomas standing over the fallen figure of Burges, staring intently down at him. The detective sergeant held the Liston knife loosely by his side, rain running off its tip and forming a puddle by his foot.

"I think you should give me that blade, sergeant," Muldoon said in a firm tone. Thomas seemed to reawaken from a dream. He looked around, startled. Then he looked at the knife in his hand.

He handed it mutely to Muldoon. The inspector took it gingerly by the blade between two fingers with the expression of a man handling the rotting carcass of a rat.

"Is he dead?" he asked.

Thomas shook his head.

"Knocked out," he said. "Just knocked out."

Sophia had come to a halt nearly ten feet from the scene. She seemed unwilling to approach any closer to the fallen Burges. And yet she was unable to take her eyes off him.

"You don't have to be afraid of him, miss," Muldoon said, looking around.

"I'm not," Sophia said in a quiet voice. "I beat him. What's going to happen to him?"

Muldoon raised a hand signalling to two approaching constables.

"He's going to wake up in one of our cells, and in the morning, we'll take him straight to Kirkdale Gaol." He pointed to the prone figure, and the two constables walked over, grabbed Burges under each arm, and hauled him upright. His head fell forward, and he mumbled quietly, his eyelids flickering.

"If he wakes up before you get him in the cell, you have my permission to put him straight back to sleep," Muldoon said. "Don't take any chances with him."

The constables grunted assent and began to haul the killer through the undergrowth towards the cemetery gates. As he was hauled past Sophia, Muldoon saw her face contort in disgust.

Arthur Burges Junior's eyelids flittered open. Hazy images swam in front of them. Headstones. Cenotaphs. The sepulchres of the city. He seemed to float past them, his muscles not under his own control anymore. The weight of the Liston knife in his belt was gone. Cooling rain soothed the pain emanating from his head. Perhaps this was the end. Had he really completed his task? He could not remember. For the briefest of moments, he saw his own name, carved in foot-high letters on a marble slab. He smiled as the abyss claimed him again. He was home.

Chapter Twenty-Seven

fter the rain, a weak autumn sun had persisted for nearly a month, giving the city of Liverpool a well-earned respite before the dark days of winter truly began. The bustle of the city had never abated, but it had been muted by fear and paranoia. Now, with the killer entombed in a cell in Kirkdale, Liverpool soon forgot its terror. Proud ships carrying timber and rum and pickled herring and fine porcelains, and a thousand other goods, entered the estuary of the Mersey. Pilots came onboard and guided them like loyal sheepdogs to the green pastures of the docks. Stevedores and dockworkers shouted and fought and jostled for a daily wage. Merchants, street sellers, and craftsmen filled their stores and stalls and emporia with the newly arrived merchandise. Factory workers, weavers, and spinners went about their business. In the tea rooms of the Adelphi, the rich and powerful discussed events in distant lands with strange names, and in the pubs, alehouses, and gin palaces, the poor spent what little coin they had on the few hours of blissful forgetfulness to be found at the bottom of a bottle.

And through it all, through all the chaos and bustle of the growing city, the constables sauntered in their navy-blue uniforms with sparkling silver buttons. Thieves were apprehended, barfights and street brawls dispersed. Skulls were cracked, informants tapped, and arrest ledgers filled out.

The last Friday in November found Detective Sergeant Thomas O'Callaghan and Detective Inspector William Haskins Muldoon leaning up against one of the courtyard walls of Kirkdale Gaol. Located between the busy thoroughfare of Walton Road to the east and the Cheshire Lines

Railway tracks to the west, the gaol had been in use for more than seventy years. Designed as a panopticon with six wings radiating from a central tower, Kirkdale was a forbidding, fortress-like structure of red brick. Low and menacing, it projected a clear message to any passers-by. Many enter here. And not all of them leave.

Within the walls of the prison, beside the heavy oak and iron double gates was a cramped cobbled courtyard. It was overlooked by two of the gaol's wings and the two detectives could see pale faces of inmates pressed to their barred windows, eager to catch a glimpse of the day's main event.

The days of public hangings attended by crowds numbering sometimes in the tens of thousands were a thing of the past. These days, capital punishment was a more private affair attended only by a handful of magistrates, officers of the law, the county coroner, and the warden of the gaol. Despite this, crowds had gathered outside the walls of the prison, and Thomas could hear the muted rumble of their excited conversations drifting across the high walls of the prison.

"I wonder what they're doing here," he said quietly. "They can't see a thing."

Muldoon took a deep puff on his pipe.

"They want to make sure the bastard's dead," he said.

Thomas fished out his battered pocket watch. Eight minutes to nine. The sun had only just emerged from the horizon, its sharp winter light chasing away the darkness and shadows of the night.

Thomas looked around. The magistrates, three of them, stood in a tight cluster, all of them in heavy black coats with stovepipe hats and heavy greying sideburns. One of them looked around, caught his eye, and nodded curtly. The warden was not yet present, but six guards had taken up station by the stairs that led to the recently constructed set of wooden gallows. A ruddy-faced man with black hair, sleeked back and shining with pomade, was busying himself by the mechanism which would, at the strike of nine, open a trap door and send Arthur Burges Junior to his eternal rest. The executioner had a business-like air about him, experienced as he was with dealing out carefully planned judicial death.

A single bell rang out from the top of the prison's central tower, signalling that the warden and his men had collected the condemned from his cell. The noise of the crowd grew in volume.

After less than two minutes, a narrow door in the east wing swung open. Two guards appeared, followed by another pair leading the condemned man between them, his hands manacled in front of him. A final pair of guards and the warden made up the rear of the procession.

"No vicar?" Thomas asked.

Muldoon shook his head.

"He spat in the face of the monsignor who was sent to take his last confession."

"Good," Thomas said. "If there was ever a soul that didn't deserve to be saved, it's his."

The monthlong stay in the gaol, the exhausting trial had changed Arthur Burges Junior. His red face was now pale grey. His mouth hung open, his neat greying hair now a straggly mane, unkempt and infested with lice. His eyes had lost none of their madness though, Thomas could see that even at this distance. Even as he walked, they rolled around wildly, seeking any escape, any reprieve.

"He's going to crack," Muldoon said.

Thomas shook his head.

"He's long gone in the head," he said. "It doesn't look like he even knows where he is."

"He'll crack," Muldoon repeated. "Trust me."

As the condemned man set foot on the first of the twelve steps leading to the gallows' central platform, a change ran through his body like an electric current. His head snapped around, his eyes focusing sharply on the noose. He let out an inarticulate gurgling cry, and for the first time since arriving in the courtyard, he began to struggle against his captors.

The guards dragged him relentlessly forward, one wooden step at a time. With each step, Burges's struggles intensified until the two burly men were carrying him, his legs flailing and kicking in the air. He did not speak, but a mixture of broken words, grunts, and screams escaped from him, the rambling of a man driven beyond the frontiers of madness by fear of the fate he had dealt out mercilessly to so many.

The guards manhandled the condemned man onto the trapdoor, but his struggles were such that they could not let him go for fear that he would throw himself off the scaffold and cheat both justice and the hangman. At a signal from the warden, another guard stepped forward, drew back his fist, and punched Arthur Burges hard in the stomach. He fell to the wooden boards, wheezing and for a moment paralysed by pain. The guards quickly pulled him to his feet, and the hangman placed a white hood over his face and the noose around his neck.

"Hats off!" the warden bellowed, and the guards and magistrates removed their hats and caps. Thomas and Muldoon remained still, making no move to show the condemned man this last respect. At the warden's command, the bell tolled again, and Thomas clearly heard a voice raised above the hubbub outside.

"Hush your gobs, they're hanging him now!"

The crowd fell silent. The guards stepped back.

In the split second before the hangman pulled his lever, Thomas saw a thin trickle of liquid soak Burges's trousers and pool on the trapdoor. Through the hood, the voice was muted, but every witness heard the plaintive cry, a haunting, hideous sound escaping from the man's throat abruptly ended by the loud metallic thud of the trapdoor slamming open.

The rope snapped taut, Burges's body twisting convulsively underneath the scaffold. He gasped, drawing the white cloth of his hood into his mouth, biting down so hard that one of his molars cracked, sending a mixture of phlegm, pus, and blood soaking into the linen. The magistrates looked away from the gruesome spectacle, but Thomas could not even blink. He needed to see the ending. Needed to know when it was done.

He never knew how long Burges struggled. Only later did he learn that the hangman had been reprimanded by the warden. A long drop execution should take seconds, not minutes of agonising wait while the condemned struggled to fill their lungs with and ever-diminishing supply of air. Perhaps the hangman, with his intricate knowledge of weights and rope length and tensile strength and the breaking point of the human neck, had decided that the killer who had terrorised his city did not deserve an easy departure from the world. There was no way to know.

Finally, twelve minutes after the trap door had opened, a young doctor stepped forward and searched for a pulse. Finding none, he nodded once to the warden. The warden stepped back, placing him in full view of the central tower. He raised a hand, and the heavy bell tolled. Just once. The crowd outside the walls and the prisoners lining their cell windows erupted into jeers and applause, catcalls and even laughter. Their monster had been slain. The world might not be fair. But at least, in this short moment of time, it was right.

Thomas felt nothing. He had expected a flood of relief, even joy, after weeks of sitting staring at Burges in the dock, speaking to magistrates and shepherding endless piles of paper and ledgers and sketches and photographs from Rose Hill to the prosecutor's chambers. But he felt no different now than when he had entered the courtyard of the gaol. He had longed for an ending. But this was not the right one.

He felt Muldoon's hand on his shoulder.

"Well," the inspector said. "It's done." He hesitated for a moment, noticing Thomas' blank expression. Then he cleared his throat. "Have you spoken to Miss Steenberg recently?" he asked.

Thomas blinked.

"N-no," he stuttered. "Not since the trial ended."

Muldoon looked him in the eyes for several moments longer than was comfortable. Thomas dropped his gaze.

"Has she left for New York yet?" Muldoon asked.

"I'm not sure," Thomas said, trying to keep his tone light and casual.

Muldoon cleared his throat and busied himself with knocking his pipe out against the brick wall.

"I must admit," he said. "I thought that you and she were perhaps…"

"No," Thomas said. "No, we just haven't had a chance to meet. It's been a busy time."

"Indeed," Muldoon said with a forced jolly tone. "My wife's certainly been complaining more than usual about my long hours."

Thomas flashed his superior a brief smile that did not reach his eyes.

"Nevertheless," Muldoon said. "Perhaps you should go to the Adelphi and ask if she is…"

"I'm certain that she will contact me if she wishes to meet," Thomas said, and Muldoon could hear from his tone that that particular avenue of conversation was blocked.

The two men waited for the crowds outside the prison to disperse before leaving. They caught a growler which took them back to Rose Hill station. They arrived in time to see the morning shift leave for their first patrol of the day. Sergeant Fraser stood by the door, enjoying the warming rays of the sun, his face turned towards the light, his eyes closed.

"Look alive, Fraser," Muldoon barked as he bustled past him. "I want to know what's been happening during the night."

Fraser snapped to attention, following the inspector into the watch room. He ducked underneath his desk and consulted his ledger.

"Been a pretty quiet night, sir," he said. "We caught a couple of house-breakers red-handed. They're both down in the cells. Then there's been a few reported thefts from those blasted pickpockets. Oh, and several barrels of rum have been lifted from one of the warehouses on Stanley Dock."

"Sounds like the Jessop Gang," Muldoon mused. "Might be worth looking into. Anything else?"

"Well, then there's been a couple of brawls and a few…"

Fraser's voice drifted into the background as Thomas looked around the low-ceilinged room with its rickety chairs and scratched tables. The watch room had always felt like home. Far more like a home than his dingy abode. That was just where he went to sleep. This room was where he lived. This room and the streets of his city. But for the first time, he felt that something was missing. He remembered the first time Sophia and he had rushed through the room heading to the dead room before Muldoon could stop them. There had been girls and women before, plenty of them. Some only for a night, but some for much longer. But never before had a few weeks felt as long.

After the final day of the trial, Sophia had excused herself. She was exhausted, both in mind and in body. The witness testimony she had been forced to give, sitting right across from the man who had tried to murder her had impacted her more greatly than she was willing to admit. Thomas could see it, and he understood it. At first, he had wanted to give her space to heal. But somehow that had turned into a wait, a wait which he subconsciously expected her to end. Perhaps he should go to the Adelphi and make enquiries. Maybe she was already long gone, strolling on the promenade deck of a trans-Atlantic steamer heading for the busy skyline of New York. An ocean, a world and a life away from him.

"Excuse me, are you Sergeant O'Callaghan?" Thomas turned around. A young lad, barely ten years old, was standing by the door to the watch room. He held a folded piece of paper in front of him like a shield.

"I am," Thomas said walking across to the boy. "Who's asking?"

"Dunno," the boy said proffering the paper. "Some posh lady just give me this, and told me to run down and find you."

Thomas reached out a hand for the paper. Behind his back, Inspector Muldoon caught Sergeant Fraser's eye and smiled.

Chapter Twenty-Eight

"And with the deed signed, the transaction will be finalised upon receipt of the final instalment." The middle-aged estate agent smiled unctuously as he took back his fountain pen and the signed contract from Sophia. "May I say what a pleasure it's been to do business with a young woman of such refined taste."

Sophia glanced at him, one eyebrow raised.

"Thank you," she said curtly, moving her gaze pointedly to the door. The agent stowed away pen and contract in his satchel, touched the brim of his hat, and hurried out. Sophia looked around the empty room. For a moment, she saw it in her mind's eye, filled with fine furniture.

After the trial, she had returned to her suite in the Adelphi. Sitting in front of the fire, she had attempted to place the experiences of not just her time in Liverpool, but the nearly six months that had elapsed since she had left her own country for good. Somehow, she seemed to have lived several busy lifetimes in that short period. She had helped catch a killer. And she had fought a killer. For all the terror, the nightmares which still haunted her, she had stood her ground. When it came to it, she had stopped running and fought back.

She did not want to be beholden to anyone ever again. She had lived her whole life being constantly reminded of how much she owed her father. This next step in her life, she would take herself. After a sleepless night, she had walked into this new city that—despite the horrors of her experiences— already felt like a new home. She had asked around and been directed to Messrs Chandler and Briggs, estate agents and landlords. She had entered their offices, described what she wanted, and before the day was out, she had placed the first instalment of cash in Mr Briggs' greasy palm.

She ran a hand along the finely carved rosewood door frame as she walked out of the reception room and into a hallway tiled in black and white. The front door was of solid oak, painted black but set with a round stained glass window depicting a flowering rose. The sunlight gleaming through it threw beams of red and green light across the walls and across her face and dress as she walked down the hallway, threw open the door, and walked down the stone steps to the pavement. She glanced at her watch.

She had waited less than fifteen minutes when she saw Thomas O'Callaghan turn the corner at the end of the street. He was walking fast, his head down and his ratty homburg hat pulled low over his scarred ear. Halfway down the street he looked up, saw her and his face broke into a wide smile.

"Sergeant," Sophia said reaching out and grasping both of his hands. "I'm so glad you came."

"I got your message," Thomas said, waving the small folded piece of paper unnecessarily. "I didn't know what to make of it."

"Do you like it?" Sophia said, beaming. Thomas frowned.

"Like what?" he asked.

"My new practice," Sophia said, waving a hand towards the property. Thomas' mouth gaped open.

"Your practice?" he said. "Do you mean…"

Sophia nodded.

"I thought to myself, why journey all the way across the Atlantic? Are there no sick people in need of a doctor in this city?"

"Plenty, I should think," Thomas said, stunned.

"Well, they will be more than welcome," Sophia said, leading Thomas up the stairs and through the front door. Showing him the reception room, five bedrooms, two parlours, kitchen, scullery and no less than three indoor washrooms took nearly half an hour. When they arrived back at the front door, Thomas looked around in amazement.

"It's a palace," he said.

"Hardly," Sophia said with a faint smile. "I'll take the rooms on the second floor as my private apartment."

"And the rest?"

"The rest will be waiting areas, surgery suites, and bedrooms for overnight patients."

"You'll need to hire help," Thomas said, his tone alarmed by the extent of her ambition. Sophia nodded.

"A nurse and a secretary to start," she said. "But more if needed."

Thomas hesitated.

"And do you think patients will come?" he asked, glancing at her, his expression embarrassed. "I mean, I'm sorry, I didn't mean to imply… Your skill is beyond question, of course…"

Sophia paused for a moment. Then her laughter rang out, echoing off the empty hallway. Thomas grinned sheepishly.

"Perhaps only women will come at first," Sophia said. "Women are, after all, rather better suited for adapting to change. We are used to it, you see. Men always talk of changing the world, and they expect us to simply learn to live with their changes, good or bad."

"Perhaps some men can change too," Thomas said quietly. Sophia put a hand lightly on his arm.

"Perhaps they can," she said, smiling warmly. Thomas looked down, but then his gaze rose to meet Sophia's. She did not turn away. Multicoloured rays of sunlight sparkled across her thick blonde hair. They stood so close he could count every one of her pale eyelashes. She smiled and raised her eyebrows questioningly. Thomas lowered his lips towards hers.

They were jolted apart by a hesitant knock on the door. Sophia, suddenly flustered, shook her head and swallowed.

"Ah," she said, a little more loudly than the situation warranted. "And speaking of hiring help, I believe this is my first employee."

Thomas, head still reeling, the taste of her lips, the smell of her soft hair still coursing through his body and mind as intoxicating as gin, blinked confused.

Sophia pushed past him and opened the front door. Thomas looked around and outlined against the winter sun, he saw the ragged figure of Skittles. The boy, as thin and light as a sparrow had a hand raised to knock again. Thomas could see that he was poised to flee, just in case the mystery house held some unpleasant surprise.

"Skittles," Sophia said stepping back and beckoning the boy inside. "I'm glad the lad I sent to find you succeeded."

"I'm easy enough to find, miss," Skittles said hesitantly. "For them as knows where to look for me."

He followed Thomas and Sophia into the reception room, staring around the large empty space with unashamed curiosity.

"Is this your house, miss?" he asked brazenly.

"Yes, it is," Thomas interrupted. "So don't get any ideas about getting a few of your thieving mates together and graduating from pickpockets to housebreakers."

Skittles grinned wickedly.

"I never would, sergeant," he said in a beatific tone. Thomas grunted noncommittedly.

Sophia turned around and looked at the urchin, her head on one side.

"I never thanked you," she said.

"For what, miss?"

"For saving my life."

The urchin looked down at his feet in their scratched and overlarge boots.

"If you had not alerted Sergeant O'Callaghan to my predicament, I have no doubt that I would have been killed."

"You're welcome, miss," Skittles said. He looked up, his eyes gleaming all the brighter in his dirt-covered face.

"I've been thinking about how to reward you," Sophia said. Thomas looked at her. Then he understood.

"I'll never say no to a shilling or two, miss," Skittles interjected with lightning speed. Sophia smiled and continued.

"This is going to be a doctor's surgery," she said. "My surgery. And when it opens, I will need a boy to fetch and carry messages," Thomas grinned, and Sophia smiled at the grubby street urchin whose eyes grew wide.

"A shilling a day, six days a week with Sundays off," she continued, and Thomas let out a bark of laughter.

"You can't say fairer than that, Skittles," he said. "Perhaps you can even find a church that'll let you in on the Sunday."

"We'll need to talk about getting you some news clothes," Sophia continued, then wrinkled her nose. "And a bath or two would not come amiss."

Skittles opened his mouth, but Sophia held up a hand to forestall his protests.

"I believe, Skittles, that if we throw you into soapy water, you may simply dissolve away to nothing, but it's a risk worth taking in the interest of markedly improving the overall hygiene of this city."

She knelt, bringing her face on a level with the boy. She reached out a hand.

"Do we have an understanding? You and I?"

Skittles hesitated for a long moment. Then his face broke into a broad grin. He spat in his palm and, before Thomas could intervene, he grabbed Sophia's hand and shook it emphatically.

In the evening, after a celebratory meal at one of the city's finer eateries on Duke Street, Sophia and Thomas walked arm in arm down St James Street. Thomas, in a fit of gallantry, had purchased a small paper bag of roasted chestnuts, so their walk was accompanied by rustling as they shared the savoury treats. They came to a halt at the end of the street. The owner of an eel-pie stall was sitting contentedly at the end of the day, finishing the last of his pies, which he had kept for his own supper. A group of kids barrelled past, their pockets jingling with pennies they would soon exchange for seats at the music hall, which lay where the street intersected Park Lane.

Sophia looked down towards the lights of the docks, clearly visible. A line of fire against the dark of the river.

"Thank you, Thomas," she said. "For trusting me."

Thomas spat out a piece of hard chestnut husk.

"You owe me no thanks at all," he said gruffly. "Without you, Burges would still be out there. Killing and maiming."

The mention of the name seemed to bring an additional chill in the air.

Sophia pressed herself closer to Thomas, an involuntary shudder running through her body.

"There's one thing you learn in this job," he said, gazing unseeing towards the river. "You can't ever destroy evil. You can only force it into a temporary retreat. It'll always return."

"But when it does," Sophia said. "You'll be there to meet it again."

Thomas looked down at her pale face and deep blue eyes and smiled.

"Aye," he said. "We'll both be there."

A lantern hoisted from the mast of an arriving schooner blended seamlessly into the star strewn sky as the ship pulled up to the dock. Life went on, the shadows of the past banished, the future unrolling bright and new, glistening with possibilities and opportunities. Liverpool was like an immense organism inhaling and exhaling the movements of its citizens and guests. Ships arrived and ships departed. Passengers came and passengers went. But some came to the city, and in it, they found their home.

About the Author

Nicky Nielsen, PhD, is originally from Denmark but moved to the United Kingdom to train as an Egyptologist. He has worked as an archaeologist on excavations in Europe and the Middle East and has written for a variety of magazines on topics related to ancient history. He lives in Liverpool.

AUTHOR WEBSITE:
  www.nickynielsen.com

SOCIAL MEDIA HANDLES:
  Twitter: @N_Nielsen4
  Instagram: nickynielsen50